Silas K. (Silas Kitto) Hocking

Tregeagle's Head

A Romance of the Cornish Cliffs

Silas K. (Silas Kitto) Hocking

Tregeagle's Head
A Romance of the Cornish Cliffs

ISBN/EAN: 9783337007942

Printed in Europe, USA, Canada, Australia, Japan

Cover: Foto ©Andreas Hilbeck / pixelio.de

More available books at **www.hansebooks.com**

TREGEAGLE'S HEAD

A Romance of the Cornish Cliffs.

BY

SILAS K. HOCKING, F.R.H.S.,

AUTHOR OF

"HER BENNY," "IVY," "FOR ABIGAIL,"

ETC., ETC.

WITH ORIGINAL ILLUSTRATIONS BY T. M. HEMY.

LONDON AND NEW YORK:

FREDERICK WARNE AND CO.

1890.

DEDICATION.

My dear Ernest,

This little book having grown out of a suggestion of yours, I dedicate it to you. Probably you have forgotten the circumstance; but some time ago you paid me the somewhat doubtful compliment of wishing I would "write a book that boys would like—a book with adventures in it, and escapes, and all that." I confess I had been labouring under the impression that boys did like my books, notwithstanding their lack of the "adventure and escape" element. I see now how easily one may be mistaken in such matters.

Still it is more than probable your suggestion would have borne no fruit, had we not soon after visited together my native county. It was while standing with you on one of the bold headlands that dot the Atlantic seaboard, watching the long rollers breaking into foam upon the rocks, and listening to their thunder as they echoed up the deep, dark caves, that the idea flashed across my mind which I have tried to work out in the following pages.

I freely confess that to myself the attempt is not very satisfactory, and I can hardly hope that it will approach your ideal of what a story ought to be. In one respect perhaps you will be pleased; there is no preaching in it, and I am not certain even, that it has a moral.

Such as it is, however, I offer for your acceptance. I know you will read it for my sake. I hope you may find it interesting. It may not come up to your expectations; but it will be at least another token of my love for you, if that you need.

I remain, dear Ernest,

Your affectionate Father,

SILAS K. HOCKING.

CONTENTS.

CHAP.   PAGE

I. INTRODUCTORY 1

II. EXPLANATIONS 9

III. SUSPICIONS 18

IV. CONCLUSIONS 26

V. THE STORM BURSTS 35

VI. THE ARREST 43

VII. A DISMAL SUNDAY 51

VIII. THE INQUIRY BEGINS 59

IX. EVIDENCE 68

X. LOVE'S RESOLVE 77

XI. THE WITCH OF CARN DULOE 85

XII. NANNY MAKES A PROMISE 93

XIII. ABEL GETS IMPATIENT 100

XIV. IN DISGUISE 109

XV. KEEPING WATCH 118

XVI. "NIL DESPERANDUM" 128

XVII. AN ANXIOUS NIGHT 135

XVIII. DISAPPOINTMENT 144

XIX. IN SIGHT OF FREEDOM ... 153

XX. EXCITEMENT 163

XXI. IN THE NIGHT ... 172

CHAP.		PAGE
XXII.	PERPLEXITY	180
XXIII.	"HE KNEW THE WORST"	190
XXIV.	"BE STRONG AND FEAR NOT"	195
XXV.	THE END OF THE STRIFE	204
XXVI.	A DISCOVERY	214
XXVII.	AN UNEXPECTED VISITOR	222
XXVIII.	SMUGGLERS AT WORK	230
XXIX.	LEFT ALONE	238
XXX.	HOPE AND DESPAIR	246
XXXI.	THE WITCH TO THE RESCUE	252
XXXII.	FOR DEAR LIFE	261
XXXIII.	HOME AGAIN	268

LIST OF ILLUSTRATIONS.

But no one paid heed to Dicky ; every eye was fixed upon a moving but headless figure out on the headland ... *To face page* 15

Soon after dawn he began to steer for home, and when on a line with Tregeagle's Head, his son Billy called his attention to some dark object in the water 70

Mary stood at the gate as the witch stalked past 121

Gladys managed to secure an early copy of the proclamation ... 169

With a curl of his lip, and quick as thought, Jack stuck the flame under Dan's nose 231

Jet and her rider were far in the distance 263

TREGEAGLE'S HEAD.

CHAPTER I.

INTRODUCTORY.

"Yet over all there hung a cloud of fear,
    A sense of mystery the spirit daunted,
And said as plain as whisper in the ear,
    The place is haunted."—HOOD.

JACK DUNSTAN and Harry Penryn went out together
on Tregeagle's Head. Several hours later Harry returned alone. He did not say what had become of his
companion; indeed he appeared anxious to avoid all
allusion to the subject. When he got home he shut
himself up in his father's study, and remained there till
Farmer Dunstan came across to the Vicarage to know
what had become of his son.

Tregeagle's Head—as every one knows who has
sailed round the Cornish coast, or tramped its seaboard
—is a huge rocky promontory, that pushes itself at
least a mile out into the Atlantic surf, and remains
at all states of the tide standing deep in the water.
In shape it is not unlike a giant's head, especially if
you can get a profile view sailing up or down the
channel.

Right and left, as well as far out in front, it is safely
guarded by an army of small rocky islands. At high
water these rocks cannot be seen, but when the tide
is low they stand up out of the water like a regiment

of black dragoons, and break the Atlantic rollers into a myriad shreds of gleaming foam.

Strange stories are told even to-day about Tregeagle's Head. But at the time of which we write—and that was long before the present century opened—every one believed it to be haunted. In stormy weather, when the night lay thick upon the angry sea, and the rocky sentinels tore the long billows into shreds, and churned them into foam, the spirit of Tregeagle might be heard calling into the darkness, and shrieking out his despair in notes so fearsome, that people felt their blood curdle in their veins.

The Rev. Leslie Penryn—who was not a super-stitious man—pooh-poohed these stories, and called them silly trash; said it was far more likely that the cries came from drowning sailors whose bark had got entangled among the rocks around Tregeagle's Head, and who were perishing with none to save.

But the fishermen of Pentudy on one side and of Porthloo on the other would have none of it. They knew better. Had not their fathers and grandfathers told them how the restless spirit of Tregeagle had been doomed to dwell in the gloomy caverns which honey-combed the great headland; to make ropes of sand, and stem the roaring tide, until by long centuries of penance he had purged away his guilt, and secured rest for his long tortured soul? What more reasonable to suppose, therefore, that when the nights were dark and wild, and the raging storm scattered his ropes of sand like dust, and the angry sea wrecked his labour, and hissed defiance in his ear—what more reasonable, that he should wail out the misery and despair of his tortured soul.

There were dozens of people in Pentudy and Porthloo who had not only heard strange cries coming across the sea from Tregeagle's Head, but had seen strange lights flickering about, as though many other spirits than that of Tregeagle's dwelt in its caves. And one or two people declared that they had in the daytime seen smoke issuing from its crown. But the majority of the fisher-folk were unable to give credence to this last statement.

Yet Sam Trewalsick, one of the most daring and reckless fellows on the whole coast, was of the opinion that there might be some truth in it.

"You never know," he said, "what those ghostes is up to. My b'leef is, the oal head is crammed full ov 'em. Me an' our Billy have heerd some strange things when we've been coastin' purty near them sent'nels."

"An' I reckon," said Dan Polslee, a little wizened man with lantern jaws and large hungry-looking eyes, "that you've a sail'd as near them rocks as any ov us."

"I've a sail'd nearer 'em than I ever intend to do again," said Sam, sweeping the little crowd of upturned faces with a meaning glance.

"It's best to give 'em a purty wide berth," said two or three voices in chorus.

"And for why?" said Sam, with a savage frown.

"Aye, give us your views," said Dan, edging his way nearer the centre of the group. "Foaks say as 'ow you've not on'y heerd things but seed things as well; ez there any truth in it?"

"Well," said Sam, emptying his mouth of a quid of tobacco and indulging in sundry preliminary oaths, "I ain't no talkin' man, and I ain't no narvus man, but some things there ain't no denyin'."

"That's true," was the general response.

"And I don't care the wuth of a pilchard what that passon over to Restormel says about it," went on Sam. "I know what I've heerd an' what I've seed, an' I tell'e, boys, I wouldn't go on Tregeagle's Head arter dark for all the gold of the Ingies."

"Nor me nuther," said Dan, with a shrug of his shoulders, and a curious leer of his hungry eyes.

"Me an' our Billy," went on Sam, without heeding

the interruption, "made up our minds one day that we 'ud defy Tregeagle an' oal his himps, the oal boilin' on 'em. So the tide being 'igh, an' most of the sent'nels under water, we hoisted sail an' made for't."

At this point Sam returned the quid to his mouth, while a visible shudder ran through his frame. The effect of this on his little audience was almost electrical. Sam Trewalsick was not the man to be "skeared" by shadows. It must have been a fearful sight that the memory of it could affect him so.

"I'd rather not tell it, boys," he said after a long pause. "But you may depend I keep as far away from Tregeagle's Head as possible."

"Oh, but you'd better tell," suggested Dan. "We be all 'daggin' to hear."

"Fact is," said Sam, shrugging his brawny shoulders and indulging in a few more oaths, "words ain't big enough to tell it. There ain't nothin' to liken it to. You've seen the mouth o' the cave from the sea?"

"Iss, iss," was the response.

"Well, far up the cave is a fire. A hawful fire, like a smeltin'-house oven—a fire as don't give no light, but burns blue, wi' strakes of yeller an' green in it, that curls and twists around like 'brakety' sarpents, and hiss wi' forked tongues red-hot. And all round, dancin' an' squirmin' with three-claw'd pikes in their hands, such imps as never afore was seen—all shapes, all sizes, all colours, jabberin', fightin', squealin'. Boys, you ain't no idee."

"That's true," said Dan, who was spokesman for the rest.

"But that ain't all," said Sam. "If me an' Billy hadn't lowered our sail sudden it 'ud a been all up wi' us."

"How d'ye make that out, Sam?" asked two or three voices.

"Well," said Sam, taking the quid out of his mouth again, and indulging in more profane language, "that's jist where I'm floored. I can't explain—I can on'y tell jist what happened. We'd got opposite the cave, an' fairly near, when we feel'd ourselves pulled, drawed, sucked like very mad. There wer'n't no wind stirring sca'ce, for nobody 'ud go near the sent'nels in windy weather; but our sails filled out, or were sucked out, in a moment, and we found ourselves going like lightning straight for the mouth of the cave. You may bet we got out of that current as soon as possible, and we ain't been near it since."

After this deliverance there was a long pause. Sam deliberately spat on the ground, then pushed his hands deep into his trousers pockets.

Then Barnicoat Tabb, or Barney, as he was always called, after a preliminary cough, remarked that "his grandfather had seed somethin' like it. And his own opinion was, that the fire went out for years an' years, then blazed up again."

"My b'lief is it's a kind o' burnin' mountain," chimed in Tommy Mudge.

"But 'ow about them limps?" queried Dan.

"They of course be after Tregeagle," said Tommy. "Everybody knows that if he ceases work for a minit till his time's up, the devil will have him. But while he keeps at it they may squirm around 'im, but they can't touch 'im."

To this deliverance there was a general nodding of heads. It was in harmony with the universal belief respecting the fate of Tregeagle.

"Any road," Sam remarked as a parting shot, "there may be somethin' in the stories 'bout the smoke coming out o' the head. But you'll not catch me tryin' to find out where it comes from."

"Nor me nuther," said Dan, with a curious leer.

And then the little company broke up to go their several ways.

In this way superstition was kept alive, and stories

grew with the frequent telling, and any man who was bold enough to express a doubt regarding their authenticity was looked upon as an infidel, or something worse.

As yet newspapers were unknown, railways were undreamed of. Even the stage-coach did not come near Porthloo and Pentudy; and for an inhabitant to receive a letter was an event to be talked about weeks and months after. The weather, pilchards, and the mysteries of Tregeagle's Head were the principal topics of conversation. Now and then some rumour of what was doing in the outer world reached their ears, but they paid little heed to it as a rule. They lived in a little world of their own—a world made fearsome by their own fancies, and darkened by gloomy superstitions.

With the inhabitants of Restormel, scarcely more than two miles away, they had little or nothing in common. Restormel was the principal village in the parish of St. Orme, and out of sight of the sea. A quaint, quiet, picturesque spot, rich in timber and all kinds of vegetation, sheltered from the Atlantic gales by a steep hill grown thick with pines, and equally sheltered on the east by the wooded slopes of Carn-Duloe. Restormel boasted a fine old church, a cosy and commodious vicarage, and three or four good residences, the principal one of which was occupied by Farmer Dunstan.

The vicar, though somewhat stern and forbidding in manner and aspect, was very popular in Restormel, but with his parishioners at Porthloo and Pentudy he was, as we have already hinted, at a decided discount. He had as good as called them fools, and that was an offence they were not likely to forget or forgive. He had told them to their face that Tregeagle was a "myth," whatever that might mean; that Nanny Flue, a reputed witch who lived in a little hut on the slope of Carn-Duloe, had no more power over men's lives or property than he had; that charms were folly and worse, and that ghosts did not exist.

Nor was that all. He had even hinted that they were cowards, because they did not man their fishing-boats—when on stormy nights they heard low cries of agony and despair coming across the sea from the direction of Tregeagle's head—and go to the rescue of those who were perishing in the storm.

"I tell you these stories about Tregeagle are all bosh," he said angrily. "My fear is that the race of wreckers has not died out yet. But I shall keep my eyes open, and any man I discover engaged in such a nefarious and dastardly practice will have to swing for it." And with a toss of his well-posed head the Rev. Leslie Penryn marched away.

But his words rankled in their memories and in their hearts. To be called fools and cowards, with a hint that they might be wreckers, was rather more than such human nature as theirs could stand.

"What do 'e know 'bout it?" they said in angry, sullen tones to each other. "He ain't no native of Restormel. He'd better mind 'iz oan business, an' look arter that big boay o' his. Keep 'iz eyes oppen, will 'e? He'd better be careful; other folks can keep their eyes oppen as well as 'e."

So it came about that the fisher folk disliked and mistrusted their vicar, refused to attend church, turned a deaf ear to his instructions, and hugged their superstitions more tenaciously than ever. He had been vicar of Restormel fifteen years. Harry, his son, was four years of age when he came; he was now a tall, muscular fellow of nineteen. Gladys, his daughter, was five years younger than Harry. The day she was born the mother died, and ever since a housekeeper had presided over the domestic arrangements of the vicarage.

Gladys was the apple of her father's eye, but Mrs.

Gaved, the housekeeper, gave nearly all her love to Harry.

"If anything should happen to Harry," she was often heard to declare, "she was quite sure it would kill her." And now something had happened, but as yet no one knew what.

CHAPTER II.

EXPLANATIONS.

"The man of pure and simple heart
Through life disdains a double part;
He never needs the screen of lies
His inward bosom to disguise."—GAY.

Mrs. GAVED opened the door in response to Farmer Dunstan's knock.

"Is our Jack here?" he asked hurriedly.

"No, he is not," she said, starting back a little, for the farmer's tone and manner alarmed her.

"Nor Harry either?" he queried.

"No, I think not," she answered; "at any rate, I've not seen him."

The farmer drew a sigh of relief, then added—

"They ought to have been back hours ago. I wonder what they can be after."

"Are you sure they are together?" Mrs. Gaved asked, for she knew the young men had not been very friendly with each other for a considerable time past.

"Quite sure," was the reply. "They patched up their quarrel yesterday, and this afternoon they started together for Tregeagle's Head, of all places in the world. I wish to my heart they would come back, for I'm getting anxious."

"Oh, I dare say they are all right," Mrs. Gaved

B

answered. "They are not like children; they know how to take care of themselves."

"Yes, that's true," said the farmer; "but I'm fidgety all the same."

"What are you fidgety about?" asked a sweet childish voice from the doorway of the dining-room.

"Is that you, Gladys?" the farmer asked cheerily.

"Yes, it's I," was the answer; "but what's fidgeting you, Mr. Dunstan?"

"Those boys," he answered; "they went out hours ago on Tregeagle's Head, and haven't returned yet."

"Oh, yes," she said, "Harry has been home a very long time."

"Home?" questioned Mrs. Gaved and the farmer in a breath.

"Yes, he came home just as it was growing dusk. He came in at the side door, and went at once to the study."

"Why did you not let me know?" Mrs. Gaved asked sharply.

"Because he said he did not want to be disturbed, as he wanted to read," was the answer.

Both Mrs. Gaved and the farmer drew a sharp breath that was almost a gasp. Perhaps the same horrible suspicion flashed through the mind of each at the same time.

Mr. Dunstan was the first to recover himself.

"I must see him at once," he said, and he marched straight past Mrs. Gaved to the study door, where he paused for a moment, then turned the handle and entered.

Harry was seated on a low chair, with his elbows on the table, and an open book before him. Two candles were lighted, and were placed one on each side the volume he was reading. He rose instantly when the door opened, gave a little start at sight of the farmer, then advanced to meet him with extended hand.

Mr. Dunstan, however, ignored the friendly sign; he was tingling to the finger-tips with excitement, and with a dread he could not shape into words. But by a manful effort he repressed his feelings, and asked in tones unnaturally calm—

"Where is my boy Jack?"

"Is he not home?" Harry asked, in a voice equally calm and passionless, but a close observer would have noticed an unusual tremor of the lips while he spoke, while a momentary pallor swept like a flash across his swarthy face.

"If he were at home I should not come here seeking him," the farmer answered, in tones that betrayed his feelings in spite of his effort to be calm.

"I am sorry he has not returned," Harry answered, meeting fearlessly the farmer's steady gaze. "I hope he has not been caught by the tide."

"Caught by the tide?" Mr. Dunstan questioned quickly. "How?—where?—in what way?"

"Well, he started to walk round Tregeagle's Head; it was low tide, you know, and he said he could get round on the rocks."

"Madness—folly! I'm sure he attempted no such thing," thundered the farmer, letting go all restraint under the force of a terrible suspicion.

"Sir?" questioned Harry, stepping back a pace, and looking at the farmer with flaming eyes.

"Yes, you may say 'sir,'" roared Mr. Dunstan; "but do you think any one will believe a story like that?"

"It's little concern of mine what people believe," was the quiet but defiant answer. "I am simply speaking the truth."

"God grant you may be," said Mr. Dunstan, quailing a little before the fearless gaze of the young man. "But go on."

"I have little to add," was the answer. "We went first to the top, and had a race across the turf, in which

he came out first; then we wrestled and I threw him;
then we went down to the beach on Pentudy side, and
walked out as far as we could get, and I never saw a
lower tide."

"Aye, it's full moon to-night," assented the farmer.

"Well, then Jack proposed we should attempt to
walk round the head upon the rocks. He said it had
been done, and could be done again, and he was going
to do it."

"And you let him ?" questioned the farmer angrily.

"I could not prevent him," was the answer.

"Did you try ?"

"Well, I said I thought the game was not worth the
candle, and that we should be foolish to run any risks;
but he would not have it that there was any risk
at all."

"Well, and what then ?"

"Then he started out alone. He said he intended to
make the acquaintance of Tregeagle, and have a peep
into his cave if he had time."

"What time would that be ? "

"About a quarter to six. He said the tide would be
at its lowest at six, and that it would be the lowest tide
for the year."

"Well ?"

"I watched him till he was out of sight. He seemed
to have no difficulty in getting from rock to rock, and
soon after he started he called back that he would be
back at Restormel as soon as I should."

"And why did you not come across to see if he had
returned ? "

"I really don't know—I had no anxiety on his
account; and besides, I had no particular wish to be
seen at your house again to-day."

The farmer heaved a long sigh, and stood for several
seconds with bent head, and eyes fixed upon the
ground.

"If what you say is true," he said at length, raising

his eyes and looking hard at Harry, "I fear my poor boy is lost. Oh! Jack, Jack!" and the farmer's voice ended in something like a sob.

"I hope he's safe somewhere," Harry answered, after a pause. "He can swim like a shark and climb like a squirrel; and as for fear—well, he doesn't know what it is."

"That may be true enough," Mr. Dunstan answered; "but if he were safe he'd have been back before this."

"He may have been caught by the tide, as I suggested," was the reply; "he may be now perched upon some ledge of the cliff, waiting for the tide to ebb again. Hadn't we better get ropes and go in search of him?"

"A very good suggestion, if we can get anybody to go with us; but who likes to go on Tregeagle's Head after dark?—tell me that!"

"It's not a question of liking, but of duty," Harry answered.

"Ah, yes, you can talk of duty now," the farmer said bitterly. "If you had minded your duty when you were with him all this might have been prevented."

For a moment the young man's eyes blazed, but he made no further answer.

Half an hour later a dozen men, bearing along with them large coils of rope, and headed by the tall form of the Vicar, might have been seen marching with long, hurried strides in the direction of Tregeagle's Head.

Mr. Penryn had returned from visiting some of his sick parishioners just as farmer Dunstan was taking his leave. It only required a few words for him to take in the whole situation, and then he started with the farmer to beat up recruits for the expedition. He had tramped nearly a dozen miles that afternoon over

his broad parish, and was now almost faint with fatigue.
But he forgot his own weariness in presence of an
emergency like this.

Moreover, he was not so dense but that he could see
how his own son was implicated. If anything had
happened to Jack Dunstan—if he were drowned, for
instance—how easy it would be for suspicion to fall on
Harry. The two boys—for they were still boys to him
—had not been friends of late, as every one knew.
Jack had shot Harry's dog, and Harry had vowed
vengeance on the slayer of his favourite. True they
had patched up their quarrel, though that was not
generally known; and people were very quick in
putting what they called two and two together.

A cold perspiration burst out over the Vicar, and
stood in big drops upon his forehead as he thought of
this. But he had a resolute will and a stout heart, and
after a few moments he put the feeling aside. There
was no time to be wasted in speculating about what
might be.

"Sufficient unto the day is the evil thereof," he muttered to himself, and with this reflection he entered
the first house in the village.

There was no great eagerness, however, to join the
expedition. Many of the men had only just got in
from the fields and stack-yards, for the harvest was late
this year; and a weary tramp out on Tregeagle's Head,
with the chance of falling over cliffs, was not a very
taking prospect. Besides, Tregeagle's Head was not
the place one cared to go after nightfall. They might
not believe all that the fisherfolk of Pentudy believed,
but they believed very much more than they cared to
confess; and if any place in the parish was haunted,
there could be no doubt it was Tregeagle's Head.
When they knew that the Vicar himself was going to
lead the expedition they were somewhat reassured.
They knew he never went out without a copy of the

Prayer-Book in his pocket, and that in itself was sufficient to exorcise even the devil.

It was a glorious night; the moon was at its full, and not a single cloud flecked the heavens. The spirit of the wind lay still as if asleep. Now and then it whispered faintly in the pine wood, or drew a deep breath, like a long-drawn sigh, that shook the pine-needles for a moment, then slept again in utter silence.

On turning the slope of the hill they came in sight of the sea, which lay like a great silver sheet in the light of the moon. Here they paused for a few moments and listened. If any one were calling for help his voice would be distinctly heard on a night like this; but only the low moan of the sea as it surged among the rocks and caves broke the stillness of the hour.

"I'm afraid it's all up with my poor boy!" moaned Farmer Dunstan. "If he were clinging to the rocks anywhere he would be calling for help."

"Let us not give up hope till we are compelled to," said the Vicar, kindly; and then the little company marched on again in silence.

Suddenly they halted with a simultaneous exclamation,—

"See! see! What's that?"

The next moment Dicky Tredinnick had fallen upon his knees, and was muttering with chattering teeth, "Our Father, 'chart in 'ebben," as fast as his tongue could give utterance to the words.

But no one paid heed to Dicky, every eye was fixed upon a moving but headless figure out on the headland. It did not seem to walk, but glided with a graceful motion across the spongy turf, then paused, stretched its ghostly figure to its full height, then slowly sank into the earth.

For several seconds after the apparition had dis-

appeared there reigned the most perfect silence, then
each member of the little company drew a long breath,
as though a great load had been suddenly lifted from
their hearts. Mr. Dunstan was the first to speak.

"It's a token," he said, "my poor boy is dead. We
need not go any further. How he has come by his
death, Heaven only knows; but it is said only the
ghosts of those who have come to their death by unfair
means ever walk the earth. But time will reveal the
secret; " and he looked hard at Harry, who stood pale,
silent, and unmoved.

"Come, friend Dunstan, no hints or insinuations,
please," said Mr. Penryn, sternly. "You are like other
folk, frightened at a shadow."

"I can't help my thoughts," said the farmer, in
subdued tones.

"You can help expressing them, at any rate," was
the reply. "But come, let us be marching, we can
learn nothing by standing here like frightened
children."

"Not a step furder for me," chattered Dicky Tredinnick. "I wouldn't go on that 'ed to-night for a million
poun's."

"Nor me nuther," said Davey Polgooth.

"Nor me!" "Nor me!" came from the lips of two
others.

"Cowards and children," said the Vicar, contempt-
uously. "I really thought the Restormel folk had got
beyond such nonsense."

"But we caan't git ovver what we've seen wi' our
own eyes," said Dicky, with his teeth still chattering.

"You've seen a man or a woman," said the vicar,
"what is there to be frightened about in that?"

"Nay but, Maister Passon, it was a sperit," said
Davey Polgooth; "real men an' wemmin don't vanish
inter the ground in that way."

"We are wasting our breath and time in talk of this

kind," the Vicar answered, shortly. " Those of you who have hearts above chickens, come on," and he marched forward, not deigning to look behind him.

But only half the little company followed his leadership, the others returned to Restormel at a rate of speed that beat all previous records, and earned for themselves thereby an undying reputation.

CHAPTER III.

SUSPICIONS.

" And shall we all condemn, and all distrust,
Because some men are false, and some unjust ?
Forbid it, Heaven ! for better 'twere to be
Duped of the fond impossibility
Of light and radiance which sleep's visions gave,
Than thus to live suspicion's bitter slave."

MRS. NORTON.

MR. PENRYN'S long and hasty strides sorely taxed the breath as well as the courage of some of those who had elected to follow him. Gladly they would have turned back with the others, but the fear of being called cowards restrained them. Moreover, if they could only face the matter out, it would be something to boast of as long as they lived. And so with loudly thumping hearts, and teeth that chattered a little now and then in spite of themselves, they followed in the wake of the Vicar and his son.

At length there was a halt.

"It was somewhere hereabouts that the figure disappeared," Mr. Penryn said, facing round on his little band of followers. "We had better spread ourselves out, and search for an explanation of the disappearance. There may be an opening into some cave, and if so it may prove a clue to many things."

"I think we'd better make for the cliffs," said Farmer Dunstan. "I don't think any good ever comes of hunting ghosts."

"We'd better be sure first it was a ghost," said the Vicar with a smile.

"There ain't no doubt about that," said two or three voices. "Everybody knows as 'ow Tregeagle's 'Ed is haunted."

"Not everybody," was the reply. "I don't know it, for one. But no harm can come of our spreading ourselves out, and making as thorough a search as possible."

After some further parleying the point was conceded, but nothing came of it. The whole crown of the headland was honeycombed with rabbits' burrows; and in all directions were holes large enough for a child to creep into, but anything like an opening into a cave was not to be found.

As they neared the termination of the headland the little party came close together again, the more timid of them falling into the rear. Now the land began to slope towards the sea, and they had to walk with cautious steps. The moon was at their back, and flung their shadows in ungainly lengths before them.

Far below in the deep shadow of the cliffs the water looked black as ink, and surged mournfully among the rocks. The sentinels were almost hidden. Here and there a white ring of foam surrounding a black speck marked the spot of some unusually tall pinnacle, but for the most part the great sea rolled over them undisturbed, and still the waters rose and swelled with a quiet strength and majesty that were even more impressive than its noisy fury when maddened by a western gale.

Now they halted again.

"Some of us," said the Vicar, "will have to go to the very edge of the cliff, and look over, and call, perhaps clamber down here and there, where there is a chance of doing so."

"It'll be rather risky," said Elisha Teague, one of the youngest men of the party; "but I'm willing to take my chance."

"And I'll be another," said Harry Penryn, who had not before spoken.

"Two will be enough," said the Vicar; "the rest of us will hold the ropes."

A minute or two later Harry and Elisha, each with a rope round his waist, were scrambling along the edge of the cliff, calling down into the darkness, and scanning with eager eye every prominent ledge. To the right went Harry, to the left Elisha, and so bit by bit they scanned the whole circle of the cliffs. Down every crevice that offered a foothold they climbed and shouted till they were hoarse. A hundred times, but for the firmly-held ropes, they would have gone head-foremost into the sea; but they never faltered in their determination to make a complete and thorough search; and when they met again at the other end of the headland they looked at each other in silence. Their efforts had proved unavailing, no answering voice had greeted their own, no human form had met their gaze. All the while the solemn sea had seemed to mock them. Like a great monster, gorged with human forms, it lay and moaned in awful mockery—as though it knew the secret and might have told, but would not, out of very cruelty and spite.

It was a silent little party that made its way back over the downs, and down by the pine wood into the wakeful village. Nobody had thought of going to bed until the searchers returned. For in the language of the modern song, "they all loved Jack." His courage and daring touched their imaginations; his uniform kindness and generosity won their hearts.

Between Harry and Jack there was no comparison in the minds of the villagers; Harry was silent and reserved, and they took, or mistook, his silence for sullenness, and his reserve for pride. They never understood him, never tried to do, in fact. He had all his father's dogged stubbornness, without his father's tact and affability. He took no one into his confidence, cared very little for company. When he was home from college he spent nearly all his time alone, loitering in the fields or woods, or rambling on the cliffs. The only people he cared to visit were the Dunstans. They were moneyed people, and lived in a good house, besides which Mary Dunstan, Jack's twin sister, was by universal consent the sweetest girl in all the parish.

There was a general impression abroad in the parish that the Vicar's son was very fond of Mary Dunstan. But none knew how much he loved her, or guessed that he was capable of such passionate devotion. They had always been friends. Mary understood him and trusted him, when others doubted and shrugged their shoulders. He opened his heart more freely to her than to any one else, except to Mrs. Gaved, or "Mammy," as he and Gladys generally called her, and so it was only natural that his liking should grow.

Yet it was only during the last few months that he became conscious of the fact that he loved her. The truth swept over his heart one Sunday morning like a flash, and of all places in the world—in the church. She came up the aisle with her father and Jack, so daintily pretty, so simply attired, so unconscious of her loveliness; her face as sweet as the June rose she wore in her bosom; her smile like the light of heaven, that as Harry gazed at her, his heart seemed to stop; then the hot blood went rushing to his face in a torrent.

He had not seen her before for several months, for his previous vacation he had spent away from home; and now her coming into the church was a complete revelation to him. The liking of years had suddenly blossomed into love; from henceforth she would fill his heart and be the inspiration of his life.

He heard nothing of the prayers or the sermon that day. He saw no one but Mary, heard no voice in the singing but hers, and wondered why her beauty and goodness had never stirred his heart until to-day. Outside the church he waited until she came out, and when she came towards him with a glad smile of welcome on

her face, his heart bounded again; and for a long while
he held her hand in his, and—foolish boy that he
was—fancied that it fluttered like a caged bird in his
hand.

What a lot he had to say to her that morning. Love
seemed to have unloosed his tongue. And when Mr.
Dunstan and Jack went towards their home, and left
them talking together in the old churchyard, it seemed
like a special stroke of good fortune.

"I will walk along with you, Mary," he said. "We
do not dine till two."

"Why where are father and Jack?" she said, looking
quickly round.

"They have run away and left you," he said, with
a laugh. "You see how much they care for your
company."

"Then I'll pay them out by not going home any
sooner than I can help," she answered, her eyes brim-
ful of mirth.

"Then we'll go the long way, round by the plant-
ation," he said. "It's a pity to be in-doors on such a
glorious day as this."

"Oh, yes, that will be delightful," she said; and they
sauntered away together.

But of his love Harry said nothing. To be with her
was enough for the present; to hear her free, un-
trammelled talk, and catch her sweet, spontaneous smile.
If he told his love she might run away from him, and
put an end to such delightful intercourse, and so he
wisely locked the secret in his own heart, and fed his
affection on the smiles she gave him in the sweet
unconsciousness of her generous nature.

But if he liked visiting at the Dunstans before, he
went more frequently than ever now, and from Mrs.
Dunstan and Mary he always received a welcome. At
least he always received a welcome from Mrs. Dunstan
when she was able to see him, for being in delicate
health, she was sometimes unable to leave her room,

and when that was the case Mary atoned for her absence by a warmer greeting than usual.

As yet the innocent heart was untouched by love's young dream. She was a year younger than Harry, and though tall and well-developed for her years, she never thought of herself in any other light than as a girl. And so the tall, dark-eyed young fellow came and went without restraint, and no one suspected for awhile—least of all Mary—what was in his heart.

At length, however, Jack began to grow suspicious, then jealous. The thought of his twin sister Mary caring more for Harry Penryn than himself almost maddened him for the moment. Mary was his all— his councillor, confidant, and friend. He loved her as perhaps few brothers love a sister, and could not brook the thought of another coming between them. Ostensibly Harry came to see him, but he knew better now. It was Mary he wanted all the while, and he resolved, if possible, it should never be.

From henceforth he began to treat Harry with marked coldness and disfavour; hinted broadly that he came to Trevose oftener than he was wanted, and finally completed the breach by shooting Harry's dog, which he found poaching in their preserves.

In justice, however, to Jack it should be said, he did not know at the time to whom the dog belonged, though it must be stated also, he made no apology to Harry until a considerable time after for what he had done. When Mary got to hear she took him severely to task for his conduct.

" You ought to go to him at once and make the most ample apology," she said.

" Which is the very thing I shall not do," he said stubbornly.

" You will not?" she said, in tones of surprise. "That is not like you, Jack. I have never known you behave ungenerously before."

"I don't care," he replied, recklessly. "I wish all intercourse between us to cease."

"Why, Jack," she said, "what can be the matter with you?"

"There's plenty the matter," he said pointedly. "If you can't see it, other folks can."

"I wish you would not talk in riddles," she replied.

"Then I will talk plainly," he answered. "Don't you see how Harry Penryn is trying to come between us?"

"Between us?" she questioned, with a look of bewilderment on her gentle face.

"Yes, between you and me. Don't you see that he is desperately in love with you, and is striving by every possible means to win your affection?"

"Oh, Jack," she said, growing pale to the very lips, "I have never dreamed of such a thing. I am but a child. I am sure you are mistaken."

"No!" he said with clenched fists, "you are eighteen, and a woman. But all the same I cannot bear the thought of any one coming between you and me—and I will not have it."

"Oh, you foolish boy," she said, trembling from head to foot. "Go and make your mind easy; no one shall come between us."

"You promise me that?" he said, a bright smile breaking over his handsome face.

"Of course I promise," she answered. "No one need ever come between us whatever happens." And then she ran away and shut herself in her own room, and tried to think.

She was still trembling violently, and very pale. Jack's words had come to her like a revelation. Suddenly her eyes had been opened, and she was able to see what he saw. A hundred little things in Harry's speech and manner, which before had no significance whatever, now flashed out with unmistakable meaning. What should she do? Should she treat him with coldness and disdain? Cut their friendship short by a sudden stroke? How could she? He had never spoken to her of love; never even hinted of such a thing.

She did not know that Jack had largely solved the problem for her. The young men had met and quarrelled violently. Hard, bitter words were spoken on both sides, and threats had been flung right and left, and for awhile the open rupture was the talk of the village. So matters went on for many weeks, then Mrs. Dunstan, when she was strong enough, interposed, and a reconciliation was effected, and Harry came once more to Trevose.

But who could have imagined such a tragic sequel? The very day after the reconciliation they had gone out together on Tregeagle's Head, and hours later Harry had returned alone, saying nothing of what had become of his companion till questioned, and apparently unconcerned about his return. And now the searchers had come back after a hopeless quest, with despair written on their faces.

What did it all mean? Had they quarrelled again? Had some of the threats been carried out? Had blood been shed? or had an accident cut short a young and hopeful life? These were questions that were debated far into the night. But the conclusion come to in most cases was the same.

CHAPTER IV.

CONCLUSIONS.

"Know, he that
Foretells his own calamity, and makes
Events before they come, twice over doth
Endure the pains of evil destiny.
But we must trust to virtue, not to fate ;
That may protect, whom cruel stars will hate."

DAVENANT.

DURING the night the wind shifted several points, and by morning was blowing half a gale from the west. Among the " sentinels " the long Atlantic rollers surged and sobbed with an ominous sound, and broke on Treg-eagle's head with a roar like distant thunder. High up the cliffs great jets of spray were shot with terrific force, and the deep, calm blue of the previous day was now a wide reach of gleaming foam.

The fishermen of Pentudy and Porthloo scanned the heavens with critical eye, and decided to keep on land for that day at least. The anxious hearts at Restormel listened to the roaring of the angry sea with feelings of dismay, for to them it was the death-knell of their last lingering hope.

Poor Mrs. Dunstan lay in her bed and shuddered ; she could hear the voice of the sea above everything else. Far off, and subdued it might be, but like a mighty pulse it seemed to shake the earth, while ever and anon it raised its voice to higher tones, and cried, " Jack is gone for ever more."

It seemed terrible to lie there in her helplessness. If she could have gone out on Tregeagle's Head, and

battled with the wind, and scanned the face of the
serrated cliffs, it would have been some relief; but to
lie there weak and helpless, listening to the cruel sea
chanting its awful dirge over the dead body of her only
son, seemed more than she could bear.

She tried to shut out the cruel voice by putting her
fingers in her ears, but all in vain; while her excited
fancy was ever picturing her handsome lad lying asleep
below the surging waves, with the slimy, tangled sea-
weed in his bright brown hair, and the great, remorse-
less billows beating his brave, manly face against the
cruel rocks. Oh, it was terrible! terrible!

Only a few hours ago he had come into her room,
his noble face lit up with smiles, his voice full of
music and cheer, and he had kissed her in his old
hearty yet tender fashion, and told her he was going
for a ramble with Harry Penryn.

"I am glad you are going," she said, laying her thin
white hand on his shining hair, "and I hope you two
lads will have no more quarrels."

"Don't you trouble on that score, you dear old
mammy," he said in his heartiest fashion; and then he
kissed her again and vanished through the doorway;
and now he was lying somewhere among the cruel rocks
dead and cold, and his dear face would never gladden
her heart again.

Meanwhile no other subject was discussed throughout
the length and breadth of the village. In all directions
little groups of men and women, and even children,
might be seen with grave, awe-stricken faces, talking in
earnest tones about the fate of Jack Dunstan. That
he was dead there was now no longer any doubt; but
how came he by his death? That was the question
which took precedence of all others.

The story of Harry Penryn seemed straightforward
enough, and under some circumstances might have
been accepted without demur; but in the present
instance there were two or three circumstances which

threw doubts upon his narrative, and which suggested
some ugly suspicions.   An almost forgotten rumour
had been revived again, that he had said, " that for
any one to harm his dog it would be as much as his
life was worth."   To whom he had spoken these
words no one could say; but that he had spoken
them no one had the slightest doubt.   How easy
therefore to put two and two together.   Jack Dunstan
had killed his dog.   That was weeks ago.   Young
Penryn had bided his time, and—— A look or a nod
told the rest.

It is true no one had ever known Harry Penryn do
an evil deed in his life, or even tell a lie; but many
people believed him quite capable of evil if the opportunity should be given.   Who could tell what wicked
passions slept beneath that calm and swarthy face?
Had he not the very look and expression of one who
would never forgive, who would nurse his wrath for
weeks or years if needs be, and deliberately take his
revenge at the last?

Nor was that all.   An apparition had been seen on
Tregeagle's Head by those who had gone to search for
Jack Dunstan.   Even the Vicar had seen it, and had
confessed that he was unable to explain the " phenomenon," whatever that might mean.   But Dicky Tredinnick had sworn that it was the very image of Jack—
just his figure, and size, and gait, everything in fact,
except the head, which was missing.   It is true several
of the others had said that the figure was not that of a
man at all.   But then everybody knew that Dicky was
the fifth son of a fifth son, and such people could see
ghosts when other people who were not so lucky as to
be fifth sons of fifth sons could see nothing.   Dicky was
therefore an authority on the question of ghosts, and
his word should be taken in preference even to that of
the Vicar, who was known to be an unbeliever in such
matters.

And then to crown all, Harry Penryn's conduct, to

say the least, was very suspicious. Why did he slink home through the twilight as though afraid any one should see him or question him? Why did he creep into his home through the side door, and shut himself up alone in his father's study? And why did he turn so pale when Farmer Dunstan challenged him to explain what had become of his son?

Taking everything into account, there could be no doubt there was a strong suspicion of foul play, if not *prima facie* evidence of the fact. The ghosts of people who came to their death by lawful means did not prowl the earth as a rule; and if no other evidence was forthcoming, this of itself was sufficient to prove that there had been foul play. That being so, who was so likely to do the deed as Harry Penryn? Indeed, there was no other who could do it. They had gone out alone together; no one had joined them; hence no hand but his could have struck the blow.

So by noon nearly every one in Restormel had reasoned himself and herself into the firm conviction that Jack Dunstan had been foully murdered, and that Harry Penryn had done the deed. Even Mr. Dunstan, in spite of all his wife and daughter could say, was not able to rid himself of the same feeling.

"Oh, husband!" Mrs. Dunstan had said, "do not add bitterness to our trouble by such a terrible suggestion. We have known Harry ever since he was a child; he has come here more than to any other house in the village, and we have never seen anything in him to warrant such a terrible suspicion."

"That may be so," the farmer replied sullenly; "but people develop murderous tendencies in a moment sometimes. It is the circumstance that makes the criminal."

"No, husband, not always," she said, wiping her eyes. "And I am sure no circumstance would lead Harry to do such a terrible deed."

"God knows, Jane," Mr. Dunstan replied, blowing his nose violently, "I have no desire to harbour such a suspicion; indeed I have been fighting against the feeling all the day. But it is of no use, I can't get over it."

"You must try, husband," Mrs. Dunstan said quietly. "You wrong the lad by such a suspicion, and you add a new bitterness to our trouble, which, God knows, is bitter enough already."

"Bitter," he said, turning away his head to hide his emotion. "Oh that I should have lived to see this day. I had hoped that Jack would have been the strength and comfort of my old age. I would that I had died instead."

"If I had been taken it would have been better still," she replied, bursting into a violent fit of weeping. "For years I have been a burden to myself and to all around me; and yet Jack loved me dearly, and said I was a great comfort to him. Oh, my son, my son!"

For several minutes no other word was spoken. Mary coming into the room, and seeing her father and mother in tears, began to cry also.

After a while the farmer rose to his feet, and hastily brushed his hand across his eyes. "We must try to bow to God's will," he said brokenly, "but it's terrible hard, terrible hard." And without waiting for any one to reply, he hurriedly left the room.

Out in the stack-yard he was greeted by several of his men.

"Foaks is a sayin' very queer things," they began. "An' we be a wondering if you bain't a goin' to take some steps 'bout it."

"Steps about what?" he said, a little bit shortly.

"Why about poor Maister Jack," was the answer.

"I can do no more than I have done already," he said huskily. "There are a dozen people on the look-out all along the shore for what this evening's tide may bring in."

"It ain't that we were meanin'," said Elisha Teague. "People say as there is clear proof there's been foul play."

"People should not talk so fast, Elisha," Mr. Dunstan answered.

"But they will talk, say what you like," said Elisha. "This mornin' they contented theirselves with nods an' looks. But this afternoon they're spaikin' straight out."

"Well, I can't help that," Mr. Dunstan replied. "I am not responsible for what they say."

"Well, it ain't our business 'zactly," said Elisha, "only justice ought to be done. And everybody a'most thinks he ought to be took up on suspicion."

"Who took up?" said Mr. Dunstan severely.

"Why the passon's son. If there's been foul play, he's at the bottom of it, an' nobody else."

"There's no proof of any foul play yet," said the farmer, bringing out the words with an effort.

"Excuse us if we think differently," was the deferential reply, and then the subject dropped.

But it was very clear how feeling was running in the village. Harry Penryn walking out alone that afternoon was treated as though he had been a leper. Even the children got out of his way, and looked at him with wondering eyes and awe-stricken faces. The women stood in their doorways and scowled at him as he passed, and the men refused him the look and nod of friendly recognition they had always been in the habit of giving.

He had never been a favourite in the village, his silent ways and uniform reserve did not suit the loquacious character of the people. They liked a young man who was frank, and friendly, and cheerful. Jack Dunstan was their ideal of what a young man ought to be.

That Harry felt keenly the changed manner of the people there could be no doubt. But he made no sign of it. He walked leisurely through the village with an air of disdainful defiance, and a look of proud contempt upon his face. He met their curious and unfriendly glances with an eye as steady as it had

ever been, and a cheek that never blanched. He knew
of what they were thinking, that in their own hearts
they had already tried and convicted him. But he was
too proud to make any sign, or offer any defence.

But all this seemed but additional evidence of his
guilt. If his hands were clean, how was it he showed
no sign of grief at the loss of his friend? Truly he
seemed a hardened offender. Indeed some of the
villagers declared he was a monster, with neither feeling
nor conscience.

On his way back through the village he met Mary
Dunstan. Her face was very pale, and her eyes red
with weeping. At sight of her his heart gave a great
bound, and for a moment sent the blood rushing in a
torrent to his face, the next moment he grew pale to
the very lips. For the first time he realized that the
beautiful dream of his life was ended, the hopes he
had cherished in secret during the last few months
must go out in despair. Mary Dunstan could never
be his. That fatal yesterday upon Tregeagle's Head,
with its unwhispered secrets, had wrecked his life—
alas! had wrecked other lives than his. All that might
have been was ended now. The world could never
be the same again to many people.

He would have passed Mary without looking at her.
What right had he to let his eyes rest on her sweet
innocent face? Better he should never look into her
eyes again. To meet her reproachful glance would
be worse a thousand times than all the cold and
suspicious looks of all the villagers combined.

But she would not let him pass. She noticed his
averted gaze, and marked too the lines of trouble and
suffering about his mouth. She knew him better
almost than any one in Restormel, better even than
his own father. He might be proud and reserved to
other people, but he had never been proud or reserved
to her; and more than all, he loved her. By an
intuition keen and true, she was as certain of this now

as though he had told her with his own lips. She had never thought of loving him, but somehow the sight of his suffering face to-day touched her heart as it had never been touched before.

"Harry," she said, stopping in front of him, "won't you call at Trevose to-day?"

Suddenly the colour came back to his face, and a mist came up before his eyes. But he could not speak; he tried to articulate some apology, but the words refused to come.

"Why do you not speak?" she asked, in tones that trembled a little, in spite of her effort to be calm.

Then he shook himself, as one coming out of a sleep, and raised his eyes to hers.

"You do not condemn me, Mary?" he asked in low tones.

"Condemn you, Harry! No. I thought you knew me better."

"How should I? The whole village has gone against me; and I have no defence."

"There is your word," she said.

"Which goes for nothing in a case like this."

"But Jack may turn up yet," she said. "I cannot give up the hope that he may still be alive."

"That is impossible, I fear," he answered. "He could not possibly live through weather such as we have been having since early this morning."

"Then you have given up hope yourself?" she asked, with trembling lips.

"Yes, I have no hope at all. And I see all the consequences. They will hang me in a month as a murderer."

"Oh, Harry, don't say such horrid words," she said in appealing tones.

"It's best to be prepared," he said. "And I don't know that it matters much. The shorter the life the less of trouble. And death is better than life without hope and without love."

"Oh, Harry, please don't talk in that way," she pleaded.

"Then I won't," he answered with a little bit of the old defiance in his tone. "But you'll remember my words when I am gone. Let us say good-bye here; to-morrow I may be in prison."

"But won't you shake hands?" she said, in a tone of surprise.

"If you wish it, yes," he said, trying to steady his voice. "I did not think of touching your hand again. Now I will kiss your fingers, Mary. The first kiss and the last. There! Good-bye, Mary, and fare——" But the word ended in a sob. He had borne up bravely, but the strain had been too much for him.

He did not give her time to speak again. He dropped her hand suddenly, and was gone.

CHAPTER V.

THE STORM BURSTS.

"Oh, now comes that bitter word—but,
Which makes of nothing what was said before,
That smooths and wounds, that strikes and dashes more
Than flat denial, or a plain disgrace."—DANIELS.

THE anxious day was drawing to a close, when a whisper ran like wildfire through the village of Restormel that the secret of Jack Dunstan's fate had been discovered, but whence the whisper originated, or how much it implied, none could guess. Every one was asking every one else "who had made the discovery, and what it amounted to?" But to these questions no one could give any answer. Yet the whisper went the rounds, and grew in the frequent telling. Surmises and speculations at length got added thereto, and were passed on as actual occurrences. Now it was that his body had been seen in the foaming surf, and a fruitless effort had been made to get at it. This whisper started at the top of the village; by the time it got to the bottom people were saying that his body had been thrown up by the tide at Pentudy, that a number of fishermen were now bringing it towards Restormel, that an ugly knife stab had been found in the neck, with other clear proof that a most foul murder had been committed.

Children listened to these stories with wondering eyes and terror-stricken faces, and thought in their hearts what a cruel monster Harry Penryn must be;

while men and women clenched their fists savagely, and said they would like to hang him there and then.

Yet for some unaccountable reason, within half an hour this rumour had entirely changed its complexion, then it was dropped altogether, for people did not know what to believe. But behind it all there remained the rooted conviction that something had come to light; some secret or clue had been unearthed. What gave colour to this conviction was the fact that Abel Tregonning the constable had been seen to leave his house very hurriedly, and to make his way across the fields in the direction of Pentudy.

Soon after nightfall another rumour began to take shape and coherence. Elisha Teague had seen a pedlar who had come from Pentudy, and who had informed him that a rumour was afloat among the fisher-folk that on the previous day two men had been seen on the top of Tregeagle's Head, the one chasing the other, that near the extreme end they met and embraced in what seemed a deadly struggle, that a few minutes later only one form was seen, who walked away alone, and appeared to descend the cliff on the Porthloo side. This scene was witnessed by some fishermen who were out in their boats at the time, but the distance was too great for them to distinguish who the combatants were.

As this story tallied in so many respects with Harry's own version of the affair, it seemed probable that a real clue had been found at last, and that the truth was sure to come out sooner or later.

Like all previous stories, it grew immensely with the telling, and in the course of two or three hours the original rumour was almost buried beneath an accumulation of startling and horrible details.

It was nearly midnight when Abel Tregonning the constable returned to his home. But late as it was quite a small crowd was awaiting his arrival. But, as became a servant of the king in such grave circumstances, Abel was very reticent. For the first time since he had been sworn in as a constable, now several years ago, did he feel that he was a real limb of the law. Hitherto his services to the king and his country had been confined chiefly to impounding stray cattle, frightening small boys who had a disposition to pilfer, and sobering one or two well-known topers who were disposed to be unruly by giving them a few hours in the stocks, in conformity with magisterial orders.

But the present case was one of mystery, perhaps of murder, and if he could successfully unravel the business it might mean a pension for him, or at least a nice little sum in the shape of blood-money. He was not therefore going to show his hand any more than he could help. He did admit, however, that the story the pedlar had told was substantially true. One or two points in it were not quite correct; but very likely the next day would bring many things to light, and clear up the whole difficulty.

So after sundry grunts and nodding of heads the little crowd dispersed to their several homes, much wondering what the morrow would unfold.

Nor were they the only people who wondered. In the vicarage there were consternation and dread, such as had never been known in it before. Even the death of his wife seemed less terrible to the Vicar than this dread suspicion that hung over his son. More than once he tried to draw Harry into a conversation on the subject, but without success.

"I have already told all I know," he said, with quiet emphasis. "If I were to talk for a month I could say no more."

But this did not altogether satisfy Mr. Penryn. He would have been better pleased if Harry had grown excited, and had protested against the insinuation. But of all the members of the household Harry seemed the most unconcerned. Poor Mrs. Gaved had cried and protested herself into hysterics; little Gladys walked about the house pale and silent as a ghost;

while the Vicar every now and then groaned aloud.
But if Harry suffered much he made little or no sign.

And yet he was as acutely sensible of the danger he
was in as any of the others. He had balanced the
probabilities, and had come to a definite conclusion.
Before getting into bed that night he carefully put his
room in order.

"The chances are this is the last night I shall be in
it," he said to himself, as he carefully straightened the
drawers, "so I had better make things tidy while I
have the chance."

For a full hour he was engaged in this occupation,
and then, after a careful survey of the room, he quietly
undressed and crept into bed. But he did not attempt
to sleep. The moon was shining brightly into the
room, so that every object in it was distinctly visible.
The silence was unbroken, save for the swish of the
wind in a row of pine-trees which grew near the house,
and an occasional moan from the distant sea.

Once the sound of a footfall in an adjoining room fell
upon his ear, and caused a swift rush of tears to his
eyes. "Poor father!" he said to himself, "it is a pity
I ever lived to be such a trouble to him, and to them
all."

But he did not indulge in reflections of this kind
for any length of time. "I must not give way to
weakness," he said to himself. "The future has to be
faced, and I must put on as bold a front as possible.
What can't be cured must be endured, and so I had
better brace myself for what is coming."

He knew that the Autumn Assizes would begin at
Bodmin on the following week. He knew that the
Restormel public had made up its mind already. He
knew that juries made light of bringing in a verdict
of guilty where there was no very strong proof of guilt.
He knew that judges sentenced men to be hanged for
poaching, and burglary, and sheep-stealing; and he
knew also that judgment was very soon carried into

effect after sentence had been passed. Hence it seemed by no means improbable that within a fortnight he might be tried, condemned, and hanged. It was certainly a grim prospect, and if his courage began to fail at thought of it, it is not to be wondered.

Then the thought flashed across his mind, why should he not escape while he had the chance? Between midnight and eight o'clock in the morning he might put five and twenty miles between himself and Restormel; or at some intermediate point he might catch the early morning coach. If he could reach Plymouth he could easily lose himself in the crowd. He could disguise himself as a sailor, and perhaps ship himself to some foreign port.

But then the question arose, for why should he do this? Was life such a precious thing, that for the mere sake of living he would be content to remain a fugitive the rest of his days? Nay, under the circumstances was not death to be preferred?

Whether he were innocent or guilty, the result would be the same. He was *believed* to be guilty, hence everything he cared for was lost to him. Mary, and Mrs. Gaved, and Gladys, and perhaps his father, believed him innocent now; but even they might lose their faith after awhile. And what then? Suppose he escaped the clutches of the law, Mary Dunstan was lost to him for ever, and life without her love, or at least the hopes of winning her, did not offer any attractions. No; all things considered, he might as well shuffle off the mortal coil as quickly as possible. In the grave there would be no aching hearts or fearful forebodings. Once under the sod, and he would be at peace.

With this reflection he turned over on his side, and soon fell fast asleep.

The next morning was a very silent and a very apprehensive one to all at the vicarage. Every one had a feeling as though a storm was gathering, and that at any moment it might burst suddenly upon them.

No one seemed to have any appetite for breakfast, or to be in any mood for conversation. At prayers the Vicar's voice very sensibly trembled, and more than once he brushed his hands hastily across his eyes to hide the traces of his emotion.

Harry was paler and much more restless than he had ever been. He seemed to be haunted by the general foreboding that brooded like a nightmare over the house; and in his heart he wished that if anything were going to happen it would happen quickly, and be done with.

After prayers the Vicar retired to his study. But he was utterly unable to read, and after one or two fruitless attempts, he put on his hat and marched forth into the village. Everywhere people looked at him with an expression of pity and commiseration. Around the little court-house, in which he occasionally sat as a magistrate, was a small crowd, chiefly of women and children; but he did not speak to them nor they to him. They ceased their conversation and stood silent until he passed, then turned and nodded significantly to each other. Perhaps they knew more than he did; perhaps some whisper had come to their ears that had not reached the vicarage.

At Trevose Mr. Penryn hesitated for a moment, then pushed open the garden gate and marched up to the house. Mary saw him coming, and opened the door before he had time to knock.

"Is your father at home?" was almost his first greeting.

"No, Mr. Penryn," she said, a little hesitatingly. "He had to go out this morning."

"And your mother, how is she?"

"She is very prostrate indeed. This trouble seems to be killing her."

"Ah, my child," and the Vicar's voice trembled as he spoke, "this is a terrible blow to us all."

"It is indeed," she said, the tears coming into her

eyes. "To me it seems like some terrible dream. I can't at all realize it yet."

"God grant we may not have to realize anything worse," he answered solemnly. "But in spite of myself, I am full of the gravest apprehension."

"But you do not believe that Harry is guilty?" she said, with an eager light in her eyes.

"No, I cannot bring myself to believe that. But I fear it is true he flung out some awkward threats, and though they might not mean much to him, they may mean a great deal in the ears of others—a jury, for instance. Ah, my child, how careful we should be of the words we speak, for even idle words shall be brought into judgment."

"The fishermen of Pentudy are prepared to swear to much," she said at length, with a little sob.

"Ah," he said, starting back, "that is something I have not heard. Is there some fresh news at hand?"

"Oh, I do not know," she said, sitting down and beginning to cry. "There are so many stories afloat that I do not know what to believe or think. It is hard enough to lose poor Jack, without having all this horrible mystery and apprehension piled upon our grief."

"But the fishermen," he said; "what are they saying?"

"Well, the latest is that a man named Dan Polslee is prepared to swear that he saw Harry push Jack over the cliff."

"Oh, no, I trust he is not prepared to swear that," said Mr. Penryn, turning pale to the very lips.

"I am only repeating what they say," she answered in a low voice.

"If any man is prepared to swear that, it is all over with my boy," he said huskily. "God help us all!" And without waiting to say good morning he strode hurriedly out of the house.

He scarcely noticed as he passed that the crowd around the court-house had considerably increased, and that there was a look of intense excitement on nearly every face.

On, on he went down the village street, increasing his speed at nearly every step. Across the churchyard he nearly ran. For the moment he lost sight of every other consideration in one consuming desire to save his son. Harry might yet escape. He might be disguised sufficiently, perhaps, to avoid detection. He should be given money enough to get away to the most distant part of the world. He could not believe his son was guilty; and to let him die when he was innocent if he could save him would be a crime. But if this were to be done there was not a moment to lose; a warrant for his arrest might be issued at any moment. He must act now, or not at all.

He had nearly reached the house when he stopped suddenly, while all the blood swept from his face, leaving him deadly pale.

" Too late ! " he groaned; and the next moment Harry descended the steps with a pair of handcuffs upon his wrists, and a constable on either side of him.

CHAPTER VI.

THE ARREST.

" The footstep of a future doom we hear,
    Against whose coming nought may e'er prevail ;
And vague presentment of some evil near
    Falls on our heart, and turns its current pale.
We tread upon the verge of mighty things—
    We grasp the veil, but with unseeing mind ;
Death hides the light the soul unconscious brings,
    And on the edge of fate we wander blind."
                                                SWAIN.

THE arrest of Harry Penryn only tended to increase the excitement that had been intense enough before. Everybody knew what was going to happen, and as a consequence nearly all work was suspended. Men and women came in from the fields and from distant farm-yards, and crowded the long village street from end to end. Even fishermen came up from Porthloo and Pentudy, and stood watchful and silent, waiting the appearance of the culprit. He came at length, his hands clasped in front of him, his wrists locked in steel. He had asked that this last indignity might not be laid upon him, but the constable was obdurate ; he must do his duty, he said, and show no respect to persons.

"You need not fear I shall attempt to run away," Harry said, and then the subject dropped.

Yet he was glad his father was not there to witness the beginning of his humiliation. He hoped he would not return until he was safely locked in his cell.

This hope, however, was nipped in the bud. Scarcely

had he descended the doorstep between the two constables than he came face to face with his father. For a moment his eyes dropped, while the hot blood rushed in a torrent to his cheeks and brow.

Mr. Penryn stood like one stricken with paralysis. He never knew till that moment how dear Harry was to him. He had lavished the wealth of his affection upon his youngest born; with Harry he had always been more or less cold and distant. The two seemed to have very little in common with each other; yet all unconsciously the hope of the father had centred in his son. Now and then he had found himself dreaming of Harry as a successful barrister, swaying courts and juries with his eloquent appeals. He would have been better pleased if his son had consented to enter the Church; but Harry would never hear of it.

"He should never be fit for a clergyman," he had always said; and at length his father had given his consent for him to study for the bar. Since that time they had occasionally talked together on the subject, and pictured the day when he would be called to the bar.

"Called to the bar!" the same thought flashed through the mind of each when they met face to face. Truly he was being called to the bar sooner than he expected, and in a way neither had anticipated. For a moment a cynical smile curled Harry's proud lip, but it vanished instantly. The humiliation was too deep for cynicism.

Yet swiftly as the smile passed Mr. Penryn saw it, and was puzzled. What did it mean? Could it be possible that Harry was guilty of the foul deed with which he was to be charged? But he put the thought from him. Not until there was some absolute proof of his guilt would he believe it.

Harry lifted his eyes and met his father's as he passed him, but no word was spoken. Had either been of a demonstrative nature there would have been a scene.

The two constables were puzzled. Were father and son so devoid of feeling that they should betray no emotion under such circumstances. If they thought of the old adage—" Still waters run deep," they did not apply it in the present case. It was rather proof that the son was guilty, and that the father believed him to be so. As a matter of fact, however, neither was able to speak. Mr. Penryn made an effort more than once; but his tongue seemed paralyzed. It was not until he got into his own study that he could speak at all, and then he poured out his heart's agony in prayer to God.

He did not attempt to follow his son through the crowded street. As yet he felt unable to witness his humiliation. Harry saw the gaping multitude, and yet he walked on as though he saw not. There was no feebleness or hesitancy in his step, nor droop in his eyelids. Straight before him he looked, and saw on either side of him the sea of faces, but he distinguished no individual face.

The people were very respectful, though scarcely sympathetic. He was their Vicar's son, and their hearts were sore for him, and yet they were very angry that this young man should bring so much trouble upon others. Now and then a low hiss was heard, followed by a few muttered sentences, but that was the only demonstration of any kind.

As soon as the trio passed the crowd closed in behind, and marched to the quick step of the constables and their prisoner. Such a procession had never been seen in Restormel before. It was a new experience even to the oldest inhabitant.

The court-house was at the extreme end of the village proper. Trevose and a few other of the better class houses were beyond it. Adjoining the court-house on the far side was the " lock-up," or what the village children called the " dark hole." Adjoining this again was the constable's house, to which was attached a joiner's shop, in which Abel Tregonning spent the greater portion of his time, for he was an industrious man, and his duties as constable took him very little from his work. The lock-up was not by any means an inviting place, for prisoners, of whatever kind, were treated with but scant courtesy in those days. John Howard had not yet commenced his philanthropic labours, and no one seems to have imagined that there was anything wrong in the English prison system.

The lock-up at Restormel was about six feet square, without chimney or any means of ventilation. The floor was composed of a mixture of lime and sand, and was as cold as clay. One small window near the roof let in a few feeble rays of light, but was never opened under any circumstances, and there is no record that it was ever cleaned. Hence the light that struggled through never dazzled the eyes of the prisoners with its brightness. A narrow oaken door, thickly studded with large square-headed nails, opened into the lobby of the court-house, from which alone access could be gained to the street. A couple of short planks stretched from end to end of the room, and pushed close against the wall opposite the door, served for a seat during the day, and a bed during the night. Beyond this the room was absolutely bare.

Harry took in the whole situation in a moment; but he made no complaint. He had made up his mind to accept his fate as stoically as possible. His sufferings would not last many weeks at the longest, " and what could not be cured would have to be endured." Such was his philosophy, and he intended to abide by it. Since he left the vicarage he had not opened his lips, but now that he was alone with his gaolers he turned to Abel and said—

" Could you not open that window a little ? this place is suffocating."

" It ain't no worse for you than for others," was the discourteous answer. " We don't have no favourites here."

"I have no wish to be made a favourite of," Harry answered with a smile.

"You wouldn't be ef you did," was the quick rejoinder. "Crimes sich as yours don't desarve no consideration."

"Exactly," said Harry; "though I think you might wait until the day of trial before you constituted yourself judge and jury."

"As for that, the jury'll make short work of 'e, an' the judge too."

"You think so?"

"I'm sure on it."

"Why are you so sure?"

"Because there be men who seed 'e with their own eyes push 'm ovver the cliff."

"They are going to swear that, are they?"

"Iss; an' what have you to say agin it?"

"Nothing to you."

"I should think not; an' nothing to nobody else, I reckon."

"That remains to be seen. But when am I to be brought before the magistrates?"

"Monday mornin'."

"And it's now Saturday forenoon; so I shall have forty-eight hours of this for a start."

"'Zactly. It'll be a little breakin' in for 'e."

"Just so. Will you allow me any books or writing materials?"

"I dunno. All depends on 'ow you behave?"

"Which, translated into plain English, means, I presume, how much am I willing to pay you for the privilege?"

"P'r'aps so, and p'r'aps not so;" and with this sententious remark the constables took their departure, Abel carefully locking the door behind him.

"Hard'n'd young 'un that," said Nathan Fraddon, the Pentudy constable, as he and Abel walked along the lobby together towards the outer door.

"Very," said Abel; "but we'll take the starch out ov 'im on Monday."

"Ay; the case is pretty clear agin 'im."

"As clear as daylight," said Abel.

"Ef we could onny find the body," said Fraddon.

"As well without," Abel replied. "Everybody knows he's dead; so whether 'is body be found or no, it won't make no defference, I'm thinkin'."

"Very likely," said Fraddon. And then the outer door was thrown open, and they found themselves in the street.

The crowd had scarcely diminished at all; but it was no longer a silent one. Every man seemed eager to give expression to his opinion, and so a hundred tongues were wagging at one and the same time.

"Didn't he look defiant?" "He never feels his position, not he." "As 'ard as stones, that's what he is." "He'll go to the gallows without wincin'." "Did you notis how bowld he kept 'is 'ed hup?" "An' actually smiled scornful." "He'll never confess." "They'll make his stiff neck longer afore he's a month owlder." "Comes of goin' to college, I reckon." "Ef 'e 'ad pity for others one could pity 'im."

These and a hundred other remarks were bandied about like shuttlecocks, some of which fell on Abel's ears as he passed, with a condescending smile on his face, through the crowd. But he made no remark, nor deigned to answer a single question.

Meanwhile Mary Dunstan had been sitting at the window of her bedroom in the warm September sunshine, feeling as though winter had suddenly dropped down upon her, and that she would never be warm again. Outside in the garden the birds were singing in the damson and cherry trees, as though there was no such thing as trouble in the world; and in the tall pine-trees which grew at the end of the house the wind was whistling musically and free. But she had no ear for the music of the wind or birds. The very brightness of the day seemed to mock her misery, and yet she kept in the sunshine for the sake of the warmth.

She had been there by the window in the same position for more than an hour. She had watched the villagers gathering in the street, first by ones and twos, then by dozens and scores, and she knew only too well for what purpose they had come. It seemed to her so like a funeral—the people were so quiet, and their faces so grave. She felt that she ought to get away from the window and draw the blinds, but a spell was on her which she could not resist. He was coming—he who loved her, a prisoner, doomed perhaps to die. Why did she think more of him at that moment than of her dead brother, who had always been the idol of her heart? She could not tell; only she felt that Harry was being wrongfully accused, insulted and degraded before all the village, with none to cast a pitying eye upon him, or bestow a glance of sympathy. And so her young heart went out to him with a thrill of compassion such as she had never felt for any one before.

Moreover, in questioning her own heart since that day, her eyes had been opened to the fact that Harry loved her. She had been almost startled at the discovery she made. He was not as a stranger to her, and never could be; nor even was "friend" the name. If he were gone, what other friend could take his place? She would not own to herself yet that she loved him; she was too young to think of love. Moreover, her heart was too full of grief for her lost brother, and too full of anxiety for her mother, to harbour such a feeling. And if they had only let Harry alone, she would scarcely have thought of him at all. But now that all the village had turned against him, and every tongue was abusing him, she could not help thinking of him, she could not help pitying him, and pity began to change her friendship into love.

It might not be seemly for her to sit there in the window staring down into the street, but she could not

help it. Though her flesh was creeping to her finger-
tips, and her heart seemed almost at a standstill, stay
she must; she must look upon his dark, handsome face
once more; she might never see him again.

At length there was a movement in the crowd, and
then—it seemed almost an age, though it could only
have been few seconds—he came into sight, walking
erect between two constables. She could see his hands
clasped in front of him, and knew that his wrists were
locked in the cruel steel. Oh, she could have gone and
struck the constables dead for subjecting him to this
indignity.

Yet *he* did not seem to mind. Onward up the long
street they came, nearer and nearer, the crowd closing
in behind. Close to the window she pressed her face.
Would he look so far, she wondered ?—would he see her
if he looked ? Alas! if he saw her he could make no
sign, for his hands were bound.

Now they have reached the court-house. See! he
pauses for a moment, and looks up towards her and
smiles. She waves her hand and smiles in reply. She
hopes he will not mistake the meaning of her smile.
She means it as a message of hope and courage to him.
Perhaps he will understand.

She draws the blind now, and goes to her bedside,
and kneels down and prays; she feels that unless God
helps her, her strength will utterly fail.

CHAPTER VII.

A DISMAL SUNDAY.

" Each Sabbath is a little pause
  Between the world and me ;
My selfish troubles it suspends,
  It makes my soul more free.
Each Sabbath, then, I turn aside,
  O world ! from thy pursuits ;
'Tis sacred to the Eternal cause,
  And sacred be its fruits."

THE day following was long remembered in Restormel as one of the most dismal Sundays ever known. From morning till night the rain came down unceasingly, while the wind wailed and moaned in the most doleful fashion. Very few people ventured out of doors. There was nothing to go out for, except to attend service at the church ; and as at the best of times they had no very burning desire for worship, very few cared to face the rain, that they might put in an appearance at church. The few who did go were impelled more by curiosity than anything else. They wanted to see how the Vicar would act under the circumstances, and whether he would conduct service as usual.

The church was dismally cold—colder than usual to-day ; for the wind crept in everywhere, and moaned around the sharp gables, with a cry almost like one in pain, and rattled the glass in the latticed windows, and called hoo-hoo-hoo-o through the big keyhole of the door.

The few people who sat in the great gloomy church,

waiting for the service to begin, listened and shivered.
They thought of the Vicar's son, sitting in his gloomy
cell, hearkening to the wind sweeping past, and the
beating of the rain. They thought, too, of handsome
Jack Dunstan, lying down among the rocks and sea-
weed, wrapped in calm and dreamless sleep, undisturbed
by wind and wave that roared above him.

Up in the tower, Ned Blight, the sexton, was still
tolling the bell, and wondering when the Vicar was
going to commence the service. Clang, clang, clang, in
monotonous regularity the sound rang out; now loud
and clear, now muffled and low, as the wind caught the
sound waves and beat them back or bore them on.

At length the bell ceased, and a moment later Mr.
Penryn's voice was heard in low, mournful tones, echoing
through the church. But he never lifted his eyes to
the few people who sat and listened. Like one in a
dream he read the prayers and lessons, for his heart
and thoughts were otherwhere all the while. He was
not a sympathetic man—indeed most people thought
him a trifle hard and cold; but what he suffered that
day no one knew. He had tried to get some one to
take service for him, but had failed, and so he was
compelled to go through with it himself.

"Would he preach?" was the question which ran
through the mind of almost every one present. They
knew he was not the man to shirk a duty if he had
strength to fulfil it. Yet when he came out of his
vestry, attired in his black gown, and slowly mounted
the tall pulpit stairs, a thrill of sympathy ran through
every heart. He looked so much paler in contrast with
the black gown; even his lips were almost livid, and
his hands trembled visibly. Much longer than usual
he bowed his head in silent prayer, and then he
announced his text, but never daring to lift his eyes.

"God is our refuge and strength : a very present help
in time of trouble."

But he had essayed an impossible task. Before he

had spoken a dozen sentences, the people were weeping silently. He tried not to heed the fact; tried to brace himself for the ordeal. In simple, sympathetic words, he went on to tell how God had been the refuge of His people in all generations; how in all their troubles He helped and sustained them; how He was as much the refuge of His people now as in ancient times, and how He was always near in their need—a present help, a present Friend.

But as one by one low sobs smote on his ear, his own voice faltered and broke. He made no allusion to his own trouble, but it was in his heart, and in the thoughts of those who listened. He tried to put away the picture of Harry sitting alone in his cell, but he could not do it. In the mournful wind that wailed around the church, and in the splash of the dismal rain against the window-panes, he seemed to hear the voice of his boy calling for help and sympathy, till at length he could no longer see the manuscript before him for the tears that filled his eyes. Then his voice failed him altogether, and ended in a sob.

A long and painful silence followed, broken only by the stifled sobs of the people; but the Vicar made no further attempt to go on with his sermon. When he had sufficiently recovered himself he pronounced the benediction, and so the service ended.

Home through the driving rain the people hurried, stopping to speak to no one; and when they got before their cheerful fires, they tried to shake off the oppression that had been upon them all the day. But the effort was a fruitless one; never seemed a Sabbath so long or so dreary. If they could have got out of doors the time would have passed swiftly enough; but to sit looking out of the window, watching the rain sweeping across the valley, and listening to the dreary autumn wind sighing round the house, was in itself enough to make them melancholy. They would have shut out from their minds all thoughts of Jack Dunstan and

Harry Penryn, had they been able to do so, but it was not possible. Every moan and surge of the sea that came borne over the hill by the melancholy wind made them think of the bright, handsome face that had been so suddenly removed from their midst.

For Harry, sitting alone in his dark cell, very little commiseration was felt. Here and there was a man or woman who could not believe he was guilty. They had seen the grave, reserved lad grow up from childhood; and though he had never been a general favourite like Jack, no one had ever known him do a wrong, and they would not believe he had done this wicked deed. But it must be confessed they were in a very small minority.

In the house of Robert Dunstan the gloom and oppression steadily deepened. Mary stood the greater part of the day pressing her hot brow against the cold window-pane, trying to collect her troubled and bewildered thoughts. In the adjoining room, her mother seemed to be growing steadily weaker, as though she had relaxed her hold upon life and was just quietly and painlessly slipping out of life. She had tried her best to be brave for her husband's and Mary's sake, but the effort had been unavailing. Jack was the idol of her heart, and now that he was gone it seemed as though life had nothing left.

No one could speak to her a hopeful word, or hint at a possibility that her son might yet be alive, for every one regarded his death as an absolute certainty, and indeed it would seem absurd to come to any other conclusion. But she had a strong hope that his body would be found; this now seemed to be all her desire. She thought if she could look once more upon his face, bruised and swollen as it might be, she would die content.

And so she waited and listened for approaching footsteps, for the steady tread of those who should bring home the body of her son. But the dreary hours of the Sabbath passed on, and the rain beat with dreary monotony against the window, but no footstep crunched the gravel on the garden walk.

Once or twice she called through the open door to her daughter—

"Are you keeping watch, Mary?"

"Yes, mother," came the answer, in tones so changed that she could hardly recognize them.

"They will surely bring my boy to me soon," she said, as though speaking to herself. "But let me know as soon as you see them coming."

"I cannot see far," Mary answered; "the rain is so thick, and is driven like a gray mist across the valley."

"But they will bring him in spite of the rain," she quietly answered. "I think they must find him to-day."

"Oh, I hope not," Mary said in low tones.

"Hope not?" said Mrs. Dunstan, quickly. "You hope they will not find him?"

"I cannot help it, mother," Mary answered with a sob. "While he cannot be found the hope lives within me that in some strange way all this mystery may be made clear."

"My foolish child," the mother answered, in low, sad tones. "We know the cruel sea has claimed him; I saw him last night standing before me with sea-weed in his shining hair, and the salt sea-water dripping from his clothes. Father thought I was asleep and dreaming. But it was no dream. I have not slept at all, and so I could not dream. Come here, Mary, and let me tell you about it."

And Mary left the window and came and stood by her mother's bed.

"Step back a little, Mary; there—stand still. That is just where he stood. I saw him as plainly as I see you now. His eyes were wide open, and bright and full of love as they used to be. His lips just a little apart, but there was nothing of death about him; his cheeks were as ruddy as when he kissed me on Thursday afternoon; but his clothes were dripping wet and clinging closely about him, and the slimy sea-weed had woven itself among the locks of his beautiful hair."

"And did he speak?" Mary asked, with a little shudder.

"No, he spoke no word. I did hope he would speak, for I was not the least afraid. I wonder at that, for I have always dreaded seeing a spirit. Yet when he stood there where you are standing I was as unmoved as I am now."

"But was it not dark?" Mary asked. "How could you see him so clearly?"

"I cannot answer that," was the reply, and Mrs. Dunstan drew her pale hand slowly across her eyes, as though the question had perplexed her. "I only know it was dark before he came and after he went away. But while he stood there it was as light as it is now."

"And did you not speak to him, mother?" Mary asked, after a pause.

"No, Mary, my tongue was holden that I could not speak; a thousand questions rushed through my mind, but I could not give utterance to them."

"That is strange," Mary said in low tones, as though speaking to herself.

"God does not let us inquire into the mysteries of the future," Mrs. Dunstan answered. "It was my persistent effort to speak that drove him away."

"I do not understand," Mary said, with a bewildered air.

"While he stood there," was the answer, "and I feasted my eyes upon his face, he smiled upon me sweetly, then raised his right hand and with his fore-finger pointed upward, and I, fearing he was going to leave me, struggled to speak, but with the first sound I uttered he vanished, leaving the room in darkness."

"I think it must have been a dream, mother," Mary answered, after a long pause.

"No, Mary. Do not say that again. I woke your

father with the sound I made, though he persists in saying he was not asleep."

But Mary was still unconvinced, though she made no further remark.

"I should not have told you this," Mrs. Dunstan went on, after a long pause, "but that I wanted to get this vain hope out of your mind. Now go to the window again and watch, and do not forget to tell me when you see them coming."

And Mary stole noiselessly out of the room and took up her position by the window again. Across the garden and down the street just a little way, she could see the gables of the old court-house, adjoining which was the lock-up, but not visible from where she stood.

Is it strange that her thoughts should constantly revert to the solitary inmate of that cold and cheerless cell, or that she should long to go to him and speak a word of hope and cheer? The knowledge that he loved her appealed to her heart in a way she could not understand, while the further knowledge that he was suffering and forsaken awoke all the sympathy of her nature.

She did not know if she loved him or not; she did not put the question to her heart. It was enough that he was her friend, and had been ever since she could remember; that he had been wrongfully accused and there was none to help him. And so in her mind she was constantly picturing him sitting, sad and desolate, listening to the swish of the wind and the splash of the rain.

Now and then she chided herself for letting her thoughts stray from her brother. But how could she help it? Thinking of one invariably suggested the other, and so, try as she would, she could not keep Harry out of her thoughts.

Down at Pentudy and Porthloo, numbers of people paced the beach from morning till night. Dressed in oilskins and with their sou'-westers pulled low over

E

their necks, they did not mind the wind and the driving rain. But when night closed round them again and the sea refused to give up her dead, they came to the conclusion that Jack would never be seen again. It was not a matter to be wondered at; the sea was deep and the currents strong around Tregeagle's Head, and a body sinking down into some deep ocean pool might be undisturbed for ever. According to the evidence to be given at to-morrow's trial, Jack had been pushed off the far end of Tregeagle's Head. Hence he would fall among the "sentinels," and sink into deep water at once. And so it was possible that neither tide nor current would ever touch him or disturb his rest. The cruel sea had claimed him and would not give him up.

It was not absolutely necessary for the requirements of law that his body should be found. The trial would go on in any case. It might simplify matters if the sea would give him up, but if she would not there was an end of it. It was clear enough he was dead, the question to be decided was—How came he by his death?

CHAPTER VIII.

THE INQUIRY BEGINS.

"Oh ! guide me through the various maze
My doubtful feet are doom'd to tread ;
And spread Thy shield's protecting blaze,
When dangers press around my head."
HAWKESWORTH.

MONDAY morning broke gray and cold. The rain
had ceased, but the clouds hung low, and trailed their
robes along the upper slopes of Carn Duloe and completely hid its crown. Soon after daybreak little knots
of people began to gather in the street near the court-
house, and to discuss the great trial which was so soon
to begin. Over the hill from Pentudy and Porthloo
they came, and from beyond Carn Duloe for many a
mile. Eager to catch a glimpse of the prisoner's face,
and hear all the story of his guilt and shame.

Mary Dunstan, looking out of her bedroom window,
and seeing the gathering crowd, shuddered and drew
down the blind. These people had come to be entertained ; to find pleasure in seeing a fellow-creature
suffer ; to lay wagers on the chances of the trial; to
get drunk, some of them, before the day was done.

The thought was sickening to her, and she tried to
banish it by shutting out the sight of the crowd. But
as the minutes dragged slowly on, their numbers
steadily increased, till by and by the street in front
of the court-house was black with a surging mass ; each
man struggling to be in front of his neighbour, and to
be near the door when it should open.

At first only a subdued murmur of voices could be heard, but this gradually gave place to shouts and loud guffaws. In their excited state they were ready to laugh at anything, or shout on the smallest provocation. Every bit of gossip was retailed with infinite gusto, and stale jokes laughed over as though they had been fresh from the mint. Each new arrival was hailed with shouts of derisive laughter, for it was quite clear he or she would have no chance of getting into the court-house or seeing the prisoner.

Now a belated clodhopper comes rolling down the street, wet to the neck, and covered with mud and slime. He had come from a village miles away, and had taken a short cut across the fields, and in attempting to leap a ditch had "landed in the water," to use his own expression, "and had come within a hace of bein' drownded, strangled, an' smothered." He had "clunked a lot of dirty water an' got nearly chuck'd" in the process.

Timothy's advent was provocative of much mirth and many comments; for a while he was the hero of the hour, and received a share of attention that was quite overpowering.

Within his narrow cell, and stretched on the hard plank bed, Harry listened and smiled—smiled bitterly and scornfully. He knew well enough what the murmur of voices and the loud guffaws meant, and in his heart there rose a feeling of indignation and scorn. "I can face them," was his reflection, "and will not quail either. But all the same I shall be glad when the business is over. There'll be a great crowd when the hanging comes off at Bodmin, but it will not last long, that's a comfort."

He had quite made up his mind as to the course the trial would take, and the verdict that would be given, and was resolved to accept the inevitable with as much composure as possible. During the forty hours and more he had shivered in that wretched cell, he had pictured the whole scene to himself a hundred times over, even to standing upon the drop with the rope about his neck.

"I think I know the worst," he said to himself, grimly. "And now all that remains is for me to go through it without flinching."

There was only one thing that disturbed his composure, and that was the thought of his father and Gladys and Mrs. Gaved. For himself he would soon be out of the disgrace, and the sooner the darkness covered him, he felt, the better. But his father had many years before him, and Gladys all her life nearly, and he knew that for them it would be a burden grievous to be borne. A burden that would crush all the joy out of their heart, and darken their life to the very last.

Of Mary Dunstan he would not think. If ever her face came up before him he put it aside by a strong effort of will. She was nothing to him now, or he to her. He had had a beautiful dream—a dream which had thrilled every fibre of his being with the most exquisite delight. But he was awake now. The dream was over and past, and could never come back again. He had seen her pale pitying face for a moment at the window on Saturday. He almost wished now he had not seen her, for it nearly unnerved him at the time, and had made it all the more difficult for him to banish her from his thoughts.

Abel Tregonning had paid him very little attention since he got him safely under lock and key, and Harry was too proud to plead for a favour.

"If 'e had been the leastest bit 'umble or penitent," said Abel to his wife, "I could feel some sympathy for 'im. But, bless you, he's 'ard as bricks. He don't seem to have no feelin', an' looks at me as though I was dirt, an' not fit to clean his shoes."

"P'r'aps he feels more than he looks," Abel's wife ventured to reply.

"Don't b'lieve it," he said. "Ef 'e were the leastest

bit sorry for young Dunstan's death, or for the trouble he's brought on both families, he wouldn't be able to 'elp showin' it a little. Everybody else in the place shows it."

"That's true," she said. "But Harry Penryn never have been in the 'abit of showin' his feelins very much."

"No, he's always been a 'arden'd cove," Abel remarked, and then the subject dropped.

Punctually at a quarter to ten the doors of the court-house were thrown open, and in about two minutes the place was crowded to its utmost capacity. Ten minutes later the magistrates filed in one by one and took their seats. Such an array of magistrates had never been seen at a trial in Restormel before. Every one who had a right to sit on the bench was there.

Below, the magistrate's clerk and his assistant were busy writing, with faces as composed as though the case about to be tried was one of everyday occurrence. To their left were a number of witnesses, including Robert Dunstan, Dan Polslee, Sam Trewalsick, and his son Billy. While over their heads, in a small gallery, were a number of ladies, whose seats had been reserved for them.

For a while a subdued murmur filled the place. The magistrates whispered and nodded and shook their heads. Then a sudden silence dropped down upon the scene, and every one held his breath and strained his eyes towards a side-door, which was seen slowly to open. The next moment Abel Tregonning appeared in sight, leading Harry Penryn by the arm. Abel glanced swiftly and proudly around the room, as though he were monarch of all he surveyed, and by far the most important figure in that little scene.

Harry, however, looked neither to the right nor the left; he walked quietly to his place in the dock, and clasping his hands behind his back, stood firm and motionless. Yet he felt that the room was crowded, and that hundreds of eyes were fixed upon his face.

It was a painful ordeal, but he made no sign; not a muscle of his face moved, nor the least suggestion of a blush tinged his cheek. By the side of Abel Tregonning's burly form, and coarse, common face, he looked very proud and handsome, and won a measure of sympathy from the occupants of the gallery at the outset.

He was very pale, paler than any one had ever seen him before, while a dark rim under his eyes told of sleepless nights. But his mouth was firm and resolute, and the glance of his eye calm and steady.

The hush that had fallen upon the court on his entrance soon gave place to a low murmur, into which a faint hiss made its way, and smote upon Harry's ear with distinct emphasis, and seemed for the moment to stab him to the heart.

He made a faint movement, as though he would face the cowardly crew, but instantly recovered himself, and the next moment Abel's stentorian tones, shouting " Silence in court," restored the equilibrium.

The preliminaries of the inquiry were soon got through. The indictment was read, or mumbled, for very few people heard a word of it, and then Abel Tregonning, with his face beaming, gave a very graphic and detailed account of what he termed the "capture" of the prisoner.

Harry glanced at him, and smiled when he uttered the word. A smile that was like a gleam of sunshine on a winter's landscape, lighting up the calm passive face, and imparting to it a touch of tenderness that was very rarely seen.

Abel was voluminous, and full to overflowing with a sense of his own importance. He never had the conduct of such a case before; the chances were he would never have such a case again. If he did not distinguish himself now, he would miss the golden opportunity of his life. It was emphatically a case of now or never, and so, like a wise man, he resolved to make the best of it.

When Abel got agoing, it was not easy to stop him. For three whole days he had been almost as silent as a sphinx, bottling up the treasures of his knowledge, till, as he expressed it to his wife, "he was fit to burst." To all and sundry who had plied him with questions he had given the briefest answers possible. Indeed, in many cases he had not condescended to give an answer at all. He had simply stared at his interlocutor as much as to say, "What business is it of yours?" and had then pompously marched away.

Yet all the while Abel had been aching all over to give vent to what he knew. It would have been worth a fortune, almost, to have got half a dozen of his chums about him in his "joinery," and talked the matter over with them. But the dignity of his position was an effectual cork to his bottled-up feelings, and kept him silent.

Now, however, the sluice-gates were thrown open, and the torrents of his talk flowed on. Much of it was utterly irrelevant, and had not the remotest connection with the question before the bench. Their worships, after a few minutes, began to grow uneasy. But they knew so little about law themselves, that they hesitated to interfere. Abel was chief constable, and ought to know what he was about. Their clerk was too far away from them to be easily consulted with, and altogether they felt that matters were beginning awkwardly.

Abel was in high feather. He flung innuendoes right and left, and intimated that he had got together an array of witnesses which would prove up to the hilt all he had said, and leave their worships no option but to commit the prisoner for trial, at the forthcoming assizes, on the charge of wilful murder.

That Abel's charge made a sensation, there could be no doubt whatever. If half of what he had hinted was true, one of the foulest murders of the century had been committed, and the prisoner before them

was a fiend incarnate, a foul reptile that should be
put out of time with all possible dispatch.

Harry listened unmoved to all that was said, and
appeared to be indifferent to the gravity of his position.
His calm impassive face revealed no secret, and gave
no hint of what was passing through his mind. The
ladies who looked at him from the gallery wondered
what this stoicism meant. Did this calmness spring
from a knowledge of his innocence, or was he the
hardened fiend that Abel Tregonning had pictured
him? He certainly had no common face. Neither
was it a bad face on which they looked. Dark he
was, almost to swarthiness, with eyes that seemed of
unfathomable depths. Large beautiful eyes, deeply
set, and hiding secrets that refused to come to the
surface. And what about that clean-cut mouth, with
its rich full lips? Was there anything cruel about it?
Strength and firmness and inflexibility were clearly
displayed. But beyond this, and a fine intelligence,
his face revealed nothing.

But the course of the inquiry left very little time
for speculation.

Robert Dunstan was the first witness called. He
was very pale, and evidently in great trouble. He
spoke in low tones, that trembled a great deal, and
once or twice his voice threatened to fail him altogether.
He stated that he had not seen his son since the
previous Thursday afternoon, and that he had not the
least shadow of a doubt that he was dead. How he
came by his death he was not prepared to offer an
opinion.

In answer to questions from the bench, he admitted
that on Thursday evening he had expressed a belief
that there had been foul play.

"Did he charge the prisoner with the murder of his
son?"

"Well no, not exactly."

"Did he hint at such a thing?"

" Very probably he did. He was very excited at the time, and he thought the circumstances looked suspicious."

" Had those suspicious circumstances been removed?"

" Well, no! he could not say they had. Still he was not prepared to stand by what he had hinted on the previous Thursday."

" Are you prepared to say that according to your belief the prisoner is not guilty ? "

" No," bringing out the word very slowly. " I am not prepared to go as far as that."

"Then you cannot say that you believe he is innocent ? "

" I am not prepared to say I believe anything," said Mr. Dunstan doggedly.

A long pause followed this remark. The chairman took off his spectacles, and held a brief consultation with his colleagues. It was very evident that Mr. Dunstan was an unwilling witness, and would not say any more than he was compelled to say.

" Silence in court," shouted Abel Tregonning, and the hum of voices instantly ceased.

The chairman put on his spectacles again, and addressed Mr. Dunstan.

" We all of us sympathize with you very much, in the painful circumstances in which you are placed," he said. " But it is very necessary, in the interests of justice, that you should state freely, and without reservation, everything you know bearing on the case."

" I am very willing to state what I *know*," was the answer. " But what I *think* is no business of anybody's."

This retort was greeted with a loud laugh, which, however, was instantly silenced. The chairman flushed to the roots of his hair, while his colleagues fidgeted uneasily in their seats.

" Very good," the chairman spoke calmly. " We will deal only with matters of fact. Now will you state clearly all that took place last Thursday afternoon, as far only as your own actual knowledge goes?"

"Yes, I don't object at all." And Mr. Dunstan proceeded to give a straightforward narrative of all the circumstances of the case as far as he had any knowledge.

He was not a very good talker, and every now and then a question was interposed from the Bench which threw him a little off his track, and considerably lengthened out the time of telling; so that by the time he had finished his story the Bench felt uncommonly dry, and was seized with an irresistible desire to retire to its private room for a "refresher." So after sundry whisperings and consultations the Bench retired behind a red curtain, and the prisoner was allowed to seek a few minutes' solace in the privacy of his cold and lonely cell.

CHAPTER IX.

EVIDENCE.

"Where then shall hope and fear their objects find?
Must dull suspense corrupt the stagnant mind?
Must helpless man, in ignorance sedate,
Roll darkling down the torrent of his fate?
Must no dislike alarm, no wishes rise,
No cries invoke the mercies of the skies?"

SAMUEL JOHNSON.

For about twenty minutes the hum of voices in the court-room rose louder and louder. Near the door, among those who had been standing all the while, there was a considerable amount of jostling, and elbowing, and angry recrimination. A few people managed to get out, though not without considerable difficulty, their egress being hindered by those who were struggling to get in. Some who were fortunate enough to secure seats stood up and stretched themselves, and tried to relieve their weariness by yawning. At the back of the room an angry discussion was in full swing, and gave promise more than once of developing into a game of fisticuffs. The ladies in the gallery fanned themselves incessantly, and even yawned occasionally, but they seemed too much interested in the scene below to talk very much.

Suddenly the hum of voices ceased, and a silence that was almost oppressive dropped upon the scene; the red curtain was drawn aside, and the Bench began to file in, looking all the more cheerful for its "refresher."

Simultaneously the side door opened, and Abel and Harry entered, the latter looking weary and jaded ; he was not supposed to require any refreshment, so none had been given. Mr. Dunstan again took his seat in the witness-box, and the inquiry re-commenced.

The Bench wished to ask through the chairman a few questions.

" Would Mr. Dunstan say if the prisoner and the deceased had been on good terms with each other ? "

Mr. Dunstan started. To hear his son Jack spoken of as " the deceased " gave him quite a shock. He had stated that he had no doubt his son was dead, nor *had* he any doubt, and yet the quiet assumption of the fact without any positive proof struck him with a painful sense of incongruity. Moreover, he felt that he was being made, against his will, to incriminate Harry ; and that he was anxious not to do. For the love he bore to his wife and Mary, both of whom believed in his innocence, and for the liking he had for the lad himself, in spite of the events of the last few days, he was anxious not to say anything that would tell against him. He hesitated so long that the chairman put the question again, and in much sharper tones.

" Will Mr. Dunstan be good enough to say if the prisoner at the bar and the deceased had been on good terms with each other ? "

" There ain't no proof, that I am aware of, that my son is deceased," said Mr. Dunstan, looking defiantly at the Bench.

What followed may be best described by the phrase " Sensation in court." The chairman fairly jumped. The oppressive silence that had preceded the farmer's answer gave place to a perfect babel of sounds. Harry stretched himself and smiled faintly, and for the first time took a swift glance round the room. The magistrates crowded round their president, and all began talking and gesticulating at the same time. The ladies in the gallery tittered.

Then Abel's voice rose strong and clear above the din, "Silence in court," and a great hush fell once more upon the scene. The clerk quietly explained that Mr. Dunstan's evidence was not essential at that stage of the inquiry, and that he might leave the witness-box, that other evidence would be put in which he hoped would enable the Bench to come to a right decision.

Then the hum of voices rose again, but was hushed a few moments later, when the sinewy figure of Sam Trewalsick was seen making his way into the witness-box. Sam came forward, however, with apparent reluctance, kissed the Bible with great unction, and started ahead without being questioned to say that "he had not a word to say agin young Maister Penryn, an' that for all he know'd to the conterary he was a very hexcellent young man."

It was not easy to stop Sam when he had started, but he was pulled up at length, and by dint of careful handling was enabled to tell a fairly straightforward story.

"As usual he and his son Billy had been out during the night fishing; he did not start out till after twelve, for he never went out fishing on a Sunday."

Sam paused on making that statement, and glanced slowly around the room, as though anxious that his virtuous conduct should be recognized, and duly appreciated.

"The rain had ceased when he hoisted sail, and the wind had died away very considerably, or he should not have gone out at all; he had caught nothing during the night."

This of course was not evidence, but it was allowed to pass.

"Soon after dawn he began to steer for home, and when on a line with Tregeagle's Head, and about two miles from the shore, his son Billy called his attention to some dark object floating in the water on their starboard side. Though there was not a great deal of wind,

"Soon after dawn he began to steer for home, and, when on a line with Tregeagle's Head, his son Billy called his attention to some dark object in the water."—P. 70.

there was a heavy swell on, and they had some difficulty
in getting near the object. However, they shortened
sail at once and put round the helm, and at length got
near enough to see that it was the body of a man
floating face downwards."

Again Sam paused and glanced slowly around him,
for he felt that his words had created a profound sensation. The stillness of the court was almost oppressive;
people held their breath to catch the words that should
follow.

"Well, and what did you do then?" The solicitor's
voice was low and somewhat husky, but every syllable
was heard distinctly.

"Well, sir," and Sam drew himself up to his full
height, "I called upon Billy to port the helm while I
got hold o' the grapplin' rod. It were a ticklish
business, for the waves was now broadside on, but at
length I hooked the body an' turned it on its back."

At this point there was more sensation in court, and
Sam paused again, and calmly surveyed the sea of faces.

"And did you recognize the face of the dead man?"
The words fell slow and distinct, and every one waited
breathlessly for the answer.

"Oh, aye, as plain as anything. Why, bless you, he
looked jist like one sleepin', wi' his brown hair floatin'
out in the water, and his lips parted as though he was
smilin'."

"And whose body do you say it was?"

"Why, Mr. Jack Dunstan's, to be sure. There ain't
no doubt on that score. Who else could it be?"

"You are prepared to swear that it was Jack
Dunstan's body?"

"Well, sir, I don't want to swear afore so many
gentry, nor use bad language of no sort, but if a bit o'
swearin' is necessary to back it up, I don't mind," and
Sam reeled off a dozen oaths before the astonished
officials could call him to order.

After some difficulty it was explained to him that

that was not the kind of oath he was required to take, and Sam expressed his regret at the mistake.

Then the question was put again, and Sam began to fence a little.

"He would not say it was impossible for him to be mistaken; their boat was rolling about, and the body was rising and falling with the swell, and the waves washing over the face. But he would describe what the body was like, and they could judge for themselves. The face was plump and fair, the hair brown and short, the teeth large and white, the body was dressed in a plum-coloured coat with brass buttons, the vest was figured over with flowers. In short, if it was not Jack Dunstan, he had never been so deceived in his life."

"Did he try to get the body into his boat?"

"He did; that was the very thing he was after. But he thought his grappling-hook must have pierced the body, all the gas escaped out of it in a moment, and it sank to the bottom like a stone."

After a few other questions had been asked and answered, "their Worships" took Sam in hand.

"Did he know the deceased well?"

"Pretty well; he had seen him a good many times in Pentudy."

"Had he any feeling against the prisoner?"

"Oh no, none at all. Why should he?"

"Nor against the prisoner's father?"

"Oh dear, no! the very opposite. He considered the Vicar a very hexcellent man."

"But had he never complained of the Vicar and his son prying into his doings?"

"Prying into his doings! Why should he?"

"That is no answer to the question."

"Well, as for that, he did not care who pried. All he did was open and above-board."

"You never intimated that it would be a good thing if the prisoner could be got out of the way?"

"Oh dear, no!—never!—that he could swear to." And he did swear to it then and there.

Harry declined to ask the prisoner any questions, and then Billy stepped into the witness-box. He corroborated all his father had said. He would not like to swear that the body he saw was Jack Dunstan's, he only caught just a glimpse of the face; but he had no doubt it was him.

Then Dan Polslee came upon the scene. Dan's lantern jaws and hungry, wolfish eyes created something like a sensation, whilst his shrill, piping voice caused a very audible titter.

"He remembered Thursday afternoon very well; he was out in a boat with Mark Jory. Between five and six o'clock he was less than a mile away from Tregeagle's Head. He saw two men running along the edge of the cliff, and called Mark's attention to them. They were running very fast, and one seemed to be chasing the other. The foremost one reached the "brow," when he tried to double, but the hindermost caught him, and they began to wrestle. He thought it very strange and dangerous, and both he and Mark got very excited. In their struggle they got to the very brink of the cliff, then one suddenly disappeared, and after a minute or two the other walked away alone."

"Did he see anything fall over the cliff?"

"Well, no! You see we was in the wrong position; if we'd been haaf a mile furder seaward we should ha' seen the body fall."

"You have no doubt that one of the men pushed or threw the other over the cliff?"

"What else could he ha' done with him?"

"That is no answer to the question; but it does not matter. You will swear that one of the men disappeared during the struggle, and that the other walked away alone?"

"Aye, that I will; and Mark'll swear the same."

"Can you identify the prisoner as one of the men you saw running?"

"No, sir, I can't do that. I reckon they was young men by the rate they runned."

"Did the prisoner wish to ask the witness any questions?"

Harry started and flushed, and for a moment his eye fell. To be addressed as "the prisoner" was terribly humiliating, but he recovered himself in a moment.

"Yes," he said, "I would like to ask the witness a few questions." Then turning to Dan, he said, "Might not the two men be running a race, instead of, as you suggest, the one chasing the other?"

"Oh, yes, of course; they might ha' been, but it hardly looked like it."

"Why so?"

Dan shuffled uneasily, but could give no answer that was at all intelligible.

"Supposing one lay flat on the ground, could you have seen him from your boat?"

"Well, no, he thought not."

"Then the mere fact of one throwing the other in a playful wrestling-match would cause the one thrown to disappear."

"Yes, for a moment; but he would pop up again into sight directly."

"Unless he chose to lie and rest awhile after running a race."

"Exactly."

"And he might have followed the other five minutes after without your noticing him?"

"Well, he was not so sure of that."

"Did he keep his eye on the cliff for some considerable time?"

"Well, yes, pretty considerable."

"How long?"

"Well, he could not say exactly, but several minutes."

A pause followed, during which Harry drew himself

up to his full height, and looking Dan straight in the eyes, he said—

" You are a great friend of Trewalsick's, I believe ? "

" Well, yes, we be fairly friendly."

" Not in partnership with him ? "

" I don't know what you mean."

" Yes, you do ; but let that go. You are away from your home a great deal ? "

" Yes, I be."

" You would not like to say how or where you spend your time when you are away ? "

Dan flushed. " That's no business of nobody's," he said, hotly.

" But it may become so."

" You're welcome to do your worst," he answered, with a triumphant leer.

" You have long regarded me as too inquisitive ? " Harry said calmly.

" Oh no, not at all ; you are welcome to inquire as much as ever yer likes," and over Dan's lantern jaws there played a most diabolical smile.

" You have a great horror of Tregeagle's Head, I'm told ? "

" I never go near it if I can 'elp it."

" And do the best you can, by retailing horrible stories, to keep other people from going near it ? "

" No, he did not. Other folks might live on it, for all he cared."

" You'll be very sorry to have me out of the way, won't you ? "

" Yes, sir, very sorry," and Dan tried to import a tone of sincerity to his voice, but with no great success.

This finished Dan's cross-examination, and he was allowed to depart. Mark Jory simply confirmed what Dan had said. Then followed several minor witnesses, who retailed a vast amount of stale gossip respecting the feud that had existed between deceased and the prisoner at the bar. Others stated how they had seen the prisoner slink into the village on the previous Thursday evening, when it was getting dusk, as though he was anxious not to be seen. These items, though of no great value in themselves, yet when added to the other evidence seemed to complete the chain.

Harry gave his own version of the story with great clearness and precision. He said he had no doubt that Jack Dunstan was dead, or that the body seen by Trewalsick was that of his friend. He had clearly been caught by the tide in his attempt to get round Treg-eagle's Head. But as for himself, he submitted that there was not a particle of evidence to support the foul charge for which he stood before them. He spoke without passion or vehemence, and when he had concluded every one drew a long breath, for the tension had been very great. And then the magistrates retired to their room to consider the verdict.

CHAPTER X.

"The brave man is not he who feels no fear :
For that were stupid and irrational ;
But he whose noble soul its fear subdues,
And bravely dares the danger nature shrinks from."

JOANNA BAILLIE.

THE result of the inquiry was a foregone conclusion. The Bench agreed with perfect unanimity, and without any hesitation at all, that this was a case for a jury. In less than five minutes after they had retired they were back in their places again, and the chairman announced, without any parleying, that the prisoner was committed for trial at the forthcoming assizes on the charge of wilful murder. No one manifested any surprise, least of all the prisoner; he looked at the magistrates with calm passionless eyes, and then quietly bowed his head. He felt thankful that the first act in the little drama was at an end, and when he reached his cell he threw himself on the hard planks with a sense of relief. To be alone again was like finding a quiet haven after a storm.

A few minutes later Abel brought him a thick slice of dry bread and a jug of cold water, and departed without a word. He had no desire to remain with his prisoner any longer than he could help; Harry's large steady eyes smote him with an uneasy feeling he could not account for; besides which, he had a fear that if he were long in the prisoner's company his pity might be excited, and that of all things he was anxious to avoid.

Outside the crowd jostled and yelled and declaimed, as though pandemonium had been let loose. They had been silent so long in the crowded and stuffy court-house, that it was a positive relief to exercise their lungs once more; besides which, such a number of topics had been suggested for debate, that it was impossible to separate without having their "say" on them. To most of them the evidence fairly bristled with curious and interesting points, and so they argued and grew angry, and talked a dozen at a time; those having the strongest voices appearing to have the greatest advantage.

Into Harry's cell the sounds came in subdued and dreamy undertone, soothing his agitated and over-strung nerves like a gentle narcotic, till by and by he fell into a sweet refreshing slumber, in which he dreamed that he was walking in the shadow of the pine wood with Mary Dunstan leaning on his arm. On the path before them, and all up the long avenue between the trees, the sunlight flickered in golden patches, which changed their shapes a thousand times as the wind shook the trees above them. From over the hill came softly and musically the subdued murmur of the sea, as it washed the shingles on the beach at Porthloo, or surged low and deep among the rocks around Treg-eagle's Head. High up in the tall trees the wind whispered and sang among the pine needles, as though to give welcome to the happy lovers who trod the sun-flecked path below.

Harry felt Mary's hand tighten on his arm as he walked, and bending down he kissed her ruby lips, and told her again how he had loved her long, but had not the courage to tell her. And for answer she raised her swimming eyes to his, and he knew he had all her heart.

Then the scene seemed to change, and he was walk-ing with Mary on Tregeagle's Head, and was telling her how he had had a horrible dream which clung to him still, and would not be shaken off. Then the wind got up, and the sea began to roar, and the tide to rise higher and higher, until it swept over Tregeagle's Head; and the wind caught Mary away from him, and swept her over the cliff into the surging sea; and he heard her cry for help, and saw her sinking into the foamy water, while he was held as in a vice, unable to move or even speak.

Then with a mighty effort he freed himself from the spell that was upon him, and awoke—awoke to the reality which was worse than the dream. It was not Mary that had been swept away and was sinking in deep water—she was safe; it was he who was sinking with no eye to pity him, no arm to save.

Meanwhile Mary was beginning to realize in a very acute sense the danger Harry was in, and Harry was her lover. That thought clung to her like a burr and would not be shaken off. And if he loved her—it did not matter whether she loved him or not—ought she to sit still and passive, making no effort to save him?

She had never fully realized his peril until now. When her father had come in and said that he had been committed to take his trial at the Assizes on the charge of wilful murder, she felt as though she had been stabbed. She had scarcely realized before the possibility of such a thing; she had talked with no one save her father and mother, and Mr. Penryn, Mrs. Gaved, and Gladys, and the servants in her own house, and they all believed that Harry was innocent except her father, and he was more than half convinced. Hence there had grown up in her heart the feeling that the magistrates would acquit Harry, or at least remand him from time to time until he was able fully to establish his innocence.

Poor child! she had not heard the evidence against him, and did not know how strong and complete was the chain. Had she known she would have been less hopeful, and the verdict would have come to her with less of a shock; as it was, she began to feel more keenly than ever how deeply and cruelly he had been wronged. If she and her mother, who had lost their all in the death of Jack, acquitted Harry, what right had those cruel magistrates to pronounce him guilty? It seemed monstrous and wicked, beyond the power of words to express.

For a full hour she paced her room, wondering if anything could be done, if there was anything she could do, if there was any possible way by which his escape might be effected.

Then a thought struck her which made her pause. She was only a girl,—timid, superstitious, frightened almost at her own shadow, and what she proposed to herself would tax her courage to the utmost. But clenching her hands tightly she whispered to herself, "Heaven help me, and I will do it."

Her mother was no worse to-day, perhaps a little better if anything, so that she would be able to leave her for an hour or two without any difficulty. She said nothing to any one of what she intended doing, for she knew that if her father got a hint of her purpose he would veto it at once. Moreover, her effort might end in failure, in which case it was well no one should know.

Tea was a very silent meal—how could it be otherwise? Two of the four chairs were empty, and over the darkened home the shadows seemed deepening all the while. Mr. Dunstan did not seem to notice his daughter at all; in his eyes there was an absent, far-away look, and around his mouth deep lines of trouble and pain. Now and then he sighed heavily, but he made no allusion to the trouble that was pressing so heavily upon his heart, nor noticed his daughter's pale lips, or the scared look that was in her eyes.

After tea he lit his pipe and drew up his chair to the fire, and began to smoke in silence, while Mary stole away to her mother's room to see that she should want for nothing during her absence. It would take her some considerable time to accomplish what was in her mind, and she was anxious if possible that her absence should not be remarked.

Mr. Dunstan had finished his pipe when she returned to the dining-room, and was sitting staring gloomily into the fire.

"Have you been up to see mother?" he asked as she came towards him, but without raising his eyes.

"Yes, pa."

"And how is she?"

"I think she is better on the whole. At least she has made a better tea than for many days."

"That's right. I think I won't go up to see her now. Tell her I'm going down to have a chat with the Vicar. Poor fellow, he must be in great trouble."

"Do you think you will be away long?" she asked, after a pause.

"An hour perhaps, or perhaps a little longer."

"All right, I will tell her;" and she quietly left the room.

A few minutes later she heard the front door bang, and looking out of her window, she saw her father walking down the garden path towards the street.

"Now is my time," was her thought; and throwing a shawl carelessly round her shoulders, and putting on her oldest bonnet, she stole quietly down the stairs and into the kitchen.

"If mother wants anything, Betty," she said, addressing one of the maids, "will you attend to her? I am going out for a little exercise and fresh air."

"And not before you need it, miss," Betty answered. "You are losing all your roses keeping in the house so much. But you should have gone out earlier, when the sun was shining."

"I must get out when I can," she answered with a smile.

And lifting the door-latch, she passed out into the

court, and from thence into the farm-yard. She was
hurrying across to the outer gate, when a faint whinny
smote upon her ears, and the next moment Jack's own
mare Jet came trotting up to her. She stopped and
rubbed her nose for a few seconds.

"Poor old Jet!" she said, the tears coming into her
eyes, "you are disconsolate, like all the rest of us, at
the loss of your master."

The mare seemed to understand, for she dropped her
head for a moment, then came a step nearer, and rested
her nose on her shoulder.

She raised her white hand and patted its face, saying
the while, " Poor old Jet !—poor old Jet ! "

She was a splendid horse, as black and shining as the
material that had suggested her name. Connoisseurs in
horse-flesh might have said that her head was a trifle
large, and her chest a little too broad; but they would
scarcely have found another fault with her. She was
just going six, and so was in her prime. For speed
there was not her equal in the parish; and in the
matter of endurance, she seemed equal to anything.

"Now, Jet, run away," she said, after a little pause.
"I cannot stay to pet you any more to-night; " and the
beautiful creature lifted her nose, and walked slowly and
dejectedly away.

Mary could not keep back her tears as she looked at
the faithful animal, and thought how never more would
his master hold her bridle-rein. But the next moment
she thought of the mission she had to fulfil, and remembered too that the day was speeding on apace, and
that the light was already beginning to fade. So dash-
ing away her tears, she hurried across the yard, passed
out into the road, along which she ran for a few hundred
yards, then turned aside and climbed over a stile, and
was soon hurrying across the fields in the direction of
Carn Duloe.

Far up its wooded and tangled slope lived Nanny
Flue, alone with her cats and frogs and lizards. About

once a week Nanny came into the village with a large basket on her arm, and when she returned her basket was always full. She had no occasion to beg; the people of the village gave her readily what she needed. They did so to keep in her favour, for Nanny was a witch, and had an evil eye. She could bewitch them or ill-wish them, or smite their cattle with murrain, or afflict their children with rickets or St. Vitus' dance. Moreover, she had the gift of healing, and knew the virtues of herbs and simples, and was a well-known charmer to boot. Hence he were a bold man who should cross Nanny's will, or offend her in any way.

She was a tall, gaunt woman, straight, strong, and active in spite of her seventy years. She had massive features, a low forehead, deep-set eyes, and a heavy lower jaw. Yet her face was by no means repulsive. Defiant and fearless it certainly was; but there was something about the eyes that redeemed it from utter brutality.

That she exercised a very unwholesome influence in Restormel there could be no doubt. The children shrank out of sight when they saw her coming, and dreaded meeting the glance of her eye. Some of the older people might be sceptical regarding her claims, but the young people had not a single doubt respecting her power.

She had been seen flying across the village more than once on the back of an enormous raven, so rumour declared; indeed no end of stories were current respecting her exploits. She was far more dreaded than the spirit of Tregeagle, which haunted the caves and rocks of Tregeagle's Head. Tregeagle could only cry and moan, and fill the darkness and the storm with terror and blood-curdling sounds. He had had his day of wickedness, and had filled his cup of iniquity to the brim while in the flesh. Now he was doomed to labour, till by his useless and unrequited toil he had purged away the guilt of his tortured soul. But he could work no more mischief in the world.

But Nanny Flue was in the zenith of her wicked and fatal strength, and could blast with ruin any one who opposed her. So she came and went, dreaded by all, yet none dared oppose her or say her nay.

It was to her lonely and gruesome dwelling that Mary Dunstan made her way on the evening in question.

CHAPTER XI.

THE WITCH OF CARN DULOE.

"Oh how this tyrant doubt torments my breast!
My thoughts, like birds, who, frightened from their nest,
Around the place where all was hushed before,
Flutter and hardly nestle any more."—OTWAY.

WHILE Mary remained in the open valley the light was good, but directly she began to climb the slope of Carn Duloe she found herself in the shadow of the trees, which were still heavy with foliage, though beginning to brown in the chill of early autumn.

At first she was half disposed to turn back. The sudden fading of the light smote her heart with an uneasy feeling, while the long gloomy avenues slanting steeply up before her, the low swish and moan of the wind, the eerie loneliness of the place, excited all her superstitious fears and made her pause. Should she go on, or should she turn back? She did not debate the question long. The issue involved was one of life or death. If Harry was to be saved he must be saved quickly, and she knew of no one but Nanny who could effect his release.

Perhaps it was beyond even Nanny's power or skill. Perhaps if she had the power she would not care to use it. Perhaps Harry was no favourite of hers. She did not know, but at least she could ascertain. She had always treated the witch kindly, always given her welcome when she called at Trevose, and sent her away full-handed. And Nanny had professed great affection for her, and more than once had promised her help if she should ever need it.

Now she needed help, and was going to put the witch's pretended friendship to the test. Yet how painfully her heart kept beating as she pushed her way up the gloomy slope, and how fearfully oppressive and solemn was the growing darkness. The great dreary forest all about her seemed full of strange and unearthly voices, as though evil spirits were whispering their secrets to each other, or were angry at their solitude being invaded by a creature of flesh and blood.

Now she paused again and pulled the shawl from her shoulders. How oppressively hot it had grown, and yet the higher she climbed the more freely the wind played through the trees and the louder the moan it made. But in spite of the wind she felt as though she were in a furnace, and was panting for a breath of fresh air.

"Oh if this terror keeps hold of me," she said to herself, "I shall have to turn back, and then I shall never forgive myself to the day of my death. But no, I will not turn back;" and setting her teeth firmly together she pushed forward again.

See knew the way quite well, for she had often been to the top of Carn Duloe, and two or three times—when her brother Jack had been with her—she had turned aside from the main path, and had pursued a narrow level track that wound round a rocky spur to have a glimpse of Nanny's dwelling.

Partly cave and partly hut, once seen it could not easily be forgotten. The hut portion Nanny had built herself, and no one had disputed her right. Stuck in front of the cave, it served as a kind of vestibule guarding the gloomy interior of the cavern. A heavy door of unplaned planks blocked the entrance. The small window was closely shuttered when Nanny was

away, and when she was at home no one would
dare to look through, so that the interior was a *terra
incognito.*

People often wondered what the inside of Nanny's
dwelling was like, but none had cared to seek admission.
Those who came to look at the outside generally kept
a convenient distance from the door. They had a
feeling that Nanny was not favourable to prying eyes,
and might "ill-wish" them if they offended her.

In the summer time young people came occasionally
to have their fortunes told, and now and then a farmer
who had a beast suffering from adder sting or "felon,"
or who had himself been "pixey led" some previous
night, would seek her aid. But Nanny seemed to
know by instinct when they were coming, and always
met them on the way. There was not a single case
on record of Nanny ever inviting any one into her
dwelling.

But the puzzle was, how did she know of the approach of people? Whether they came in the brightest
day or blackest night, whether with noisy feet or
muffled tread, she always knew, if she was at home, and
came out to meet them. But then this was only one
puzzle out of a great many. How did she know a
hundred other things?

Mary reached the narrow track which led away from
the main path at length, and paused again before
pursuing further the lonesome way. Her fears had not
subsided in the smallest degree; her heart was beating
so fast she could hardly breathe. But she had come so
far that it would be worse than cowardly to turn back
now, though the loneliest bit of the road still lay
before her.

The wind that had sprung up at sunset was by this
time making wild music in the interlacing branches
above her, and the tall trees were waving ghostly arms
in the gathering darkness. But the thought of Harry's
danger made her brave. Clenching her hands tightly

she hurried forward again, not daring to look to the right hand or to the left. The path was level now, and she increased her speed at every step. On, on, still on, as though all the imps of darkness were in hot pursuit. Then suddenly she stopped, overcome by a great horror, and with a low cry sank to the ground.

Before her, as though she had risen out of the ground, was the tall gaunt form of the witch. Mary hid her face in her hands, trembling and sobbing, but she made no attempt to rise. Nanny stood looking at her, silent and impassive. The wind wailed and moaned in the trees above them, and the darkness deepened all the while. But neither spoke for many seconds.

Then Nanny reached out her stick and touched the prostrate figure of the girl.

"Get up, child," she said, "and look at me."

Slowly and tremblingly Mary obeyed.

"Art afraid, child?" she asked, in not unkindly tones.

"Yes, I am terribly frightened," Mary answered.

"Then why didst thou come here, and alone?"

"I came to ask a favour, to crave your help," Mary answered, with clasped hands and downcast eyes. "I am in great perplexity."

"And in love," said the witch, with a touch of scorn in her voice.

"Oh, I know not," Mary answered, trembling violently. "I know I am in great trouble. Sorrow has broken all our hearts."

"Hearts don't break in these times," the witch answered with a laugh. "But enough, I knew thou wert coming, and came to meet thee. The way is lonesome, and thou art young."

"You knew I was coming?" Mary asked in astonishment.

"Of course I knew. But ask no prying questions, or it may be worse for thee."

"Pardon me," Mary said humbly; "I did not wish to be rude. Now let me tell my story."

"Nay, not here, though there is none to listen save the spirits of the dead, who are all about us; but thou art ready to faint, and wilt take cold if thou remainest here."

"I am feeling better now," Mary answered.

"Then follow me, and fear nothing, for not a hair of thy beautiful head shall be harmed."

"You speak kindly. Oh! I hope you will help me."

"Thou hast been kind to me, many times and oft; kind because thou fearedst me, perhaps, but chiefly because thy heart is kind."

"Oh, I know not what my heart is, save that it is nearly broken."

"Aye, thou hast a double sorrow. To lose thy brother is hard, and to lose thy lover is perhaps harder still."

"But Harry is not my lover," Mary interposed. "He has never spoken to me of love."

"And what matters that? Thou knowest he loves thee, and thou, poor silly child, has given thy heart in return."

"He has been my friend for years," Mary said, "and I would save him if I could."

"I know thou wouldst; and for this thou hast come to me. But hurry thy steps, and we will speak together within." And Nanny strode away into the gloom, Mary quickly following. For a couple of hundred yards or so the path was quite straight, then it took a sudden bend round a spur of rock, and ended on a small plateau, surrounded on three sides by frowning and precipitous rocks.

Here Nanny paused before the door of her hut, while three or four black cats came and rubbed themselves against her skirts, and a tame magpie called to her from a ledge of rock high above her head. Mary shuddered as the sepulchral croak of the magpie fell on

her ears, and for the first time the question swept across
her mind, whether or no she had done right in coming
to seek the aid of a witch.

It was generally supposed that Nanny had no deal-
ings with heaven; that she was in league with evil
spirits; that she derived her power from the nether
regions. Hence, could it be right to associate with her
in any way—even in an attempt to do what was just
and right? But Nanny gave her no time to debate the
question. Turning suddenly round, she raised her long
bony arm, and said in a hoarse voice,

"Listen!"

Mary placed her hand upon her side to steady her
heart's loud beating, but no sound fell upon her ears
save the moaning in the trees, or the deep undertone of
the sea.

"You notice we are above the tree tops here," said
Nanny, speaking again, "and above the pine forest on
the other side of Restormel. On moonlight nights, as
well as in the day time, I can see Tregeagle's Head, and
the white waves surging round the sentinels."

Mary shuddered, but did not speak.

"I am farther away from the sea than you at Restormel," Nanny went on, "and yet I can hear its voice
when to you it is still; and when the lone spirit of
Tregeagle cries in the night, his voice floats across to
me. You are below the pine forest, and hear nothing,
but every sound floats up to me."

"And are you never afraid?" Mary asked, tremblingly.

"Afraid!—no. What have I to be afraid of? Think,
child, and remember in the years to come what the
witch tells thee to-night. Nothing outside can harm
thee; nothing but thyself can do thee mischief. Keep
down the evil within, and thou art safe. But hist! I
thought I heard it again."

"Heard what?" Mary asked, with a startled look in
her eyes.

"That is what puzzles me. Borne soft on the wind, a voice comes sometimes which I do not recognize."

"Is it not the voice of Tregeagle?" Mary asked.

"It may be, but I doubt it; I have thought it must be thy brother's voice. Nay, do not tremble; the secret will be unearthed in time."

"But oh! my brother is dead!" Mary said, with a sob. "Sam Trewalsick saw his body floating in the sea; that came out in evidence to-day."

"That may be quite true; and if true, it may be his spirit crying for vengeance that I hear."

"Oh, no, no; do not say that. There has been no foul play in his death, of that I am sure. He and Harry had a quarrel, I know, but what of that? Harry would no more harm him than he would harm me."

"So I would fain believe," said the witch, musingly; "and if he wished to win thy love, and make thee his wife, he would hardly begin by killing thy brother."

"He would not have killed my brother if he could have won the world by it," Mary answered impulsively.

But the witch was silent; she stood with head bent and hand outstretched in a listening attitude. All down the forest slope, and right and left, the roar of the wind could be heard, but no other sound fell on their ears.

"I confess I am puzzled," the witch said at length, raising her head.

"But I thought you knew everything," Mary replied.

"Child, no one knows everything save God. But come, I am taking you where no one has ever been before."

Mary shuddered and stood still.

"Nay, do not fear; I have already promised thee that not a hair of thy beautiful head shall be harmed. And thou art faint, and art beginning to feel the cold; thou hast been too long already outside."

"But I must not stay long," Mary said. "My mother

is ill, and if I am long away she will wonder and get concerned."

"I will not keep thee a moment longer than is necessary. Now follow me;" and touching a spring, the heavy door flew open, and the witch disappeared in the darkness.

CHAPTER XII.

NANNY MAKES A PROMISE.

"Heaven may not grant thee all thy mind,
Yet say not thou that Heaven's unkind.
God is alike both good and wise,
In what He grants and what denies;
Perhaps what Goodness gives to-day,
To-morrow Goodness takes away."—COTTON.

As soon as Mary got within the hut the door was instantly shut, and she found herself in darkness so dense that not a single object was visible; but trusting in the witch's word that no harm should befall her, she repressed the cry that rose to her lips, and stood quite still, waiting for what was to follow. At length a dull red gleam pierced the darkness, as the witch stirred the embers on her hearth, and a moment later a candle was lighted, and stuck in a rude bracket fastened to the wall; and Mary, with a sigh of relief, began to look around her.

The room was about ten feet square, with a low roof, exposing all the rafters. The chimney was in the left-hand corner farthest from the door. To the right of the chimney was hung a heavy curtain, hiding the entrance to the cave beyond; to the left of the chimney, against the wall, was the witch's bed, a narrow and extremely primitive arrangement, which answered the double purpose of sofa and bed. The floor was covered with a thick mat of woven rushes. The walls were adorned with skeletons of rats, cats, birds, and fishes of various sorts and sizes, while two skulls occupied conspicuous positions on the window-ledge. From the rafters were suspended large bunches of mugwort, bitany, henbane, hemlock, poppy-heads, and various other herbs. A small round table occupied a convenient position between the fireplace and the head of the witch's bed, and almost in the centre of the room was a rocking-chair. This completed the furniture of the place.

As soon as Nanny had stuck the candle into the bracket, she turned to Mary, and pointing to the rocking-chair, said—"Sit thee down and wait." Then lighting another candle, she disappeared behind the curtain.

Mary sat herself down in the chair and shuddered. The sight of the skulls made her flesh creep, while the silence of the place was more oppressive than the moaning of the wind outside. Moreover, the atmosphere was heavy with the smell of dry herbs and stale turf smoke, while the light of the solitary dip was only enough to make the darkness visible.

The witch had not left her three minutes ere she felt she could have screamed with terror. It seemed to her as though the whole atmosphere was full of invisible spirits, and nameless terrors pressed upon her heart and almost stopped its beating. She began to wonder where the witch had gone, why she had gone, and what mystery lay behind that curtain, yet she dared not get up and look.

The silence was oppressive. She might be in a tomb, so still and hushed was everything. Would the witch never return? It seemed hours since she went away, though in truth not more than five minutes had elapsed. The vague terror that was weighing upon her heart was becoming intolerable. She must scream if she would save herself from fainting.

The next moment a voice, clear, distinct, but far off, broke the silence. It disturbed the sleeping echoes of the cavern, and wailed away in the distance, and died at last in silence.

Mary started to her feet, trembling and affrighted. The next moment the voice was heard again, still far away behind the curtain, but she recognized it now as belonging to the witch. Some strange doggerel she was chanting in a clear, shrill voice. Mary listened intently and caught some of the words, many of which were repeated over and over again—

" The earth is full of mystery ;
The deeps are dark, I cannot see.
I send my cry into the night,
I wait, I pine, I long for light.
The forests bellow in my ear ;
The thunder's roll I do not fear.
Death and the dead walk through my cave ;
I sleep above my own cold grave.
I hold discourse with death and hell,
And round the living weave my spell.
       And yet, and yet
       I chafe and fret :
       How little light
       Greets my poor sight ;
       My hands are tied,
       Hell mocks my pride—
And heaven has hurled me from her gate,
And thundered in my ears ' Too late.'
       But what care I ?
       I will not cry,
       I will not sigh,
       I will not die.
I laugh and sing and work my will,
And weave my charms in darkness still.
A queen in darkness reigneth I,
A queen enwrapped in mystery.
Here in my cave serene I sleep ;
Here in the darkness vigil keep.
I listen to thy song, oh sea ;
I hear the night wind moaning free.
   I hear the lash of wintry waves ;
   I hear the crash when ships find graves.

I hear Tregeagle's sad lament,
Bemoaning life so badly spent.
　Ah-ha, Ah-ha, I sing and laugh ;
　Ah-ha, Ah-ha, my drink I quaff,
Distilled from adder's flattened head,
And tongue of lizard three months dead.
I mix with care, and add a mite
Of hemlock leaf and aconite,
And then I quaff till care is gone,
And I am happy all alone.
　　Ah ha, ho ho,
　　I love it so.
　　I am the queen
　　Of Carn Duloe.

When the chanting ceased a long-drawn sigh followed, which echoed mournfully through the cavern, then all was still again.

Mary dropped into the chair and pressed her hand against her side to still the wild beating of her heart. A few seconds of intense silence followed. Then the curtain parted in the middle, and the witch appeared again, followed by her cats.

"The charm works beautifully," she said. "The night is favourable. The spirits are holding revel. Now open your heart freely, and let me know your will."

"It is that you release Harry from prison, and help him to escape," Mary said with a blush.

"I can release him from the dark hole in which he is now lodged," she answered, "but more than that I cannot do, will not do. If he is guilty there is no escape for him."

"But he is not guilty, I am sure of that," Mary answered.

"Nothing is sure," said the witch, gravely. "I have questioned the spirits, but they will not answer, and the voice I have heard puzzles me."

"But you can guess ?"

"Guesses are as often wrong as right, and I prefer to wait before giving an opinion."

"But you will try to find out?"

"Try? I *shall* find out, and until then the lad should have a chance."

"You mean Harry?"

"I mean the Vicar's son."

"But he will be taken to Bodmin gaol to-morrow, and what is done for him must be done quickly," Mary answered, wringing her hands.

"I have not forgotten that," was the reply; "and no time has been wasted yet."

"Oh, it seems as if I had been here a very long time, and I fear they will be getting anxious about me at home."

"Thou hast no need to fear. But come, we will delay no longer."

"You will go with me?" Mary asked eagerly.

"Of course, child. Thou sayest there is no time for delay, and I am ready," and the witch went to the door and opened it, and Mary passed out into the breezy darkness.

Oh, what a relief it was to breathe the fresh air again after the stifling atmosphere of the witch's house. The wind was still soughing in the great forest all around her, and the trees were swaying their ghostly arms in the darkness, but the "outer" night had no longer any terrors for her. In a few moments the witch was by her side, having extinguished her light and fastened the door.

"Now follow me," she said, and instantly strode away along the level track.

Mary followed close upon her heels, only too eager to get out of that gloomy forest and away from its fearsome associations. Very few words were spoken until they emerged from the shadow of the trees and began to cross the level valley. Then the witch paused a moment that Mary might walk by her side.

"Thou hast no desire that thy visit to me be made known, I expect?" she asked.

"Oh, no, I would not like any one to know of it."

"Not even thy lover?"

"Oh, please, I have no lover," she said appealingly.

"Tut, tut. But thou hast no wish that I tell the lad that I visit him at thy request."

"Oh, no, I would not that he should know for the world."

"Very well. Thou art a heap of contradictions, like all thy sex." And the witch marched on ahead again. At the stile against the road she paused again. "Now, thee get thee to thy home at once," she said. "Aye, and get thee to bed as soon as possible. I will wait here till thou art out of sight."

"And you will do your best to release Harry?" she asked again.

"Fear nothing, I *will* release him, unless he refuses to leave his present quarters. Now go home and say thy prayers, and get to sleep."

"Nay, sleep will be impossible; but I will go home and pray."

"As thou wilt; and if thou hast faith in thy prayers, put up a petition for me."

"I will pray for you always."

"That is kind. Now begone."

And without more words Mary climbed lightly over the stile, and was soon bounding down the road towards Trevose. No one seemed to be abroad, for she did not meet a single creature. Nevertheless she drew a sigh of relief when she got inside the yard-gate, and heard it click behind her. Her step was heard and recognized as she crossed the court, and the door was opened from within.

"Oh, miss," said the maid, "we was gettin' quite hurried 'bout you. We couldn't tell what 'ad become of you."

"Is it so very late?" Mary asked.

"No, not so very; but it's been dark some time."

"Yes, I know; but I have been detained. Has mother asked for me?"

"No, she's been having quite a long sleep."

"Oh, that is right. And father?"

"He ain't got home yet, miss."

"Then I expect he will stay supper with the Vicar. At any rate you need not get it ready unless I tell you."

And Mary passed quickly into the hall and up the stairs to her own room. Here she instantly removed her bonnet and shawl, and then fell on her knees by her bedside and began to pray.

Her conscience was not altogether easy. She was not at all certain whether she had done the right thing in consulting the witch of Carn Duloe and seeking her aid. If Harry was innocent God could release him without the witch's assistance.

And yet God did not always interfere in such matters. He seemed to leave such affairs in human hands, and if men failed to do what was in their power, they must take the consequences of such neglect.

She felt happier when she rose from her knees; and when a few minutes later she stood by her mother's bedside, her face bore no trace of what she had passed through during that evening.

CHAPTER XIII.

ABEL GETS IMPATIENT.

" Let me then in peace depart,—
    Let me quit this world for ever !
Earthly pleasures leave a smart,—
    Time all earthly ties must sever ;
And its charms are empty show,
Vain deceit, which ends in woe."

                            FROM THE GERMAN.

ABEL TREGONNING was considerably astonished that evening when, in response to a loud knock, he opened the door, and found himself face to face with the witch of Carn Duloe.

" What, Mrs. Flue ! " he said, starting back.

He did not know whether Nanny was Mrs. or Miss ; but, like most of the villagers, he was intensely superstitious, and would not offend Nanny for the world if he could help it, and he thought " Mrs." was the most respectful term he could apply to her.

" Yes, Mrs. Flue," said Nanny scornfully. " Stand back and let me come in, for I want to talk with thee."

" I am at your sarvice," said Abel, deferentially, " though I be very busy, as you can well understand."

" Busy ! What has thou to be busy over ? Thy prisoner is safe under lock and key, I suppose ? "

" Oh yes, he's safe enough, an' likely to remain so for the rest of his natural life," and Abel laughed grimly.

"Aye, thou'rt a trusty jailer, Abel. This'll mean promotion for thee, and perhaps a pension."

"I hope so," said Abel, with a smile. "I've made a lot of labour over the case."

"And proved it up to the hilt, eh, Abel?"

"That I have; there's no doubt of his guilt."

"Then he ought to swing."

"And swing he will," said Abel. "I wish I was as sure of promotion as he is of a hempen cord."

"They say the evidence left no loophole," said the witch, with a curious leer in her dark eyes.

"They say what's true," assented Abel. "Fact is, there never was a clearer case."

"A man that murders a friend, and in cold blood too, deserves no pity, Abel."

"That's what I say."

"You keep him fast, I warrant?"

"That I do."

"That's right, Abel; and let none of his friends visit him?"

"Not one on 'em. His father came this evening, just as it was growing dusk. Pleaded 'ard to see 'im, but I was firm."

"Thou art a model jailer, Abel. I commend thee."

Abel smiled broadly. "It don't do to be soft in a case o' this sort."

"Soft! I should think not. I despise soft men of all things. Now, Abel, get out thy keys and a light, and come with me. I want to see thy prisoner."

"But, but—" began Abel, growing white, then red.

"No 'buts,' man," said the witch. "Thou surely art not going to turn soft?"

"No, not if I know it," asserted Abel; "but it's agin rules, and everything is made tight for the night. I'm bound to refuse."

"Thou'rt bound to make thyself an ass," said the witch, in a tone of ineffable scorn.

"I'm willin' to oblige you in most things, Mrs. Flue,"

said Abel, bringing out the words with an effort; "but in a case like this you will excuse me, I'm sure."

"I'm sure I shall do nothing of the sort," was the reply. "I have come on purpose to see thy prisoner, and I'm going to see him. Now get out thy keys."

"An' what ef I refuse?" said Abel, straightening himself up and trying to look brave, but feeling dreadfully frightened all the while.

The witch laughed. "What if I smite thee with St. Vitus' dance, or double thee up in a fit, or paralyze thy hands that thou canst not move, or shake thee for ever in a palsy? But no, I wish thee no harm. Now, man, no more parleying, but obey."

Abel hesitated for a moment, then sulkily got out his lantern and his keys.

"Now thou art wise," she said; "and do not again hesitate as though I were thine enemy; and if thou makes me thine enemy it will be worse for thee."

"I don't know why you should want to see the prisoner, and at this time o' night too," Abel muttered.

"That's no business of thine. Now march, and cease thy chatter."

A few minutes later they stood before the door of Harry's cell.

"He's fast asleep by this, like enough," Abel muttered.

"And what if he is? Open the door, and be quick about it."

Reluctantly Abel inserted the key and turned it, then pushed open the heavy door.

"Thou canst wait outside, and lock the door upon us if thou wilt. Thou wilt have both of us safe then."

"I'd rather remain with you," Abel said.

"I do not wish to harm thee," the witch said impatiently; "but if thou wilt be a fool, thou wilt have to pay the penalty. Now give me the lantern, and when I knock, open the door and let me out, and see to it that thou asks no questions."

Abel hesitated no longer. Without a word he handed her the lantern, then slammed the door behind her and locked it, and for the next half-hour he paced uneasily up and down the dark corridor. Once or twice he paused before the door and placed his ear against it, but he could hear no sound. If they were engaged in conversation, the sound of it was completely muffled by the heavy door.

He was in a very uneasy frame of mind. Angry that a woman should so completely master him, and compel him, in spite of himself, to act in direct opposition to his better judgment; suspicious lest she meant mischief, and should contrive by means of her diabolical incantations to release the prisoner. And yet he did not see how that could possibly be. There was no way out of the cell except by the door through which she had entered, and that at present was securely locked, and he held the key.

"I'm a fool for fidgeting," he said to himself. "She can't go through a stone wall, nor he neither; she must come out o' the door, an' I'll see to it that only one comes out."

And with this reflection he began to pace more rapidly the long corridor. But time went very slowly; every minute seemed as long as ten. He would have opened the door and gone into the cell if he had dared, but fear of incurring the anger of the witch kept him outside.

"She might 'ill-wish' me," he reflected; "that evil eye o' hers could do 'most anything that's bad. There's Jonas Trethurgy, he's never looked up since that day he call'd her an old hag. They say she never spoke to him, but just look'd at 'im straight wi' those hawful eyes of hers, an' he felt it all go through 'im down to his toe-nails. He was creepy an' shivery all over as though poison 'ad got into his blood, an' soon after he was took wi' a seizure; then his gray mare was knocked over wi' blind staggers; then his best cow was chucked wi' eating a swede turmut; then his old sow lay on three vears (farrows) one night. And so it's gone on, an' the poor old chap have never 'ad no luck never since. No, I'd better keep on the lew side o' her, or it may be worse for me."

And so he continued to pace up and down the corridor, but getting more and more impatient all the while.

Meanwhile the inmates of the cell were not inactive. Harry was very much astonished when the tall, gaunt form of the witch stood before him, holding in her hand the constable's lantern. He had heard no voices or footsteps in the corridor outside, and when the sound of the key grating in the lock fell on his ear he supposed that it was Abel coming to see that he was safe for the night. He had been trying to make himself as comfortable as his plank bed would allow, and to keep away as far as possible all unpleasant thoughts. He fully believed that his days were numbered, that he was doomed to die. But no good could come of brooding over the matter; better make the present as pleasant as possible with sunny memories of the past. So he lay there in the darkness, trying to imagine that he was in his own room at the vicarage, or else wandering in the quiet lanes with Mary Dunstan.

Yesterday and the day before he had succeeded in keeping Mary very largely out of his thoughts. He thought it would save him pain if he could forget her; but to-night a different feeling had come over him. Might he not live in a sort of dreamland for the rest of his days? He could give his imagination play; he could dwell with Mary and Gladys, and his father, and Mrs. Gaved, and all those he loved, and forget the bare walls that surrounded him, and the awful doom that awaited him. And so he lay there on the hard boards with wide-open eyes, peopling the darkness with the forms and faces of those he loved, and filling his brain with memories of the past. The light from the lantern brought him back to himself, and with a start he sat up and stared hard at his visitor.

"Thou didst not expect to see me?" she said, laying the lantern on the floor, and proceeding to take off her big coal-scuttle bonnet and long heavy cloak.

"I did not," he answered.

"Well, I did not come of my own free will," she replied; "I came at the urgent request of another."

"Of another?" he asked, with up-lifted brows.

"Aye, at the request of one who loves thee."

"My father?" he questioned eagerly.

"Dost think thy father would seek the aid of a witch?" she questioned.

"You are right," he answered; "and yet I do not know who else would ask you to come."

"And don't inquire," she said, "for I am not going to tell thee. And now to business."

"What business?" he asked.

"Thou mayst well ask that," she said with a cynical laugh; "but there's no time for parleying. Thy friend believes that thou art innocent. I know not if thou art or not—"

"But I thought you knew everything," Harry interposed, a little bit maliciously.

"Don't sneer," she said, "or I will leave thee to thy fate. I came to release thee if I can persuade myself that thou art innocent."

"What evidence do you want?" he asked.

"That is not an easy question to answer," she said. "Three times in my little home on lone Carn Duloe's slope I have heard a voice calling across from Tregeagle's Head. It has sounded like a cry for help, and in tone it was like his voice."

"Like whose voice?"

"Jack Dunstan's."

Harry started to his feet, and breathed hard.

"And what do you make of it?" he asked.

"I hardly know," she said. "If he has been murdered I can understand it. It is his spirit calling for vengeance. And yet I am loth to believe thee guilty."

"Tush!" he said, "you do not believe in spirits. Don't try to impose on me with talk of that kind."

She started a little, and looked at him steadily. "Thou knowest," she said, "that Tregeagle is often heard on stormy nights."

"I know nothing of Tregeagle," he said, "and don't believe the talk; and I'm of opinion that you don't believe it either. It may suit your purpose to make people think so."

"Thou hast amazing impudence," she said, evidently taken a little aback. "Art thou not afraid of what I may do to thee?"

"Afraid?" he questioned, with a bitter laugh. "What have I to be afraid of? If you could smite me dead here and now I should be grateful. Nothing worse can come to me than has already come. Have I not lost all—liberty, love, home, friends? and life is nearly ended. Come, witch, do thy worst or thy best."

"Nay, nay," she said, "I came not to kill, but to set thee at liberty."

"You cannot," he answered; "and if you could, to what end? Life has nothing to offer me. Is mere existence so precious that I would be willing to be hunted as a fugitive, and live in terror the rest of my days? No, no; go your way, and leave me in peace. I am dead to the world, and the world is nearly dead to me."

"But for the sake of others," said the witch, "for the sake of those who love thee. And if thou art innocent thou oughtest to be eager to live in the hope of proving thy innocence."

"Ah, if I could do that!" he said, with sudden energy.

"Then thou art innocent?" she questioned.

"The magistrates say no," he answered bitterly.

"Come," she said with temper, "this is a game of

cross purposes; and but that I promised one who loves thee that I would help thee to escape, I would go and say no more. Perhaps thou art guilty. I have heard his voice three times—there is no mistaking that."

Harry started again. " Are you not fooling me ? " he said.

" I am speaking the sober truth," she answered, " so help me, God."

For a moment or two he paced his cell in silence. Then stopping before her he said slowly,

" This is a solemn matter. Do not deceive me, as you hope for heaven."

" I am not deceiving thee," she answered. " I have nothing to gain by deceiving thee."

" And you have heard what seemed his voice ? "

" Three several times," she answered, " borne by the night wind across the valley to my lonely eyrie among the rocks."

" You are sure you were not dreaming ? "

" Quite sure. Dost think I'm a love-sick maiden ? I've heard voices before—blood-curdling cries—perhaps Tregeagle's—perhaps the cries of drowning men."

" And the tones seemed those of Jack Dunstan's voice ? "

" Yes ; but in that I may have been mistaken."

" Oh that I were free ! " he said, as if speaking to himself, " that I might probe this matter to the bottom."

" So thou art coming to thy senses, eh ? " she said cynically.

" Coming to my senses ? No, it is idle to talk of freedom."

" It is not idle," she said. " Obey my instructions, and in ten minutes from now thou shalt be under the stars, in the free air of heaven."

" Freedom for a few days would be welcome," he said,

"to search, to prove. If what you say is true there is
no cowardice in desiring to be free."

"Then you will obey me ?"

"Yes, I will."

"Good. Now listen ;" and the witch dropped her
voice to a whisper while she unfolded her plan.

CHAPTER XIV.

IN DISGUISE.

"And is it that the haze of grief
Hath stretched my former joy so great?
The lowness of the present state,
That sets the past in this relief?
Or that the past will always win
A glory from its being far;
And orb into the perfect star
We saw not, when we moved therein?"

TENNYSON.

"Thou art just a little taller than I am," whispered the witch, "but not sufficient to be noticed. Thy face is bare, and with the aid of this bit of charcoal I can put in all the wrinkles necessary. Now be still, and I will make thee the very image of myself."

"There," she chuckled at length, "the likeness is nearly perfect. Now get on this old dress of mine which I have brought for the purpose. But thou art clumsy. Art excited?"

"No, I'm as cool as a cucumber," he whispered.

"That's right. Never mind if it doesn't fit around the waist, the cloak will cover that. Now for the bonnet;" and she lifted up her coal-scuttle and placed it on his head.

"Good heavens!" she chuckled; "I never saw anything better in my life. The disguise is absolutely perfect. If I were to meet thee and did not know, I should swear thou wert my double."

"I feel as though I were," he said, with a low laugh. "At least I don't feel myself at all."

"So much the better," she replied. "Now take two or three turns round the cell to get used to walking in skirts."

"All right," he said, following out her instructions.

"But thou art taking much too long strides. Now bow thy head forwards so. That's better."

"Anything else?" he whispered.

"Yes; keep thy mouth shut when thou art passing out. He will never recognize thee unless thou speaks. When he opens the street-door let the lantern drop, and while he is picking it up take thyself off as fast as possible."

"But what of you?" he questioned.

"Never mind me," was the answer. "I can spend a night here very comfortably, and it will be easier than toiling up to Carn Duloe. When he comes in the morning he will be glad enough to let me out. He is so frightened of me that he will do nearly anything I tell him."

"Poor man!"

"Aye, poor man! But art thou ready?"

"Quite."

"Then knock at the door and keep thy mouth shut. I will do all the talking."

Instantly Harry raised his foot, and gave the door two or three vigorous kicks; while the next moment he was startled by hearing the witch's voice almost close to his ear saying,

"Come, make haste, thou model jailer, I want to get out of this hole."

"And I'll be glad eno' to have you out," muttered Abel. "I thowt you were goin' to stay all night."

"Hold thy clatter and obey, or it will be worse for thee."

"I caan't be no quicker," growled Abel, turning the rusty key slowly in the lock. That done, he cautiously pushed open the door, until there was just space enough for one to pass out.

"Thou need not fear any one will attempt to come out with me," spoke the witch; and the next moment a cloaked and stooping figure came through the narrow opening.

Abel was still holding the door firmly, and quickly pulled it to, and closed it with a snick.

"I feared he might ha' tried to come through at the same time," muttered Abel; but the cloaked figure marched quickly towards the outer door without vouchsafing a reply.

Abel seemed quite as eager to get into the open air as was his prisoner. Indeed he was thoroughly out of temper at having to wait so long, and all the more so because he knew his supper was waiting for him, and he feared was spoiling.

He wasted no time, therefore, in unlocking and throwing open the street-door, and Harry, dropping the lantern as he had been instructed, passed swiftly out into the night.

By the time Abel had picked up the lantern and locked the door the supposed witch had vanished into the darkness. Abel paused for a moment and looked up and down the street, then with something like a sigh he strode towards his own door, and soon forgot his worries in the odour of boiled hake, which greeted his nostrils.

In the meanwhile Harry was striding rapidly in the direction of the vicarage. Where else could he go but to his own home? He had no thought of escaping to some distant part of the country, or of putting the ocean between himself and his pursuers. Indeed he had no formulated plan of any sort. His escape had been so sudden and unexpected, that he had had no time to think of what he should do when he found himself at liberty.

His first feeling was one of intense relief at finding himself free. It seemed an age since he had been led away to prison. He had counted almost every moment of the time, and could hardly persuade himself that it was less than three days ago since he was apprehended.

When he reached the churchyard he paused, and took off the huge bonnet that enveloped his head, and turned his face towards the west. He wanted to breathe again the fresh sea-breeze, and feel its strong cool breath playing round his neck and face. After the stuffy atmosphere of his cell, it seemed like new life to him; and throwing back his shoulders, he took deep inspirations, as though it were nectar.

Around the old church the wind wailed and whistled, and across the grassy hillocks it swept with a low swish, as though it would hush into a deeper sleep those who lay beneath the turf.

He had no fear of being discovered, none of the villagers ever crossed the churchyard at night-time. It was too suggestive of ghosts to be frequented after sunset. And even should some adventurous native cross his path, he felt sure that his disguise would be a perfect protection. So he loitered among the graves for fully ten minutes. The time and the place suited his mood. Moreover, now that he was close to his own home an unaccountable nervousness came over him— a fear lest he might not be welcome, or lest his unexpected appearance should be too great a shock to their nerves.

Once the idea suggested itself to him of going at once to Tregeagle's Head and spending the night there, trying to fathom the mystery of that cry of which the witch had spoken; but he dismissed it after a moment's consideration. He was too weary and exhausted yet for such a vigil. Evidently his first duty was to get a good night's rest and sleep.

So replacing his bonnet at length, he struck out for the vicarage, and soon felt the gravel of the path crunching beneath his feet. He saw a light in the dining-room window, which tempted him to go close up to it and listen. Perhaps he might be able to get a peep within. He did not know why he should act in this way. He was a puzzle to himself. He felt like a stranger rather than a son.

At one corner the blind was not quite down, so that nearly all the room was exposed to his view. At the head of the table sat his father, with an open Bible before him; near the door sat the two serving-maids; close to the fire was Mrs. Gaved, with her back towards him; and by her side was Gladys, sitting on a low stool hugging her knees.

He could not help noticing how haggard and troubled his father looked. He seemed to have added ten years to his life during the last few days. Very mournfully, too, his voice sounded as the words fell distinctly on Harry's ear—

"Why art thou cast down, O my soul, and why art thou disquieted within me?"

"Poor father!" Harry thought, as the tears welled up into his eyes and nearly blinded him. But he hastily brushed them away, and fixed his gaze upon Gladys, who, though pale and hollow-eyed, had a strangely resolute look upon her face. Gladys too looked older, as though she had put away childish thoughts and things, and was now going to face the world with a woman's heart and will.

The psalm ended, they all knelt down to pray.

"I'm glad I did not disturb them at prayers," he said to himself, as he bowed his head and listened.

It was a beautiful prayer his father offered, full of tenderness and sympathy. Evidently grief and anxiety had already begun to soften his austere nature, and to bring him more into touch with those who suffered and sorrowed around him.

Harry could not keep back his tears when allusion was made to himself.

"Father in heaven, bless my boy," the Vicar pleaded. "Alone in silence and darkness he pines to-night; be very near to him, and grant him Thy peace. We may

not see him or speak to him a word of hope; but bolted
doors are no barrier to Thee. Oh, let my poor boy feel
that Thou art near him, and know that he is not forsaken. We yearn to give him comfort, while a sight of
his face would be like medicine to our sorely-stricken
soul. Oh, Father of mercies, reveal Thy mercy to him
and to us, unravel this tangled skein, if it please Thee,
and let light arise upon our darkness, and hope take
the place of our despair."

Harry felt no longer like a stranger when the prayer
was ended. Going quickly up to the door, he gave
three distinct raps, and a moment after it was opened
by one of the maids. But at sight of him she started
back with a little cry of alarm, which instantly brought
the Vicar to her side.

"You can go to the kitchen, Jane," he said; "I will
attend to Mrs. Flue." And nothing loth, Jane instantly
retreated with an alacrity that was most unusual with
her. Meanwhile Harry had come into the hall, and
closed the door behind him.

"And now, madam," said the Vicar, turning to Harry,
"to what am I indebted——" Then he suddenly paused,
and stared hard at his visitor. "Ah," he said sternly,
"and who are you? I see I am mistaken; this is an
unwarrant——" But he did not finish the word.

"Yes, father," Harry interposed, "you are mistaken
this time."

"W—w—w—hat. W—w—hat!" he exclaimed,
stammering as though seized with an attack of ague.
But before Harry could again reply he had grasped the
truth, and seizing Harry by the arm he dragged him
into the dining-room, much to the astonishment and
even consternation of Mrs. Gaved and Gladys.

"Why, look at him!" he exclaimed, laughing and
crying at the same time. "Isn't it fine? I think it is
just splendid," and he stood back a little from Harry,
and laughed again till his sides ached.

But Mrs. Gaved and Gladys could not see where the

laugh came in. To have the witch of Carn Duloe
thrust upon them in this unceremonious manner was
not a laughing matter. Indeed, Mrs. Gaved resented it
most unmistakably. She got up from her chair with an
ominous frown upon her brow, and was about to march
out of the room, when Harry, who could no longer
maintain his gravity, burst into peals of laughter.

Instantly Gladys leaped to her feet, exclaiming,
"Why, it's Harry. Oh, you dear, blessed old Harry."
And the next moment her brother had caught her in
his arms, and had half smothered her with kisses.

Mrs. Gaved stared hard at the intruder, then dropped
into a chair and began to cry. But a kiss and a kind
word from her heart's idol soon comforted her.

"Now, Mammy," he said, "dry your tears, and get me
a good supper; we'll talk after. I'm hungry enough at
present to eat a gravestone."

"My poor boy, I wonder you are not dead," sobbed
Mrs. Gaved. "But, oh dear! how did you get here,
and are you quite safe?"

"I'm safe enough for to-night, at any rate," he
answered. "For the rest you must wait till I have had
some supper. Meanwhile you can draw down that
blind at the corner, and I will have a wash and a
change of raiment," and he rushed away up-stairs to
his own room.

"Oh, papa!" exclaimed Gladys, climbing on the
Vicar's knee. "What does it mean?"

"I don't know, my child," said the Vicar, blowing
his nose violently. "He has evidently duped his jailer,
but how he has managed it I can't tell; we must wait
till he explains."

In a few minutes a substantial supper of cold meat
was laid on the table, and Harry proceeded to attack it
with a vigour that left nothing to be desired.

The Vicar was greatly affected as he sat watching his
son, and more than once stealthily wiped away the tears
that rushed unbidden to his eyes. It seemed almost

an age since he had looked upon his face, and even now he felt it was only a stolen glimpse he got; any moment he might be marched away again to prison, perhaps to death.

Harry seemed the most unconcerned of the little group, and when he had satisfied his hunger, he pulled up his chair nearer the fire, and proceeded to tell the story of his escape.

"I think Nanny is an old brick," he said with a laugh. "If she has done nothing else, she has secured me a good supper, and that I sorely needed, and I fancy I shall sleep to-night without rocking."

"But what object can she have had in interposing," the Vicar asked. "She has run considerable risk, and even now she may find herself in jail in consequence."

"Well," said Harry, after a pause, "I am more than a little puzzled over that matter myself. She told me she came at the urgent request of some one who loved me. For the moment I thought she meant you; but of course you would not seek the aid of such a woman."

"Not I indeed," said the Vicar.

A moment's pause followed this remark, during which Mrs. Gaved began to poke the fire in an unusually vigorous manner.

"I should not have attempted to escape," Harry went on, "but that I felt I should like to probe to the bottom the secret of this cry Nanny declares she has heard."

"Do you think it possible Jack Dunstan may be yet alive?" Gladys asked suddenly, with an eager light in her eyes.

"I don't know what I think," he answered slowly. "It seems impossible that he can be still living. But the witch is positive she has heard a voice like his. I am not superstitious, but I am certainly curious."

"Harry," said the Vicar, getting up from his chair, and looking very white, "you will excuse me, I am sure, for seeming to doubt you, but it would satisfy me to hear it from your lips, that neither by accident or design has Jack suffered harm at your hands."

"Forgive me, father, if I have been too reticent. But I am as innocent as you are."

"My boy, that is enough," the Vicar said, blowing his nose violently. "And now what about the future?"

"I don't know. I have had no time to think yet. Suppose we let matters drift until to-morrow. I want a good night's sleep, that will clear my brain; to-morrow we can put our heads together. At present I have no desire to 'cut the country,' as they say. I'd rather be hanged than be hunted like a fugitive all my life. My only hope lies in the secret of Tregeagle's Head."

"We are in God's hands, my boy—in God's hands," said the Vicar solemnly.

Then silence fell upon the little group. After a while Harry got up, and kissing them all good night, betook himself to bed.

"And so dear old Mammy Gaved is the friend who got the witch of Carn Duloe to interest herself in my behalf," he said to himself, as he closed the door behind him. "Well, well, she played her cards very well. Her professed indignation at the presence of the supposed witch in the dining-room was well put on; but she should not have poked the fire so vigorously—that let the cat out of the bag. Well, well; here I am, safe in this dear old room once more. Now for a soft bed and some refreshing sleep."

CHAPTER XV.

KEEPING WATCH.

"With me, youth led. . . I will speak now,
    No longer watch you as you sit
Reading by firelight, that great brow
And the spirit-small hand propping it
Mutely, my heart knows how."—R. BROWNING.

ABEL was in no hurry to visit his prisoner next morning, for he had decided that Harry should have the luxury of a day's rest in Restormel "lock-up" between his trial before the magistrates, and his removal to Bodmin gaol.

"He kep' me for near a hour without my supper las' night," Abel soliloquized ; "he can wait for his breakfas' this morning."

So Abel took his time over his griddled pilchards, and appeared to enjoy the performance. Perhaps the thought of Harry pining for his stale crust gave an added relish to his own toothsome meal.

After six pilchards and a small loaf of bread had disappeared down his capacious throat, Abel paused, wiped his lips with the back of his hand, spat out sundry small bones that adhered to the sides of the cavity he called his mouth, and finally rose from his chair, kicked the cat under the "dresser," and then called to his wife.

"Iss, Abel," she answered, from a small room at the rear of the house.

"I'm agoin' down to Pentudy after I've took the

prisoner his breakfas'," he said, "so you needn't wait denner for me."

"All right, Abel," she replied.

"There's more in Sam Trewalsick then he's let out," Abel said, "so I'm agoin' to pump 'im."

"I would, Abel."

"I've got to see Nathan Fraddon to come along wi' me to Bodmin to-morrow; we'd better be two of us."

"Yes, Abel."

"Nothin' like bein' on the safe side, so 'ere's off."

And Abel put on his hat, unhung his bunch of keys, and departed, taking a small basket with him which contained the prisoner's breakfast.

As usual, he opened the cell door with great caution, and took a peep before venturing inside. He hardly knew why he did so, for Harry had manifested no desire whatever to escape.

The prisoner was lying full length on the hard bed, his head wrapped in the solitary blanket which was his nightly covering. Abel grunted to himself, pushed the door a little farther open, and entered.

Scarcely had he done so, however, than he found himself seized by the throat, and swung to the further end of the cell, while over him there loomed—not Harry Penryn—but the witch of Carn Duloe.

In a perfect agony of fright Abel sank trembling upon the floor. He was too terror-stricken to speak or even to move; his teeth chattered as though he had been smitten with ague, his legs refused to support him, his brain was in a whirl. What did it mean? But before he had time to frame an answer to the question, the witch, ghost, or whatever it was, disappeared, slamming the door behind her.

Abel did not try to get up. The whole proceeding had been so sudden and startling, that his slow brain could not grasp the situation.

Was he awake or dreaming? Was he drunk, or pixey

led? or had he been ill-wished or bewitched? He
staggered to his feet at length, and sat down on the
plank bed, trying the while to think out the problem.
But he was not able to make head or tail of it.
Evidently the whole thing was a piece of diabolical
witchcraft.

That he had let the witch out of the cell the previous
night he was quite certain. He had taken particular
notice of her appearance, had seen her face with the
light of the lantern shining upon it, had noticed the
deep furrows on her cheeks. That much was quite
clear. And yet that only made the more mysterious
the present mystery. How did she get back into the
cell again, and how did the prisoner get out? He had
locked the doors carefully enough, and no one had
touched his keys during the night.

Long Abel sat upon the bed knitting his brows, and
scratching his pate; then suddenly leaping to his feet,
he said to himself,

"I have it! It weren't her at all, it weren't; it were
'im. She's given him some drug as have transmuggri-
fied 'im, that's what she's done. I've heerd about sich
things afore; elixir, of hemp seed distilled wi' mundic
water 'll do it, so they say. He'll look like somebody
else, likely as not, an' nobody 'll know 'im. But, good
Lord, what be I to do?"

And Abel went to the door and began to tug at it
with might and main, then he commenced kicking at
it, and finally he shouted, "Help! murder!" at the top
of his voice. Getting exhausted at length, he lay down
on the bed with a feeling gnawing at his heart akin to
despair.

All his dreams of blood-money and promotion
vanished into thin air. Would the magistrates and the
officials at Bodmin believe his story when he told it
them? He feared not. The chances were he would
be charged with neglect of duty, if not with a criminal
defiance of prison rules and regulations.

"Mary stood at the gate as the witch stalked past."—P. 121.

" I may as well li» 'ere quiet till they come searching for me," he said to himself. " P'raps I'd better say nothin' 'bout the witch ; say as 'ow the prisoner jumped up as I was a bringin' in his breakfas' all of a sudden, an' knocked me down afore I know'd what I was about, and 'ow I lied 'ere unconscious for several hours, knowin' nothin' 'bout nothin'. Iss, iss, I think that'll be the best way out ov the mess arter all." And having come to this conclusion, Abel turned over on his side and tried to make himself as comfortable as the circumstances would permit.

Meanwhile, Nanny was making her way with all possible haste towards her home on the slope of Carn Duloe. She knew that once there she would be safe from observation, while in the labyrinths of her cave she would be able to defy pursuit.

Mary Dunstan had been on the look out for her all the morning. She had been in a fever of fear and anxiety all the night, courting sleep in vain, and watching eagerly for the dawn.

Nanny was nearly opposite Trevose when Mary caught sight of her, and running out at the back without a bonnet, she crossed the farm-yard, and stood at the gate as the witch passed. Nanny did not appear to notice her, she stalked straight on, but whispered as she passed the young girl,—" I have set him free."

Mary's heart gave a great bound, but she forbore to ask any questions, as she saw plainly enough that Nanny did not wish to be noticed.

For several minutes longer Mary remained at the gate, then quietly retraced her steps across the yard, and stood for a moment or two to stroke Jet's nose, who had eagerly trotted up to her.

The farmstead was very quiet—all the hands were out in the fields gathering in the remnants of the late harvest. The work must go on, however heavy the trouble that pressed upon their hearts. But all the joy

1

had gone out of the work. Duties were done because they must be done, and not because there was any pleasure in the doing of them. Everything about the place seemed to feel the general depression. Down in the pool the ducks quacked in a subdued kind of way, as though there was something in the atmosphere which checked a full expression of their feelings; the peacock had not spread its tail for four whole days—perhaps the lack of sunshine had something to do with that, for the sky had kept persistently overcast, while the wind moaned sadly all day long.

Yet while Mary stood stroking Jet's nose, the sunshine broke through a rift in the clouds just for a moment or two, and flooded the old farmyard with a golden light.

"Oh, Jet," she said, turning a moment to look up at the sky, "we will not give up hope yet. Harry is free, and oh! nobody knows what is going to happen. The light is behind the clouds," and with eyes beaming with hope she tripped lightly across the yard and disappeared through the doorway.

About noon the men came in from the fields, and the children crowded out of school with laugh and whoop and shout, and for a few minutes the sleepy old village seemed wide awake; but it soon settled down again into its normal state of somnolence. Mary wondered that nothing was said about the escape of Harry. It seemed strange, if what the witch had told her was true, that no one had heard of it. Several times while the "hands" were getting their dinner in the large kitchen she made some excuse for going amongst them, in the hope of gleaning some fragment of information; but their conversation turned on "crops," "cattle," and "the weather," and not a single word was said respecting the matter which lay nearest her heart. She began to fear after a while that Nanny had deceived her, and to consider how or in what manner she could prove the truth or falsehood of the old woman's words.

She longed to question her father on the subject, but had not the courage, so as usual the meal passed in silence.

Directly dinner was over he went up-stairs, and sat for nearly an hour with his wife.

" Oh, I wish I knew," she said, as she busied herself clearing the dinner-table. " This strange silence and uncertainty is becoming oppressive. I must summon up courage to ask father when he comes down if he has heard anything."

She was shaking the table-cloth out in " the court," surrounded by a flock of chickens, when her father came out.

"I think mother is a little brighter to-day, Mary; don't you think so ? " he said.

" Yes, she has seemed a little more cheerful, but she is very weak and prostrate."

" No wonder, no wonder," he said, absently. " But perhaps time will soften the pain."

" Time seems to go very slowly," she answered. " I seem to have lived through a lifetime in these last five days."

" Aye," he said, his voice shaking just a little, " it seems five weeks ago since this trouble came."

" Do you know if they have taken Harry to Bodmin, to-day ? " she said, after a moment's pause.

He was looking away out across the fields with an absent stare in his eyes, and so he did not notice her heightened colour as she spoke; indeed, he did not seem to heed her words at all, though he heard them distinctly enough. The silence that followed the question brought him back to himself.

" What were you saying, Mary ? " he said. " Oh, yes, I remember. No, they have not taken him to Bodmin, to-day, they start early to-morrow morning," and with a sigh the farmer turned on his heel and walked slowly away.

Mary went back to the house feeling more perplexed

than ever. It seemed incredible that Harry should have escaped and no one in the village know of it. And yet the witch had distinctly told her that he was free. And so she alternated between hope and fear, until the uncertainty seemed almost unbearable, and she resolved to pay a visit to the vicarage ostensibly to see Gladys, but really with the hope of gaining some information respecting Harry.

At the vicarage the nervous tension was even more acute; to all callers the Vicar was " not at home." He had resolved that he would see no one. He was a very conscientious man, and was afraid that some one would ask him *point blank* if he knew anything of his son's whereabouts. And he felt that such a question would offer a very strong temptation to equivocate, and under the circumstances he was not at all certain if he would be able to resist the temptation. In the seclusion of his own study he found himself debating the question, whether or not, under certain circumstances, an untruth was not justifiable. If telling the truth, for instance, would condemn an innocent man to death, and telling a lie would save his life, would not telling a lie be justifiable, and telling the truth a moral wrong?

For a long time he wrestled with this problem without arriving at any satisfactory conclusion. In truth the question had never come home to him in this way before. He had been very fond of quoting the old adage, " Speak the truth and shame the devil," but to-day he felt that there might be circumstances in which, to say the very least, the truth ought not to be spoken. So he resolved he would see no one; he would as far as possible keep out of the way of temptation.

He had had a long talk with Harry during the morning, and had strongly urged him to consider some plan of escaping out of the country. But Harry only shook his head. He had thought of the same thing himself during the night, but the difficulties seemed so great, and the chances of escape so feeble, that he put the idea aside as not worthy of consideration.

Moreover, he had availed himself of Nanny Flue's aid with the distinct and definite purpose of probing the mystery of the cry which the witch had heard coming from Tregeagle's Head, and to run away now, he felt, would be to be false to himself, and disloyal to the memory of his friend.

"No, father," he said, "I will not run away; my duty is here for the present. Nothing may come of it, but I shall have the consciousness that I have done my best."

"As you will, my boy," the Vicar answered, with a sad look in his eyes; "but I have no faith in the witch's story. And even though we keep you safe for a few days, we shall have to give you up again."

"If nothing comes of this matter, yes," Harry answered, slowly; "I am not building much on it. The shadow of the scaffold is still over me, but I am not afraid."

The Vicar did not reply, but he walked away to hide his emotion.

"I must give him up," he said to himself; "I don't think he could escape if he were to try, and he evidently does not want to try. But oh, it is very hard!"

Down-stairs a sharp look-out was kept, both at the back and the front. Every moment they expected to see Abel approaching armed with a search warrant; and they had duly prepared themselves for his advent.

In the best bedroom was a huge old-fashioned wardrobe, which had been constructed with what was known as a false back; behind this partition was quite sufficient standing room for two or three persons. And it was arranged that at a given signal Harry should touch a secret spring, by which access was gained to this cavity, and hide there till the search was concluded.

But as the hours of the morning passed away, and the village remained free from all excitement, and Abel did not put in an appearance, they began to wonder what it could all mean. The tension of watching and waiting and listening became almost intolerable. Every one moved about the house with muffled steps, and spoke only in the softest whispers. The oppression was similar to that which precedes a thunderstorm. They knew it was coming, and waited almost impatiently for the first peal to break the solemn stillness.

And still the minutes dragged slowly along, and lengthened into hours. Harry at length ventured down-stairs. He looked pale and worn, and in his eyes there was an anxious, apprehensive look, but otherwise he was quite composed. Hearing his footsteps, the Vicar came out of his study and stretched himself, and yawned two or three times—a most unusual thing with him—and then began to walk up and down the hall with slow and somewhat uncertain steps.

About noon Gladys was despatched into the village, to gather up what items of news might be floating about. But she returned in about half an hour, to say that everything was unusually quiet and free from excitement, and that neither among the workmen who were returning home to dinner, or among the school children, did she hear a single syllable respecting either Harry or Abel Tregonning. And then as a last resource she had gone into John Dickery's shop, and had purchased two ounces of sweets, and nothing was mentioned there; and so she had come home, not knowing what to make of the unusual calm and silence.

"Evidently Abel is keeping the matter to himself," Harry said. "I dare say he is off on the search somewhere. Up at Carn Duloe, very likely. But he will be turning up here before the day is out."

But the watch was not relaxed for a moment, and still the day wore on, till by and by Gladys clapped her hands, and ran towards the door, exclaiming, " Here comes Mary Dunstan ! I am delighted." While Harry stood in the middle of the room irresolute, not knowing whether to rush out of sight or stay.

CHAPTER XVI.

"NIL DESPERANDUM."

"I am not concerned to know
What to-morrow's fate will do ;
'Tis enough that I can say,
I've possessed myself to-day ;
Then if haply midnight death
Seize my flesh and stop my breath,
Yet to-morrow I shall be
Heir to the best part of me."—WATTS.

HARRY'S hesitancy did not rise from any fear that
Mary would betray him; for that matter he could
readily trust his life in her hands. He knew that she
would guard his secret as carefully as any member of
his own family. He hesitated, because he did not
know if it would be wise to look upon her face again.
He had given her up, as he had given up everything
else that he held dear on earth. And in his bitter
fight this had been the hardest part of it. To give
up Gladys, and his father, and Mrs. Gaved, had been
hard enough; but to give up Mary, none knew what
that meant. But then the struggle was over, and he
had won the victory. He had no longer any dread of
death ; all the beauty of life had been taken away
since she was lost to him. She was only a dream now
—a dream to be lived over and over again, as long as
his brief life should last. But nothing more than that.

But if he saw her again, looked into her eyes, and
touched her hands, might it not unman him ?—awaken

again all the old love and the old longing, and send
him back to his prison to fight the battle over again?
The sound of her footstep on the gravel had set his
heart throbbing wildly, and he found himself over-
mastered, almost with a passionate desire to look upon
her sweet pure face, and listen to the music of her voice.

And yet, and yet, was it not foolish? Had he not
better run away and hide himself until she had gone?
put his fingers in his ears until the low-toned music
of her voice had ceased? But while he hesitated the
matter was decided for him. He could not escape
except through the hall, and Gladys had already opened
the door, and Mary had entered.

On the whole he was not sorry; nay, in truth he
was very glad. His judgment might condemn him,
and pronounce his hesitancy foolish; but his heart
upheld him;—and perhaps it is well that our hearts
should rule us sometimes. It is our habit to decry
sentiment and emotion, and to pronounce for reason
on every occasion; but cold, calculating reason may
sometimes lead us as far wrong in one direction as
the impulse of a generous heart may lead us wrong
in the other.

Harry walked up to the mantel-piece, and stood
leaning with his elbow upon it when Mary entered.
He appeared to be very cool and collected, but it was
more in appearance than reality. Mary was dressed
in black—in mourning for her brother—and by contrast
she looked unusually pale. Harry started at these
symbols of grief, and clenched his hands tightly; while
Mary uttered a little cry of alarm, and grasped a chair
for support.

"Don't be alarmed, Mary," he said with a smile, that
had just a touch of bitterness in it; "I will not harm
you."

"Oh, I am not afraid," she answered cheerfully. "But
you did astonish me! How did you get here?"

"Well, that's too long a story to tell in a sentence,"

he said. "Anyhow here I am, and have been here since last evening."

"Oh, I am so thankful," she said, speaking straight out from the heart. "But why do you stay here? Why don't you try to escape to some place where you are not known?"

"Sit down, Mary, and I will tell you," he said, in tones that sounded strangely tender; and looking up, she caught a look in his eyes she could not fail to interpret aright, and which sent the warm blood rushing to her fair neck and face.

"Thank you," she said, dropping into a chair, and dropping her eyes at the same time.

"Keep a sharp look-out, Gladys," he said to his sister, who had again taken up her station at the window. "Abel may pounce upon us at any moment, so we must be careful not to be off our guard."

"Of course when night comes you will get away under cover of darkness?" Mary questioned.

"No," he answered. "I intend to spend the night on Tregeagle's Head. What secrets its caves may hold I know not; but while I remain at liberty I intend to do all I can to discover them."

"Oh, Harry," she said, growing very white, and leaning forward in her chair with an eager look in her eyes, "have you any hope? that is, is there any real grounds—? Oh, I do not know how to shape the question, but you know what I mean."

"I will tell you all I know, Mary," he said tenderly. And then in simple language, and without betraying any emotion, he told her all the story of his escape, and what the witch had said about the voice she had heard.

She might have said that the witch had told her the same story, but she discreetly held her peace. She gathered from his manner that he did not suspect her of interceding with the witch, and as a consequence her heart was lightened of a considerable load of apprehension.

"Do you think it wise," she said at length, "to pay any heed to what Nanny says?"

"Yes, I do," he said in decided tones. "The old woman has shown an interest in me in very practical fashion, and she could gain nothing by attempting to fool me in this matter."

"Yes, that is true," Mary answered slowly. "But Nanny is a strange creature, there is no accounting for what she does or says."

"I believe the old woman is a great deal better than people generally believe her to be," he said quickly. "And my only fear is, that she is kept under lock and key at the present time on my account."

"Oh, no, she is not," Mary said quickly. "I saw her passing Trevose this morning."

"You saw her?"

"Yes."

"Are you sure?"

"Quite sure."

"Did you speak to her?"

"No, Harry, I did not. But I am quite certain it was her."

"Well, I am glad," he said. "But I wonder what can have become of Abel? You have not seen him about, have you?"

"No, I have neither seen him nor heard of him."

"Well, this is the strangest affair I ever heard of," he said. "But he'll turn up, there's not the least doubt, and perhaps when he's least expected."

"Yes, you are running great risks by remaining at Restormel," she said; "and yet I cannot blame you. Oh, I do hope that something will be brought to light that will clear you of this foul charge."

"I do not expect to remain at liberty many days," he said. "If I can discover nothing I shall be glad for this drawn-out agony to end quickly. I have given up everything, and in imagination have gone through all the agony of execution."

"Oh, Harry, dear Harry!" exclaimed Gladys, running up to him and putting her arms about his neck. "It cannot be, it must not be; nay, it will not be. I have prayed for you night and day, and into my heart God has put a great peace, and I know now that He will not let you die."

"My little Gladys," he said, stroking her long wavy hair, "you must not buoy yourself up with hopes that may never be realized."

"I don't," she said, with a bright smile; "but are we not to believe what God tells us?"

But Harry remained silent; he did not like damping the child's faith and hope with his own fears and doubts. Better, he thought, that she should remain in the light of hope as long as possible.

"Ah, you don't believe me," she said playfully; "but you will believe me some day."

"I hope so," said Mary, with a little sigh; while Harry looked at her with a wistful smile, but did not speak.

A few minutes later Mary rose to go. Harry went with her into the hall, while Gladys kept watch at the window.

"We shall probably never meet again, Mary," he said, as he closed the door softly behind him, "so I will say farewell to you here."

His voice was low, but very steady; he had evidently nerved himself for this farewell, and his strong will was not likely to fail him.

"Oh no, not farewell," she said, with a little gasp; "I cannot help hoping that something will happen to lift from your name this terrible suspicion."

"Then you believe in me still, Mary, in spite of the evidence given yesterday?"

"Of course I believe in you, Harry; have I not known you all my life?"

"Thank you," he said, with eyes bent upon the floor; "it is a comfort to think that there are a few people who will think kindly of me when I am dead."

"You should not speak in that way," she said; "you know that while there's life there's hope."

"Ah," he said, after a pause, "I had hopes once till this trouble came—hopes so beautiful that they made earth an Eden to me; but they are gone now. Like flowers nipped by an early frost, they have faded and fallen. Let me not talk of them; perhaps in another world I may find again what here I have lost."

She knew what he referred to, and so was unable to speak; but she felt the warm blood rush to her neck and face, and the tears leap to her eyes, while her hands trembled visibly.

"Oh, Harry, I must go now," she said at length; "and oh, please don't despair."

She would like to have said more; she longed to comfort him, for in his deep trouble and distress all her heart had gone out to him; she knew now but too well that she loved him with all the strength of her nature.

He took her hand in his and held it firmly; he felt it tremble like a caged bird, and then her eyes drooped. Should he tell her his love? He was half assured that she was not indifferent to him. And would it not comfort him to have the assurance of her affection? Would it not soften the slow misery of imprisonment, and the sharp agony of death? Would he not be able to face what lay before him with a braver heart, knowing that her heart was his, and that she would be true to his memory to the last? It was a hard struggle, and he nearly bit his lip through in trying to keep silence; but he mastered himself at last.

"No," he said to himself, "it would be a cowardly thing to speak of love under such circumstances. Even if she loves me, it would be mean of me to ask her to confess it. I, a criminal, hiding from what is called justice, may at any moment be pounced upon, and dragged to prison and to death. No, no! Heaven help me, no!"

He pressed her hand firmly, then dropped it. She

glanced timidly up into his face. It was hard and cold, and in his eyes there was a stony look which made her almost shudder.

"Oh, Harry," she said, "please don't despair."

"Despair!" he said, after a pause; "no, Mary, I won't. I will go out on Tregeagle's Head to-night buoyed up with hope," and back into his eyes there came a softer light, like that which follows the clearing of rain-clouds after a storm.

"That is right," she said, hopefully; "and I will pray for you all the night."

"Will you pray for me?" he asked simply.

"Indeed I will," she said, her face beaming with the light of a lofty purpose.

"Then I will not despair," he answered. "And now, Mary, good-bye. We may meet again—God only knows. But if not——"

"If not we will meet in heaven," she answered.

For a moment he looked at her steadily, then raised her hand to his lips and kissed it, and without another word turned and walked quickly up the stairs to his own room.

Mary waited for a moment, then quietly let herself out, and was soon speeding across the old churchyard in the direction of her home.

CHAPTER XVII.

AN ANXIOUS NIGHT.

" Midnight was come, and every vital thing
  With sweet sound sleep their weary limbs did rest;
  The beasts were still, the little birds that sing,
  Now sweetly slept beside their mother's breast;
  The waters calm, the cruel seas did cease,
  The woods, and fields, and all things held their peace."
                                            SACKVILLE.

ABOUT ten o'clock Harry left the vicarage to keep
his lonely watch on Tregeagle's Head. The night was
cloudy and dark, with a fretful and intermittent breeze
blowing in from the west, and a dampness in the atmosphere that was anything but exhilarating. He had
spent the two hours previous to his departure in per-
fecting his disguise. Nanny had been so clever with
her charcoal, that he thought he might do something
in the same direction by the aid of burnt cork. His
efforts did not quite come up to his satisfaction, though
Gladys, who kept him company, declared that the
graduated series of wrinkles he produced were just
perfection; and when he put on a large wide-awake
hat, with a fringe of white hair attached to the inside
of the crown, she laughed till the tears ran down her
face.

" Why, Nanny herself would not know you now," she
said; " you look the full three score years and ten.

Mr. Penryn had kept in his study most of the day,

but he came out into the hall to say good night to
Harry. For a moment he stood still, with a curious
look upon his face.

"Why, Harry," he said, "I should not have recognized
you!" and he smiled sadly while he spoke.

"And so you think I have been fairly successful with
my disguise?"

"Successful! the fact is, I never saw a better. Indeed, I am sure with a disguise like that you might
safely get away from here. Think of it again, my
lad——"

"I'll keep watch on Tregeagle's Head to-night, at
any rate," Harry answered quickly. "In fact, there
lies my only hope at present."

"But not mine," Mr. Penryn answered. "I feel
certain nothing can come of your watch."

"But I shall not be satisfied until I have probed this
matter to the utmost," Harry answered.

"Don't think I wish to prevent you," the Vicar said
quickly. "Do what you think best; but if nothing
comes of it, let us plan to-morrow some way of escape
for you."

But Harry only shook his head.

"Nay, do not shake your head," the Vicar said,
dejectedly; "I am sure it is not impossible."

"Perhaps not," Harry answered, gloomily; "but life
under such conditions is hardly worth having."

"Well, think of it, my son," the Vicar said, kindly;
"and the Lord be with you to-night."

But Harry did not reply again. His father's tenderness and solicitude were so new, and withal so
pathetic, that it almost unmanned him, so he pulled
his hat low over his eyes, and marched forth into the
night.

Outside the gate he paused for a moment and
listened, but there was no sound save for the wind
complaining in the trees. He knew that the villagers
would be all a-bed by ten o'clock, and so he had no

anticipation of encountering a single soul. And even
if he did, he thought his disguise would be a sufficient
protection.

Having satisfied himself that no one was near, he
straightened himself from his stooping posture, and
started on a brisk walk. For some distance the road
was level, then it began to wind up and around the
pine wood. Just at the bend there was a stile, with a
footpath across the fields, which led to the opposite end
of the village.

After he had passed the stile he began to walk more
slowly, for the road began to ascend in the shadow of
tall pine trees. Suddenly he started and grew pale, for
very distinctly there was the sound of a quick footstep
behind him. His first thought was to plunge into the
darkness of the wood, but he dismissed it after a
moment's reflection. If it were somebody in pursuit
of him, such an act would awaken suspicion in a
moment.

"No," he said to himself, "I must put a bold face on
the matter, and trust to my disguise."

So leaning on his stick, and bending his shoulders
into a very pronounced stoop, he slowly hobbled on.
Steadily the quick footsteps neared him, then suddenly
stopped.

"Hm!" he muttered between his set lips; "I'm
observed at last, so I must make the best of it." And
stopping short, he began to cough in a decidedly
wheezing and asthmatic fashion.

Then the footsteps came on again, quicker than
before, and gained upon him every moment. Harry
was deep in the shadow of the wood, and the figure
passed him on the outer side of the road.

"A woman, eh!" he said to himself, still persisting
in his cough. "And, by Jupiter, Abel Tregonning's
wife. I wonder what's up; and where can she be
hurrying to at this time of night?"

Mrs. Tregonning looked hard at him as she passed,

K

but she could only discern the outline of what seemed
a very old man.

"Well, I needn't ha' been skeared," she said to herself, as she hurried on. "But I wonder who he can be.
I don't know any old man 'creabouts as is bothered wi'
a cough like that."

But neither the old man nor his cough occupied her
thoughts for very long; she was too concerned about
her husband to trouble herself about any other matter.
She had got him some fresh pilchards for tea, and had
even made him a potato cake "to finish up with," as
she said to herself.

But tea-time came and went, and hour after hour
passed away, and still Abel did not come; until when
the clock struck ten she could bear it no longer, but
resolved to go off to Pentudy in search of him. She
was not a particularly nervous or apprehensive woman;
and had it not been that there was a prisoner locked
up in the cell, she would not have been nearly so much
concerned; but she felt sure that Abel would not have
left the prisoner so long without food unless something
very unusual had happened.

She dared not go to the cell herself, and indeed, when
she came to think about the matter, Abel had never
returned to the house with the keys. Evidently he
had taken them with him—a most unusual thing for
him to do. Hence there was nothing left for her to do
but make her way to Pentudy with all possible haste.
This suspense was becoming unbearable, and if anything had happened to her husband, the sooner she
knew of it the better. Every step of the way she
kept hoping she would meet him. On the brow of
the hill beyond the pine-wood she paused for a few
moments. Straight ahead, with the sea surging round
its rocky base, was Tregeagle's Head, a place to be
shunned night and day—a place given up to Tregeagle's
gloomy spirit, and made gruesome by his despairing
cries.

To-night, however, the restless ghost was silent; no
sound floated on the chill damp air, but the surge of
the restless sea. Very frequently she prayed that she
might not see Tregeagle, nor hear his cry.

"If I was to see his ghost I should faint and die,"
she said to herself; "and since the murder—oh dear!"
and the poor woman shuddered visibly.

But anxiety about her husband kept her brave; not
even the fear of Tregeagle could keep him out of her
thoughts, and drawing a long breath, she hurried along
the road that now gradually slanted downwards into the
village of Pentudy.

The little hamlet seemed quite asleep when she
reached it; not a solitary light burned in any cottage
window. The narrow and circuitous street that threaded
its way down to the little harbour was completely
deserted, and almost as dark as a dungeon.

How loudly her footsteps echoed as she hurried along
the narrow causeway. How oppressive was the silence.
Most of the men were out in their fishing-boats, and
would not return till dawn; the women and children
were fast asleep.

"But where was Abel?"—that thought haunted
her like a restless ghost, and filled her with the wildest
alarm.

Nathan Fraddon, the constable, lived at the far end
of the village. If her husband were still with him a
light would be burning in his window; but when she
got near his house her heart almost stopped—all was
dark and silent as the grave.

"What could have become of Abel?" Before
Nathan's door she stood still and wrung her hands in
silent misery; she hardly dared knock, lest she should
learn that her worst fears were realized. Still, certainty
was better than this agonizing suspense, and after she
had eased her heart by a few silent tears, she went up
to the door and gave a loud rat-tat-tat.

She heard its echoes ring through the silent cottage,

but no voice came out of the darkness, so she knocked again, louder than before. A moment later a small window was opened just over her head, and the shrill piping voice of a woman inquired,

"Who be you? an' what do you want?"

"I want to know if Abel Tregonning is here," was the quick and anxious reply.

"Abel Tregonning here? I should think not," was the somewhat indignant answer.

"Not here? This is Nathan Fraddon's house, ain't it?"

"Iss, it es; but what of that?"

"Well, Abel came here to see Nathan this morning, an' he's never returned yet."

"I think you be mistook," said the woman; "Abel Tregonning ain't been in Pentudy to-day."

By this time Nathan himself was at the window.

"Is that you, Mrs. Tregonning?" he said. "What's up?"

"Abel's lost, or got hurt, or something," was the quick reply. "He started off directly he 'ad his break-fas' to come 'ere to see you; he wanted you to go wi' 'im to Bodmin to-morrow."

"Humph! he ain't been 'ere," was the deliberate answer.

"Not been here?" she questioned.

"No; he ain't been in Pentudy to-day, or I should ha' seen 'im or heard ov 'im."

"Oh, dear! what *can* ha' become of him?" the woman almost wailed. "And there's the prisoner a'most starvin', I expect."

"This is very serious," said Nathan, rubbing his bristly chin with his hard palm. "But wait a minute, an' I'll come down; this must be looked into at once. If Abel's out o' the way, why—"

But Nathan did not complete the sentence. Instantly there loomed up before his imagination a vision of blood-money, promotion, a pension perhaps, and many other good things. Abel being out of the way, he would come to the front in this murder case, which was now the talk of the county.

In a few minutes Nathan was dressed and downstairs, and Mrs. Tregonning was seated in the only comfortable chair the cottage contained, looking a picture of misery and despair.

"I'll go back with you," said Nathan, struggling hard to get into his shoes. "The prisoner must be 'tended to, any'ow; I'm feared we can't do much for Abel till mornin'."

But Susan Tregonning did not reply; she simply rocked herself to and fro in her chair. She cared little at the moment what became of the prisoner; all her thought was of Abel.

"You can come down an' bar the door after me," Nathan at length shouted to his wife; "I may not be back till mornin'. Now, Mrs. Tregonning," he said, "I'm at your sarvice."

Susan rose without a word, and followed him out of the house. Along the crooked and deserted street they walked in single file. Neither was in the mood for speech; Nathan just then was too full of his own importance, and Susan too full of trouble.

At length Tregeagle's Head loomed into sight, cutting a fairly distinct outline against the sky. The night was not quite so dark as it had been, and in the north and west a few stars had come out, and glimmered faintly in the deep vault of night.

Steadily the road wound upward, till by and by their heads came into line with the highest point of the cliff. Suddenly Nathan paused, with an exclamation that was a cut between a grunt and a cry.

"Mrs. Tregonning," he said, "d'ye see yon?" pointing with his large forefinger in the direction of Tregeagle's Head.

"See what?" she exclaimed quickly.

"You!" he ejaculated, still pointing with his shaking finger.

Mrs. Tregonning seized his arm in her terror with a grip that made him wince.

"It's Tregeagle!" she gasped, in a hoarse whisper.

"Aye, it's him," Nathan said, with chattering teeth. "There's a storm a-brewin'—he always comes afore a storm."

Far out on the highest point of the headland, and dimly outlined against the clearing sky, was the motionless figure of a man, or rather of an immensely magnified giant; his height appeared not an inch less than twenty feet, with breadth in proportion.

"What a monster!" gasped Susan.

But Nathan did not speak; he stood as if rooted to the ground, with his eyes fixed upon the terrible apparition.

Suddenly the figure changed its shape, and there stood out a blurred dark mass against the sky; this gradually grew smaller and smaller, till by and by only the broken outline of the cliff was seen against the sky.

Nathan drew a long breath, and made an effort to pull himself together.

"I've heerd Tregeagle many and many a time," he said at length; "now I've seed 'im, an' 'tes a sight, sure 'nough."

Susan Tregonning clung to Nathan's arm the rest of the way to Restormel; the journey was a slow and silent one, but the distance was covered at length.

There was still one hope in Susan's heart, that her husband had returned during her absence; he had a key which would unlock the door. Perhaps he was now sitting in his chair, waiting for her. Her heart beat very fast as she neared her own home, and when she tried to unlock the door, her hand shook so much that she could with difficulty insert the key; but this was accomplished at last, and pushing open the door, she plunged into the darkness. In a moment she had reached Abel's chair; alas! it was empty, and she dropped into it herself with a low cry.

"Abel's dead," she sobbed; "Abel's dead."

CHAPTER XVIII.

DISAPPOINTMENT.

" Out, out, brief candle !
Life's but a walking shadow ! A poor player,
That struts and frets his hour upon the stage,
And then is heard no more : it is a tale
Told by an idiot, full of sound and fury,
Signifying nothing."—SHAKESPEARE.

IT was a dreary and disappointing night which
Harry spent on Tregeagle's Head. He had hoped
almost against hope that he would hear that cry of
which the witch had spoken, but it was not to be. No
sound broke the silence save the low sob of the sea,
and the fretful voice of the complaining wind. Across
the headland he stalked in all directions; along the
cliffs he crept on hands and knees; on the spongy turf
he lay still and listened, but no human cry pierced the
silence, or trembled on the startled air.

The night was painfully long to him. Every minute
seemed as long as ten, while the hours appeared interminable. Yet that lonely vigil was not without its
influence upon him. He realized as he had scarcely
ever done before the joy of freedom, while the prospect
of imprisonment and death, to which he thought he had
become reconciled, became horribly sickening and repulsive. Out there under the free heaven, and with
the boundless sea chanting its dirges all about him,
mere existence seemed a joy. Almost any kind of

life was to be preferred to the cruel fate which he had looked upon as inevitable.

"Perhaps father is right," he said, "in wishing me to make an effort to escape. Life is from God, and I ought not to yield it up any sooner than I can help. We will discuss the matter when I get home."

Long before the gray of the morning began to steal up the eastern sky, the hope of solving the mystery of Tregeagle's Head—if mystery existed—had almost died out of his heart.

"Nanny may have heard a cry," he said to himself, "or many cries. She may have fancied that it sounded like his voice. But fancies are not facts. She is not to blame; but clearly there is no hope in this direction."

The cotters of Restormel were early abroad in the fields, and as Harry had no wish to be seen, he stole homeward ere the night began to melt, sadly disappointed with the result of his watch, and much perplexed about the next step he should take.

Meanwhile Abel Tregonning was raving and fuming like a man possessed. His taste of solitary confinement produced anything but a softening effect upon him; the gnawings of hunger were not as yet a means of grace. He was angry at everybody and everything, himself included, and in his frenzy he shouted himself hoarse, and beat the door until his hands were bruised and bleeding.

"She must be a born fool," he said to himself, "that she don't come here and look me up, and see that everything is straight; but if ever I get out o' this hole, she shall feel the rough side of my tongue, if not something wuss."

He did not consider that he had taken the key with him, and had told her that he was going to Pentudy to see Nathan Faddon and Sam Trewalsick. He thought her own common-sense should lead her to the lock-up

directly she discovered he did not turn up when
expected.

"But there," he groaned, "women ain't got no common-sense. You might as well expec' sense out ov a
spar stone. An' nobody knows what stupid things
she'll be a-doin', an' 'ere be I forsook ; an' only the Lord
knows what'll become ov me."

By the time night had closed round him he was
almost exhausted, and too hoarse to shout. He could
only sit, like Bunyan's Giant, grinding his teeth and
biting his nails, and threatening unutterable things to
all and sundry who had helped him into his present
predicament.

It was considerably after midnight when Nathan,
after doing his best to encourage Mrs. Tregonning,
began to consider how he could best get at the prisoner.
He had some keys of his own, and he resolved he would
do what he could with these as a first attempt. Much
was his surprise, therefore, in trying the street-door, to
find that it was unlocked. For Nanny, in her eagerness
to escape unobserved, had not waited to turn the key
in the door.

"Hello," said Nathan to himself, " what in the name
ov Moses is the meanin' of this!" But he did not stay
to debate the question. Marching along the corridor
to the cell door, he tried that also.

"Hum," he grunted to himself, " Abel's not—— "

But he never finished the sentence. The next moment
he was startled by a hoarse voice calling from within.

"Is that you, Susan? Do let me out, for God's
sake."

"Let you out!" called Nathan, nearly letting the
lantern fall in his terror. "Who be you?"

"Who be I?" snarled Abel from within. "Why I
be Abel Tregonning, you fool. Who be you?"

But without waiting to reply Nathan rushed out of
the place, and bursting in on Mrs. Tregonning, shouted,

"Abel's locked up in the cell. Come this very minute."

Bewildered and incredulous Susan followed him, and was soon pounding on the cell door with her hands, calling—

"Be you really there, Abel?"

"Of course I be here," he snarled. "Where else should I be? Do let me out."

"But where's the key?" she asked.

"How do I know?" he snapped. "Dost tha think I've locked myself in for the fun ov it?"

"Then who locked you in?" she called.

"The Lord knows, I don't," he groaned. "But see about getting me out, and don't chatter so much."

"But 'ow are 'ee to be got out?" she asked. "We caan't undo the door without a key."

Abel groaned savagely, then after a moment said—

"Ain't Nathan there?"

"Aye," Nathan answered, with a touch of disappointment in his tone, for the hope of stepping into Abel's shoes had vanished since he discovered that he was alive and well.

"Can't you get me out?" Abel asked querulously.

"I don't know," said Nathan, a little bit sulkily. "Where's your prisoner?"

"Bolted," snarled Abel.

"Then there's two on you bolted," chuckled Nathan with a sudden inspiration of wit, which was an astonishment to him for the rest of his natural life.

"Don't be a hass, Nathan," snarled Abel.

"No need," said Nathan. "One ass in this place is enough at a time."

Abel ground his teeth, but did not reply, for he felt that the rebuke was only too well merited.

"What are 'ee agoin' to do?" he asked at length in a milder tone.

"I'm trying my keys," said Nathan, "but they'll none on 'em fit."

"Can't you get a crowbar and prize the door open?" asked Abel.

"Do 'ee think I carry a crowbar round wi' me in my waistcoat pocket?" Nathan asked maliciously. "Where be I to get a crowbar?"

"Moses Dingle will lend 'e one," said Abel.

"Moses Dingle be in bed an' asleep hours agone," Nathan answered.

"Then go an' rouse 'im up," roared Abel.

"And let all the place know you've made a fool o' yourself, and let your prisoner 'scape?" said Nathan.

Abel groaned, but did not reply.

"'Ain't you a bar about the place as 'll answer the purpose?" Nathan asked at length.

"No," grunted Abel.

"Then you'll 'ave to bide the consequences," was the retort.

"Good Lord, 'ain't I bided the consequences long enough already?" growled Abel. "Why, man, I'm nearly famished, and as sore as Jerry Fidler's cow."

"Sarve 'e right," said Nathan. "A purty mess you've got the constabulary into, for we'll all be blamed for it."

"What's the use o' rakin' that up?" complained Abel. "Why don't 'e do somethin', and jaw less?"

"I be doin' what I can," said Nathan, "so how'd thy noise."

For the next couple of hours Nathan, assisted by Abel's wife, tried every method they could think of for the purpose of getting the cell door open, while Abel waited within in a fever of impatience. But nothing came of the attempt.

"It's as firm as a hact of Parliament," said Nathan; "and nothin' less than a batterin' ram 'll bring it down, in my opinion."

"Oh dear," sighed Susan Tregonning in reply. "I don't know what poor Abel 'll do; I'm 'fraid he'll faint."

"Not he," said Nathan, "he's too mad to faint; but we may as well let the cat out ov the bag first as last, and get Moses down with a crowbar an' some wedges."

"Aye," assented Susan. "Shall I go an' fetch him?"

"No; you stay 'ere an' comfort Abel. Moses 'll be sleepin' as sound as a church by this time, so I'll go myself."

And Nathan started off to wake up the village black-smith, and enlist his assistance if not his sympathy.

Moses was not the most amiable of men at the best of times, and so it may be taken for granted that to be roused out of a sound sleep between two and three in the morning did not tend to improve his temper. But when he learned the object for which he had been called, he first swore, then laughed, and finally declared that Abel might remain in the cell till his ears grew moss, for all he cared.

"But won't you come an' try open the door?" said Nathan.

"I'll eat my ears off fust," said Moses. "He clapped me in that lock-up once when I was a little over the Lay, an' I ain't forgotten it yet, nor ain't likely to this year."

"But the prisoner's 'scaped," pleaded Nathan.

"I'm glad of it," said Moses. "An' what's more, I hope you'll never catch him again."

"What!" said Nathan, aghast. "Do 'e rejoice in the 'scape ov a murderer?"

"Get away, man, and shut up thy tatey chopper," roared Moses. "He's no more a murderer than thou art."

"But," pleaded Nathan, "Abel's been in the lock-up since yesterday mornin' with nothin' to ait."

"I'm glad to hear it," said Moses, with a great burst of laughter.

"But he'll starve," said Nathan.

"Well, let him," was the reply. "He's been so mighty perky of late, that it's quite time somethin' took down his conceit."

"And so you'll not come?" questioned Nathan, making a last appeal.

"Come?—no!" roared Moses, growing angry again. "But if you are not gone, and that mighty soon, you'll repent it." And he shut the window with a bang, while Nathan stole away into the darkness in the direction of the court-house.

Both Abel and Susan were getting very impatient at his long absence, and when at length he returned, and told the result of his errand, Abel began to swear and his wife to cry.

"Now, you may as well hush," said Nathan, feeling very much out of temper himself. "Neither swearin' nor blubberin' is agoin' to mend matters; we'll 'ave to 'bide till mornin'; we'll get help then, and batter down the door."

"But I'll be dead wi' hunger afore that," groaned Abel.

"Caan't 'elp it," said Nathan, indifferently; "I'm dead beat wi' tiredness an' want ov sleep, so I'm goin' in to your 'ouse and try an' get a nap," and without waiting to hear Abel's reply he marched away.

Susan followed him a few minutes later and fetched a chair, which she placed close to the cell door, that she might keep her husband company. But she soon fell into a sound sleep, for Abel was too angry and hungry to talk, besides which, she was almost worn out with anxiety and fatigue.

When she awoke the light of day was all about her, and Nathan was standing before her with the missing key in his hand.

"Come, get out o' the way," he said; "I want to unlock the door."

"Unlock the door!" she said, starting up with a look of bewilderment in her eyes.

"Aye," he said, "look spry. Don't 'e see you're blocking the keyhole?"

"Have you got the key?" she said excitedly. "Where did 'e find it?"

"Didn't find it at all," he said. "Davey Polgooth found it as he was goin' to his work."

"Where?" she asked quickly.

"In one ov the fields on the way to Carn Duloe," he said.

The next moment the door was thrown open, and Abel staggered forth out of the foul reeking atmosphere, looking as worn and haggard as though he had risen from a bed of sickness. He did not say anything, he was too faint and dejected to speak. Slowly and unsteadily he walked between his wife and Nathan to his own house, where he dropped into a chair with a gasp, muttering,

"Do get me something to eat, Sue, or I shall die."

The potato cake which had been prepared for the previous evening was soon fished out of the turf ashes where it had been kept warm, and Abel proceeded to attack it with a vigour that left nothing to be desired, washing down large junks of it with deep draughts of warm milk and water.

When he had appeased his hunger he washed himself, then staggered up-stairs to bed; half-way up the stairs he paused, and called to Nathan.

"Don't go away," he said. "Send somebody's boy down to Pentudy to let your wife know you're not coming home just yet; I'll have just an hour's sleep, an' then, Nathan, we must tackle this business."

"All right," Nathan answered.

"And meantime," said Abel, "you can go over to

Squire Trelawney's an' get a search warrant; we caan't afford to lose no more time than necessary."

" We've lost a purty mess ov time a'ready," Nathan answered.

" Aye, that's true 'nough," Abel said, with a groan. "But we'll get the best o' this affair yet."

" I hope so," was the reply.

" Well, thee start for the squire's," said Abel. " Tell him the whole story; how as I was a enterin' the cell wi' his breakfas' in my hand, he springed upon me sudden, an' knocked me down, an' while I was lyin' senseless he walked off, slammin' the door behind 'im."

" He'll be purty mad," said Nathan.

" He can't be no madder than I be," Abel replied.

" Dunno 'bout that," said Nathan. " Anyhow I'll do as you say," and he picked up his hat and stick and walked away.

CHAPTER XIX.

IN SIGHT OF FREEDOM.

" Thou, who hast a vague foreboding
  That a peril may be near,
Even when nature smiles around thee,
  And thy conscience holds thee clear—
Trust the warning—look before thee,—
  Angels may the mirror show,
Dimly still, but sent to guide thee,
  We are wiser than we know."

CHARLES MACKAY.

MR. PENRYN was waiting up for Harry's return. He recognized his knock, and let him in without a word; then securely bolting the door, he followed him into the study, where a bright fire was burning, and a tempting meal spread on the table.

Harry threw himself wearily into a deep wicker chair before the fire and sighed.

"Come, my boy," said his father, "you had better get something to eat while you have the chance of having it in peace."

"Yes, you are right," he said absently. "I don't know when I may be able to get another good meal."

"We are in God's hands," said his father solemnly. "The issues of life and death alike are with Him."

"I've discovered nothing," Harry said after a pause.

" I expected as much," was the answer.

Then silence fell between them while Harry resolutely attacked the joint of cold meat before him. Mr. Penryn sat and watched him with an anxious look in his eyes

L

and deep lines of care upon his brow. He was wishful that Harry should be the first to allude to any future plans.

"I do not think any good can come of my going on Tregeagle's Head again," Harry said at length.

"I am of the same opinion," his father answered.

"Yet liberty is very sweet, father."

"It is, my boy."

"And life is a precious thing, after all."

"It is from God," the Vicar said solemnly.

"Perhaps I ought not to yield it up lightly," Harry said after a few moments of silence.

"Not unless some great and good purpose is to be accomplished thereby," his father answered.

"Just so. But by hanging me I don't know that good will come to anybody."

"That is true, my boy. And that is why I have been wishful you should try to get away from here to some place of safety."

"Have you thought of any plan of escape?" Harry asked after a pause.

"I have thought of many," the Vicar replied, "but only one of them seems feasible."

"And that one?"

"That when night comes on you start and walk to Lugger Sands."

"It's a long walk," said Harry.

"It's just twelve miles," said his father. "You can walk it easily in four hours; that is, if you start from here at midnight, you will get there about four in the morning."

"And when I get there?" he asked.

"When you get there board Captain Will Paterson's brig, the *Gipsy*, which is lying close up to the quay. You can't miss her, for she's the only brig there. There are two or three small schooners besides, so that you can't possibly make a mistake."

"And what then?"

"Ask for Captain Will if you don't see him, and give a letter into his hand which I will give you."

"Well," said Harry, "and what will that lead to?"

"Will Paterson, as you know, is an old friend of mine," said the Vicar. "He came to see me ten days ago, you may remember him. He walked all the way from Lugger Sands for the sake of old times."

"Yes, I remember him," said Harry.

"Well, I have learned that the *Gipsy* sails to-morrow morning. It will be high tide about six; and as he has only ballast on board he'll weigh anchor perhaps an hour before that. Now I know Will would do anything in reason to oblige me, and when he discovers who you are, he'll be only too glad to help you."

"Do you mean that I remain on board, and go to sea with him?"

"That's just what I do mean," the Vicar replied. "He owns the *Gipsy;* he is bound to no port in particular, and if he likes he can run you across to the Irish coast, or the Welsh coast, or the French coast, anywhere where you and he may think best."

"It looks feasible, though not unattended with risk," Harry said after a pause.

"There's risk whatever you do or don't do," the Vicar said quickly. "It's risky remaining here."

"I never thought at one time I could entertain such a proposal," Harry said, as if speaking to himself; then raising his eyes suddenly to his father's, he said, "Do you think it's cowardly to try to skulk off in this way?"

"If I thought so I should not propose it," was the quick reply.

"Then I'll make the attempt," Harry said, with a touch of passion and energy in his voice. "I can but fail; and now for bed and forty winks."

When Harry had gone up-stairs the Vicar drew up his chair to the fire and for a long time sat perfectly-

still, gazing into the grate. Though he had sat up the
whole of the night he was not in the least sleepy. He
sometimes felt that he would never sleep soundly again.

He did not notice the daylight beginning to peep
through the joints of the window-shutters. He was
thinking of some future time when, Harry having got
safe to some distant land, he and Gladys would join
him. To continue to live in Restormel, he felt, would
be an impossibility. Whether Harry escaped or was
re-taken, the fact remained that the majority of his
parishioners believed, and would ever believe, that he
was guilty of the murder of Jack Dunstan. Hence
to dwell amongst them as their minister while they
cherished such a belief would be more than he could
endure. He was roused at length by Mrs. Gaved coming
into the room.

"You should have gone to bed and got a few hours'
sleep," she said, beginning to open the shutters. "You'll
be knocking yourself up at this rate."

"I will have a bath," he said, "that will do me more
good," and he left the room at once.

Mrs. Gaved sighed, then marched away into the
kitchen, and soon the usual stir and bustle began to
make themselves felt all through the house.

Mr. Penryn had just completed his toilet when there
came a loud rat-tat at the door. Gladys sprang up in
bed, her heart beating wildly, while Mrs. Gaved ran
into the dining-room, that she might get a peep at
their early visitor before letting him in. Harry slept
on undisturbed.

"It's Mr. Dunstan," said Mrs. Gaved to the Vicar,
who was hurriedly descending the stair.

Mr. Penryn gave a sigh of relief.

"I feared it was the constable," he said. "But open
the door, Mrs. Gaved, and show him into the study."

A moment later Mr. Penryn and the farmer stood
face to face.

"Have you heard the news?" the farmer burst out, without waiting even to say good-morning.

"What news?" said the Vicar, quietly.

"Why, the village is in an uproar," said Mr. Dunstan. "Your son has escaped, and Abel's been discovered locked up in his cell."

"Abel locked up in the place of my son?" questioned the Vicar, with a curious twinkle in his eye.

"Aye! he says as how yesterday mornin' he took in his breakfas' as usual, when Harry sprang upon him like a tiger, knocked him down and nearly killed him, and that while he lay stunned, made his escape, locking the door behind him."

The Vicar laughed, while the farmer regarded him with a puzzled expression.

"It's awful curious," went on the farmer, after a pause. "It seems Davey Polgooth, going to his work as soon as it was dawn, found the lock-up key in a field on the way to Carn Duloe. Of course he didn't know who the key belonged to, so he thought he'd return it to Abel, but when he got to the house he found Fraddon there. Abel was locked up, Fraddon said, and he had been trying all night to prize open the door, but without success. Of course when they got the key Abel was liberated directly."

"It *is* a curious story," said the Vicar, reflectively, "very curious."

"I'm precious glad he's escaped all the same," said Mr. Dunstan, "for I fear he'd have no chance before a jury. And they haven't had a hanging at Bodmin for such a long time that they'd be glad of the chance of convicting him."

"Don't say that, Dunstan," said the Vicar. "We must try not to be ungenerous."

"I do try," said the farmer, "but it's hard work sometimes. I do hope Harry'll get safe away. It's hard enough for me to lose my boy; I don't want you, Vicar, to lose yours also;" and Mr. Dunstan blew his nose violently.

For a few minutes there was silence in the room. The Vicar hesitated whether he should tell the farmer the whole truth about the matter, but finally decided that the fewer the people who know the secret the better.

"I expect Abel'll be here directly," said the farmer, jerking out the words abruptly.

"What makes you think so?" said Mr. Penryn, with a touch of anxiety in his voice.

"Well, I saw Fraddon hurrying off to Squire Trelawney's for a search warrant," said Mr. Dunstan; "so I expect he'll search your house first off."

"He is quite welcome," said the Vicar, calmly. "I shall put no obstacle in his way."

"Mother's quite delighted," said Mr. Dunstan, after a pause. "The news has been like medicine to her. Next to the news that Jack was living, nothing could have done her more good."

"I am glad she is better," said Mr. Penryn, with evident sincerity, "very glad."

"I hope she'll not get bad news to knock her down again, that's all."

"I hope not, indeed."

"Well, I must be going," said the farmer, sidling towards the door. "Work can't stop, whatever happens."

"That's quite true," said the Vicar.

"Oh, by the bye," said Mr. Dunstan, pausing with his hand on the door-knob, "I forgot to tell you that Tregeagle's been seen again."

"Nonsense and fiddlesticks!" said the Vicar, impatiently.

"You always say that," answered the farmer, "but I believe there is something in it. Both Fraddon and Susan Tregonning declare they saw him as plain as ever they saw anything in their lives. He was standing on the farthest point of the headland, clear and distinct against the sky, and they say he was as tall as four ordinary men."

"Hem!" said the Vicar, suddenly remembering that they might have seen Harry.

"You say 'hem!'" said the farmer, "but you see if there ain't a storm after this; he never appears except before a storm."

"Dunstan," said the Vicar, seriously, "you ought to know better than to give credence to such silly superstitions."

"Perhaps I ought," he said; "but time'll tell, all the same." And the next moment he was gone.

Two hours later Abel and Nathan were espied by Gladys coming across the churchyard at a rapid rate. Harry had been up some little time, and all the beds were made, and everything about the house was neat and orderly.

"Quick, Harry," said the Vicar, "there is not a minute to be lost."

"All right," was the reply; "but if you look as excited as you do now, they will begin to suspect something."

"Don't trouble about me," was the answer, "but get into hiding at once."

A few minutes later there was a loud double knock at the door. One of the maids opened it, while the Vicar remained in his study. Gladys and Mrs. Gaved were by this time in the dining-room.

"Is Mr. Penryn in?" said Abel in surly tones, and in his most pompous manner.

"I believe so," said the maid. "I will go to his study and see."

Abel and Nathan followed her.

"Excuse us not standin' on ceremony," said Abel, trying to look defiant. "Your son have escaped, an' we've come here to search for'n."

"You say my son has escaped?" said the Vicar, pre-
tending to look incredulous, a guilty kind of feeling
coming over him at the same time.

"We do, sir; an' now you'll excuse us if we search
your house."

"Of course I will excuse you," said the Vicar, blandly.
"And be assured of this, I will not put the least obstacle
in your way."

Abel's face fell, while Nathan whispered to him—

"I towld 'e 'twern't no use comin' 'ere. We'd 'ave
better made for Carn Duloe first thing."

"Hold thy voice," said Abel, angrily.

"Thee hold thine," snarled Nathan; while Mr. Penryn looked on with an amused smile upon his face.

The next moment the search began. They started
with the cellars, and steadily mounted upwards, carefully
examining each room in turn. At length they came to
the Vicar's bed-room. Harry in his place of hiding
could hear every word that was said. And now that
they were so near him, and he knew that the least
sound or movement would betray his presence, he became painfully nervous. He badly wanted to sneeze,
the dust of the old wardrobe had got into his nose, and
the irritation was becoming unbearable.

What a position to be in—life trembling upon the
ability or otherwise to suppress a sneeze. Oh, the torture of those moments! He could hear Abel and his
companion pulling out drawers, and the almost noiseless
sound of heaps of clothes being thrown on the floor. Oh,
how he wished that Gladys and Mrs. Gaved would come
in and start up a clatter of conversation, or make a noise
of any kind, under cover of which this dreaded sneeze
might have play. But the room was almost painfully
silent. He knew that his father was there watching
the proceedings, but he was evidently in no mood for
conversation.

"It is of no use," he said to himself at length. "I

shall be compelled to sneeze in spite of myself, and then my doom is sealed."

Never did life seem more sweet than at that moment; never did liberty seem more worth an effort. He was already, he thought, within sight of freedom. Once on board Paterson's boat, and he would defy all the constables of England to recapture him; and in another land perhaps Mary might come to him, and all his hopes be realized.

He pinched his nose until it ached, but the irritation would not cease. In spite of every effort it seemed to be steadily growing worse. Could he hold out? He feared not.

Now they had reached the wardrobe. He heard the twist of the handle, but the door was not opened. Then Abel spoke in very pompous tones.

"Will you kindly unlock this door, Mr. Vicar?"

"With pleasure," he heard his father say; "though I really do not think it is locked."

"Excuse me, but I say 'tes," said Abel.

"Perhaps you are right," said Mr. Penryn; "but let me try it. There,"—as the door flew open—"it only sticks a little. I thought it was not locked."

Harry's heart thumped so loudly that he thought they would be certain to hear it.

"Unhang those clothes," said Abel to Nathan, "an' bundle 'em out."

"It's no use ruckin' up all the gentleman's clo's," said Nathan. "He caan't git into the pockits, an' he ain't 'ere, that's sartin."

"Well, stand aside, an' let me have a look," said Abel.

"Look as much as thee hast a mind to," Nathan said, standing aside for Abel to make an inspection.

Abel evidently had no scruples about "ruckin' up the gentleman's clo's." He flung coats and vests right and left, and finally, with something like an oath, he banged the door to and marched out of the room.

But he had scarcely reached the door when the sound of a suppressed sneeze fell distinctly upon his ear. Nathan was close upon his heels. In a moment both men paused, and turned quickly on their heels.

But with a rare bit of diplomacy the Vicar, who was standing close to the wardrobe, was ready for them. He too had heard the sneeze, and quick as thought had pulled his handkerchief out of his pocket, puckered up his face, bent his shoulders forward, and was in the act of applying the handkerchief to his nose when the constables turned round. They did not speak, they looked at him for a moment, while he seemed to be preparing for a second paroxysm of the nasal membranes, then turned and marched away.

The Vicar followed them through the other rooms and up into the attic, and finally led the way downstairs, opened the front door for them, and politely bowed them out. A moment or two later Gladys put on her hat and followed them. She came back again after about ten minutes.

"They're off across the fields in the direction of Carn Duloe," she said; "so I think they won't trouble us any more to-day."

CHAPTER XX.

EXCITEMENT.

"And though he posted e'er so fast,
His fear was greater than his haste;
For fear, though fleeter than the wind,
Believes 'tis always left behind."—BUTLER.

NANNY's reception of the constables was characteristic. In harmony with her invariable custom, she came to meet her visitors.

"I knew thou wert coming," she said to Abel, "so I came to meet thee."

"How did 'e know?" said Abel; "did 'e see us?"

"Nay," she said, with a scornful toss of her head, "I did not see thee. Dost think I can see through a stone wall?"

"I don't know what you can see through, or what you can do, except mischief," said Abel, sullenly.

The witch laughed.

"A purty scrape you've got me into," Abel said.

"Me?" she said, lifting her eyebrows in seeming astonishment.

"Yes, you," said Abel, while Nathan listened in surprise.

"Ah, Abel!" she said mockingly, "thou art a trusty jailer—a very trusty jailer. But why art thou so down in the mouth? Has thy bird flown?"

"You needn't ask that," Abel answered bitterly; "it

was you as transmuggerified 'im with your drugs an' witchery."

"Thou believes that?" she said in a tone of triumph.

"I'm sure on it," he answered savagely.

"Well, and if I did?" she asked, "what then? Have I not the right to exercise my power sometimes. Come with me into my house, and I will exercise my power over thee!"

"Not if I know it," said Abel, starting back.

"But thou camest to search my dwelling, and brought this fool with thee" (with a scornful look at Nathan), "because thou hadst not courage to come thyself."

"Who said so?" said Abel, looking dreadfully frightened; while Nathan literally shook in his shoes.

"Who said so?" she asked, in a tone of ineffable scorn. "I said so, man. Dost think because thou art a fool, that everybody else is equally devoid of sense? But come, and I will lead the way."

But neither of the men moved.

"Art afraid?" she said, mockingly.

"P'r'aps we be an' p'r'aps we bain't," said Abel in a sudden inspiration of lucidity.

"Ah, Abel," she said with a smile, "thy caution is worthy thy intelligence, and both do thee credit."

"I don't know," said Abel, looking puzzled, "but you are sich a old hand."

The witch laughed again.

"Me an' Nathan, 'tes true, 'ave come up here searchin' for the prisoner; but if you'll swear on the Bible as he ain't 'ere we'll be satisfied."

"Aye," said Nathan, speaking for the first time. "We don't want to search your house, Mrs. Flue; indeed, we don't want to give you no trouble at all. We'll take your word giv'd on oath."

"How very considerate," she said, with a curl of her lip. "But come a little further, for no harm shall come to you while you remain in the open air;" and she turned on her heel and walked away toward her house.

After some considerable hesitation Abel and Nathan decided to follow, and by and by found themselves on the little plateau on which the witch's house stood. It was an eerie spot even in the daytime. Perched on a ledge of rock was a raven, which began to croak in most sepulchral tones, while any number of magpies were hopping and chattering about the place.

" Don't 'e think we'd better go ? " whispered Nathan. " I don't like the look ov this shop at all."

" We'll be all right 'ere," said Abel; " keep your heart up an' put a bold face on it."

" Easier said than done," Nathan replied.

" Ah," said the witch, looking at them with a curious twinkle in her eyes ; " you are a worthy pair of guardians of the peace. Your courage does you infinite credit."

But neither Abel nor Nathan replied.

" Well, come, you are wasting time," she said at length. " There is my dwelling—enter, make diligent search ; mayhap your prisoner is there. I will not say he is not."

" If we go in and search, will you promise no harm shall come to us ? " Abel asked.

" Nay, I will promise thee nothing," was the reply. " Whoso enters there does so at his own risk."

Nathan shuddered.

" This much, however, I will tell thee, that if thou crossest that threshold thy search will not end to-day. My house is but the vestibule of a cavern. Whither it extends, what it contains, I will not disclose. Search for thyself, I give thee permission."

But Abel only shook his head.

" Afraid ! and thou a constable ? " she said mockingly. " Come, I will lead the way, and find thee tapers."

" No, not to-day, Mrs. Flue," Abel said, drawing back a pace or two.

"But you came for this purpose," she said, with a scornful glance at the two men.

"Well, no, not exactly," said Abel; "we did not want to do any searching; but we thought if you had the prisoner 'ere you might give him up to us, or that if he was not 'ere you'd say so on oath."

"Weak cowards, away with you," she said, with a curl of the lip. "And let your pace be rapid, lest evil overtake you. I give you five minutes to be out of the forest; and if—"

But neither waited to hear the end of the sentence. Nathan was the first to take to his heels. Abel's step was more measured at the outset, but as soon as he had turned the spur of rock he started off like the wind.

"That woman's the very devil," he said, as he tore ahead of his panting and affrighted comrade.

"I know it," gasped Nathan, quickening his pace; "but don't leave me, Abel."

"Every man for himself these times, an' the devil take the hindmost," Abel called back, without in any degree slackening his pace.

"No, don't say that," gasped Nathan, "for I believe she's after me."

"Caan't help it," was the only reply he got, and a minute or two later Abel was out of sight.

At the foot of the hill, however, he waited for Nathan, and side by side, with very measured steps, they made their way into the village.

"We've been made purty fools of," remarked Nathan, as soon as he had recovered his breath.

"Aye, but say nothin' 'bout it," Abel replied. "If she's got him there she won't keep him long; he'll be trying to clear off some ov these nights, so we mus' be on the look-out."

It was the wakeful dinner-time when they got into the village, and the whole place was in a ferment of excitement. Everybody was in the open air, and everybody was discussing the strange and unexpected turn in the tide of affairs. Abel and Nathan were surrounded by an eager and inquiring crowd directly they came into sight. They would gladly have escaped if they could, but there was no chance for them; so they stood their ground, and answered the torrent of questions poured upon them to the best of their ability. Abel had to give his version of the escape of the prisoner, and Nathan had to tell the story of the appearance of Tregeagle on the headland. And to this was added the further mystery of the old man Susan Tregonning had seen under the shadow of the pine wood, and which now she firmly believed was a ghost, though she did not think so at the time.

Abel had his own theory about this ghost, which, however, he kept to himself. He had no doubt in his own mind that Nanny, by means of drugs or incantations, or perhaps both, had what he called "transmuggerified" the prisoner. Hence it was as likely as not that this old man his wife had seen was none other than Harry Penryn, stealing off under cover of darkness to some place of hiding. It is true that against this theory there were a great many objections, but this was equally true of nearly every other theory. In fact the whole affair at present was shrouded in mystery. Still he was resolved that if he ever came across this old man he would arrest him on suspicion.

At an informal meeting of magistrates that morning it was resolved to offer a reward on their own account for the apprehension of the prisoner, and an hour later Peter Guy's printing establishment was in a state of great excitement. To receive an order for a hundred bills during the forenoon, and expect them to be posted during the afternoon, was an unheard-of thing in Restormel. To begin with, Peter was not at all certain that he had paper enough in stock to meet such a large demand. Then his type had got considerably mixed, for he scarcely got a printing order once in three months. In the present case, however, there was no time to be wasted in excuses or regrets—the thing must be done, so while Peter and his boys struggled to decipher the "copy" and set up the type, Peter's wife and the girls cleaned the "press," mixed the ink, and cut the paper into lengths.

By three o'clock in the afternoon the first bill was posted on the door of the court-house. It was a unique specimen of the printer's art. On the top of the page in large type was the word "murder," followed by the announcement of ten pounds reward; but in the unusual hurry of production it was only natural perhaps that a few mistakes should have crept in unobserved. Moreover, some of Peter's sons, who lent a helping hand, had never attempted type-setting before, and so were not to blame for getting in a few letters upside down. Indeed, the wonder is that they got in the letters at all. The crowd that soon gathered round the door of the court-house found not a little difficulty in reading the placard, of which we append a copy.

MUᴚDƎR ?

ᗡᴚ∀MƎᴚ 01£

WhERas on THE morNinG oƎ tHe 13th DAy of sEPtemBer onƎ HEnRy PeNRYn diD aɟter wiL ɟully malTᴚƎ∀Tiug his J∀iler Esↄ∀dE Fᴚom ԀRison HƎ BeeiNG CoMMiTƎT For triAL On ThE cH∀ᴚGe of WillfɐLL muRdER AnD sincƎ SAH noT Seen BeeN or HƎ∀ᴚD of. ThE ABove ᴚEW∀ᴚD wil Be ԀAiD TO YNA onE wHo shALl CAPʇƎR Him or gIve ScH iMfoREMatun as shAL LEaᗡ to hIs aRreST.

By Order.

" Gladys managed to secure an early copy of the proclamation."—P. 169.

By ten minutes past three four more copies had been struck off, after which time, the machine having got into working order, the rate of production was much more rapid.

The posting of these placards produced intense excitement, not only in Restormel, but also in Porthloo and Pentudy, where they were conspicuously displayed.

Gladys, who was always on the look-out for news, managed to secure an early copy of the proclamation, and hurried off home with it with all possible haste. Harry, who was the first to inspect it, laughed till the tears ran down his face, notwithstanding the increased gravity of the situation.

" Peter deserves a gold medal for this," he said; " and if it does not secure him immortal fame, then all I can say is, that this is an ungrateful world."

The Vicar, however, only saw the serious side of the question. A hundred people would now be on the look-out instead of two, and so the difficulties in the way of Harry's escape would be increased a hundredfold.

" This is a very grave matter, my son," he said to Harry, after he had glanced over the bill, " a very grave matter."

" Yes, it makes escape more difficult," Harry replied; " but I think we shall manage to outwit them."

" I hope so ! I hope so !" said the Vicar, gravely; " but my heart begins to misgive me."

" Nay, nay, father," Harry answered, cheerfully, " don't despair so soon. And even if the worst comes to the worst, why it won't matter much; a few years more or less of life is not worth troubling about."

But the Vicar did not reply; he walked away into his study with a sadly troubled face, and an oppressive foreboding in his heart.

The remainder of the day wore slowly on. When tea-time came no one had any appetite for it. The nervous tension was becoming very painful; on every face there

M

was a look of apprehension; while poor little Gladys declared she had a feeling as though there was a great stone in her heart.

Each one felt that a crisis had come. At twelve o'clock Harry would go out from the Vicarage to return to it no more. If he escaped he would be an exile for the rest of his days, and years might pass before they looked upon his face again. If he were retaken, two or three weeks at most, in all probability, would be the measure of his life. Hence it was impossible to be cheerful under the circumstances.

Slowly the hands travelled round the white dial of the clock, bringing nearer and nearer the time when the long farewell would be spoken. Mrs. Gaved tried to sew; the Vicar tried to read, but the effort in each case was a fruitless one. Harry paced up and down the hall, restless and excited. He was eager for freedom now, anxious to live; to go back to prison again would be a thousand times worse than at the first. Better never to have escaped than to be retaken.

By eleven o'clock Harry had completed his disguise, and packed the small bundle of things he would take with him. Then all the lights were put out, and to all outward appearance the vicarage was wrapped in slumber. Yet every eye was wide awake. Close together in the dim firelight they sat, Harry holding his sister's hand. It was a pathetic picture. What the future had in store no one could tell; but even the most hopeful out-look seemed full of pain. The Vicar's mouth worked painfully all the while; Mrs. Gaved wept silently, letting the tears fall into her lap without an effort to wipe them away. Harry's face was stern and resolute; but every now and then he pressed his sister's hand, while a tender, pleading look stole into his eyes. Gladys seemed the most hopeful of the four.

" I have been praying to God for you," she whispered

to him, "and He has put the peace into my heart again; so I know, dear Harry, it will be all right."

For answer he pressed her hand again, then all was silent once more, save for the ticking of the clock, and the pitiful moan of the wind up the chimney.

So the minutes wore slowly on till close upon the stroke of midnight; then Harry rose, and without a word went up to his father's chair and kissed him.

"Good-bye, my son," the Vicar said in a choking voice, "and God be with thee."

But Harry did not answer. In silence he kissed Mrs. Gaved, and then he gave Gladys a great hug; he tried to speak to her, but the words would not come.

"My darling Harry, don't be down-hearted," she said with a plaintive smile. And for answer he kissed her again and again.

Then he stole quietly into the hall, where he donned his hat and shouldered his bundle. The others came after him, and the Vicar noiselessly opened the back door and held it ajar.

"Good-bye, and God bless you all," he struggled to say, then stepped out into the night.

For a moment he stood on the threshold, then turned for one last glance, and without a word plunged into the darkness.

CHAPTER XXI.

IN THE NIGHT.

"Well may dreams present us fictions,
  Since our waking moments teem
With such fanciful convictions,
  As make life itself a dream.
Half our daylight faith's a fable ;
  Sleep disports with shadows too,
Seeming in their turn as stable
  As the world we wake to view."—CAMPBELL.

HARRY'S heart beat fast when the door had closed
behind him, and he found himself once more alone in
the night. He never before felt the sense of forsaken-
ness as he felt it now. Home, kindred, friends—all
were lost to him again, and he was once more adrift
with but one glimmering star of hope to guide him. At
the gate he paused for a moment, and looked back at
his old home dimly outlined against the cloudy sky.
It seemed a strange fate that he should be leaving it
thus. What had he done that he should have to creep
away like a thief in the night, startled by his own footsteps and trembling at his own shadow ? He had often
heard his father preach about Providence, but somehow
the memory of his father's words brought him very
little comfort now. He had a feeling that Providence
had forsaken him, and gone into league with a cruel fate
to blight his life.

All that was dear to him he was leaving behind,

never perhaps to see again. How cosy and restful and warm seemed that home-nest to him now! How peaceful its daily uneventful life! How loving its embrace! And yet he would never, he thought, enter that door again, nor sleep in that cosy room doubly dear to him now—where he had slept almost ever since he could remember, lulled to slumber ofttimes by the dreamy wind singing in the pines.

"Dear old home," he said to himself. "We never value our blessings till they are lost to us. Oh, to be free again, to go and come as I used to do; to ramble with Mary Dunstan up through the sloping pine wood, and dream of bliss which was once within my reach, but now is lost to me for ever." And he drew his hand quickly across his eyes to wipe away the unbidden tears.

Suddenly he started back. Was that the figure of a man lurking in the shadow of the tall hazel-grown hedge on the opposite side of the road, or was it mere fancy? Long and eagerly he looked with heart beating fast; but the heavier shadow—if shadow it was—against the hedge did not move.

"It is my excited fancy playing me tricks," he said to himself. "I wonder if all my life is to be haunted by wretched fears like this? If so the game will be hardly worth the candle."

A moment later he pressed his hat a little more tightly on his head, lifted his bundle a little higher on his shoulders, pushed open the gate, and stepped cautiously out into the lane. All was silent and motionless. For a moment he paused to listen, but no sound broke the stillness, and with a sigh of relief he started down the lane at a swinging pace. On either side were tall hedges covered with hazel bushes, which often overhung the road, making it exceedingly dark. He rather rejoiced in this than otherwise. Darkness seemed a protection to him; and night, which as a lad he used to dread so much, had become his best friend.

On, on he went—then paused! Was that the soft
patter of feet behind him, or but the echo of his own
firm steps. He turned on his heel and tried to pierce
the darkness behind him, but neither sight nor sound
greeted him.

"It is my foolish fancy," he said, wiping away the
perspiration that gathered suddenly upon his brow. "I
shall waste all my strength in foolish fears at this rate,"
and he turned on his heel once more and resolutely
strode on.

To divert his thoughts from all unnecessary fears,
he began to picture the long and lonely road he
would have to travel before he reached Lugger Sands.
Half a mile further on, Restormel valley took a sudden
bend, and lost itself at length in a little creek to the
south of Porthloo. His road, however, lay straight on
over the hill and across a wide stretch of "downs," or
moorland, then down into the valley of the Lugger,
whose tortuous course he would follow till it found the
sea.

"I wish I was there, at any rate," he said to himself;
"for with this promise of ten pounds, I do not know
who may be on the watch. But hist!"

A shrill whistle sounded clear and distinct, and went
echoing down the valley. Harry felt his heart give a
great bound, then it seemed to stop. "Can it be that
some one is on my track," he muttered between his
clenched teeth. "If so, there shall be a run for it."
But no other sound startled the midnight silence, and
after a few moments he pressed forward again.

"I expect some smugglers are about," he said to himself. "This is just the night for them, and very likely
the sound I heard is a signal."

Yet all the while he kept fancying he heard the
sound of footsteps behind him. Not loud and firm, but
soft and muffled, as though a dog were following him.
Fifty yards further on the road took a quick bend to

the right, with a stile on the left, or, more correctly, straight in front, leading to some farm-houses not far away.

Harry had nearly reached this stile, when suddenly a man bounded over it into the road and confronted him, while very distinctly now came the sound of the footsteps behind him.

"Trapped!" was the word that leaped to his lips; but before he had time to utter it he felt himself grasped by the collar of his coat, and a voice, which he easily recognized as Abel Tregonning's, hissed in his ear,

"You're a prisoner!"

He did not speak, but quick as thought he slipped out of his coat, which was loose and unbuttoned; and ere Abel's slow brain could grasp what had happened, he found himself grasping an empty coat, while Harry was bounding away at the speed of the wind.

"What! 'scaped again?" said Nathan, running up, his feet well muffled in old stockings.

"Curse 'im, iss!" said Abel, pulling his whistle out of his pocket and blowing it vigorously, an example which Nathan quickly followed. Then both set off at a run after their prisoner, shouting in gasps, and at the top of their voices, "Stop! Murder! Stop! Murder!"

Scattered all over the country side were lonely farm-houses and secluded cottages, and many a light sleeper that night was startled by these unusual sounds, and sprang up in bed, and threw up their windows to know what they meant; while farmers who happened to be in their farmsteads attending to sick cattle rushed off in the direction from whence the sounds came, and so almost unwittingly joined in the chase.

Harry felt that his chance was hopeless from the first, but he was resolved not to give in without a struggle. He had not gone far when he met a farmer rushing to meet him with a pitchfork in his hand.

"What's up?" shouted the farmer. But instead of replying Harry leaped the hedge, and went bounding across the fields. In a few minutes there was a great hue and cry behind him, and the thud of many feet on the grassy sward.

"It's like a game of hunt the fox," he said to himself, with a touch of his old cynicism, as he bounded on like a startled hare.

"There he is!" shouted a voice.

"Where? Where?" cried two or three other voices.

"Yonder against the thicket." And then the chase became fast and furious.

Harry plunged into the thicket, cut across a corner of it, and then doubled back in the shadow of a tall hedge. This gave him a momentary advantage, for his pursuers began to search the thicket, thinking he had sought it as a place of hiding.

Meanwhile he was steadily creeping back towards the spot where the chase began. He had given up all thought of reaching Lugger Sands, nor did he think of trying to make his way back to the vicarage; but if he could reach Nanny Flue's hut on the slope of Carn Duloe, he thought for the time being at least he would be safe.

For a few moments he paused to recover his breath, then ran on again, still keeping in the shadow of the hedge. He had no real hope that any good would come of it. If he were not captured to-day, he would be to-morrow, or the day after that. Yet there was some small satisfaction in foiling his pursuers. All his nervousness by this time had passed away, and he was as cool as he ever had been. To extract a little fun out of Abel and Nathan, and those who had joined in the fray, was the most he expected to accomplish.

Now a broad open field had to be crossed. Could he gain the other side without observation? It seemed exceedingly doubtful. His pursuers were still beating the thicket, but from various sounds which greeted his ears, recruits were joining them in all directions, and so his chances of escape were diminishing every minute. Still "nothing venture, nothing win," was the thought which passed through his mind, and stooping till his hands touched the ground, he began to creep on hands and feet across the open field.

Half way across the field and still unobserved, and a feeble hope began to steal into his heart and to stir his pulse to quicker motion. If he could gain the shelter of the wood which sloped up the hill-side, he might under its friendly cover steal round to Carn Duloe, and find a refuge in Nanny Flue's cavern. It was worth the effort, if only for the pleasure of foiling the blood-thirsty dogs who were at his heels.

Still on, and three-fourths of the distance cleared. " I shall do it now," he said to himself. "Once in the shelter of the wood I shall defy them."

The next moment he was startled by a loud whoop, and a moment later the thud of running feet, coming, it seemed to him, from all directions, fell upon his ear.

"Trapped again !" he ejaculated. "Now I must run for it," and rising to his feet, he bounded forward in the hope of reaching the wood before he was overtaken.

But it was not to be. He saw a dark figure running up the field with the evident purpose of intercepting him ere he could reach the slope ; so he veered suddenly to the left, and kept straight up the open valley, in full view of his pursuers. It was now a race for life pure and simple. But the odds were against him. Many of the runners were fresh to the work, besides which, they knew the ground better than he did. Still while *they* were running for a share of a paltry ten-pound note, *he* was running for life—and life was sweet even yet, notwithstanding all he had passed through.

He still had a hope of reaching the wood and baffling them in its darkness ; if he failed in that his fate was sealed. Evidently, from the sounds which fell upon his ears, all his pursuers were now behind him. He could hear their laboured breathing, and the quick thud of their feet on the turf.

Still on, and, judging by sounds alone, he was holding his own. Some of his pursuers might be fresher than he, but he was lighter and more active than they, and so clearly they were not gaining upon him. This gave him a measure of confidence, and he began gradually to shape his course in the direction of Carn Duloe.

But the race was beginning to tell upon him. There was not the same spring and elasticity in his step as at the first, and yet the chances are he would have won the race but for a wooden hurdle that lay across his path, and which in the darkness he did not see. Coming suddenly upon this he fell heavily forward, and for a moment lay stunned and bewildered; and when at length he scrambled to his feet his pursuers were all about him.

Yet no man seemed to have the courage to touch him, but they closed round in a compact ring, and waited for Abel, who had been left far in the rear, to come up.

"So you have caught me," he said, staring at them with a look of defiance.

But no one answered him.

"Cowards," he hissed between his teeth. "You might have given a man a chance to escape."

But they growled sullenly and shook their heads. Then some one called out, "Here comes Abel!" and the next moment the constable, angry and exhausted, broke through the ring and gripped Harry by the throat. But the next moment he had cause to regret his savage passion.

Harry would have submitted to the handcuffs without a word, but this unprovoked assault was more than his

English blood could bear; and shaking himself free, he doubled his fist and dealt Abel such a blow between the eyes that the guardian of the peace fell to the ground like a log, and would have remained there for a considerable while had not friendly hands lifted him up.

"You shall pay for this," muttered Abel, shaking with rage. "My turn will come next."

"You are welcome to do your worst," Harry said, defiantly, "and all these other cowards can help you if they like."

By this time Nathan had slipped a pair of handcuffs on Harry's wrists, and the march commenced towards Restormel. Half an hour later he was alone in his cell once more, a prey to keener misery and deeper despair than he had ever known before.

CHAPTER XXII.

PERPLEXITY.

"I stand like one who has lost
IIis way, and no man near him to inquire of;
Yet there's a providence above that knows
The road which ill-men tread, and can direct
Inquiring justice."—SIR R. HOWARD.

HARRY's second period of detention in the lock-up
was of short duration. No sooner had Abel got him
safely under lock and key once more, than he began to
make preparations for their journey to Bodmin. First
and foremost he fortified himself and Nathan with a
substantial meal of potato cake and fried ling, washed
down with frequent draughts of herb beer. This was
followed by nearly an hour's sound sleep. Then Abel
started up, washed himself, put on a bran new worsted
muffler, and started out, followed by Nathan. Nathan,
however, was in a very complaining humour, and very
much disposed to quarrel with Abel, for being in what
he termed "sich a tearin' 'urry."

But Abel was not to be deterred from his purpose.
He would " clear out wi' the dawn," he said, " an afore
the foaks were stirrin'."

The morning was raw and chilly, with a tendency to
rain. The wind blew in from the west in fitful gusts,
and moaned sadly up the long deserted street of the
quaint old village.

Nathan yawned incessantly, and grumbled at every

step, but he assisted nevertheless in getting the horse
and trap ready, and drove round to the court-house
door, while Abel went to apprise the prisoner of the
next step in the little drama.

Harry, in spite of weariness and disappointed hopes,
had dropped off into an uneasy slumber, from which
Abel had some little difficulty in awaking him.

"Come, stir yerself," said Abel, in his gruffest tones.
But Harry only turned over on his side, muttering
incoherently as he did so.

Abel held up his lantern that the light might fall
full on the prisoner's face, which was now turned towards
him. For a moment or two he looked at it without
moving. It was a handsome face spite the swarthy
skin, and a somewhat scornful curl of the lip.

Abel was in no sense a tender-hearted man, and yet
the sight of this doomed youth—his wrists still locked
in the cruel steel, his brown hair falling in heavy waves
over his noble forehead, his eyes closed in deep forgetful
sleep—touched him strangely.

He forgot for a moment the pain and humiliation he
had been made to suffer, forgot even the blow that had
felled him to the earth, and from which he had not yet
fully recovered, forgot the crime of which he deemed
him guilty. He only saw the still more tragic side. It
did seem a pity to bruise that shapely neck with the
hangman's rope, and hurry a youth of so much promise
so suddenly out of time.

"Poor young beggar, it do seem 'ard," he said to
himself, "for I reckon he won't 'ave much more sleep
till the hangman 'as finished wi' him. Well, he'll 'ave
sleep enough arter that to make up for't, so 'ere
goes."

And he went and took hold of the chain that united
the two wristbands, and pulled gently but firmly, saying
at the same time,

"Come, wak' up now, you 'ave to be out ov this."

Harry moaned uneasily, but did not open his eyes.

"Come, wak' up," repeated Abel, tugging at the chain he held.

Slowly the large dark eyes opened, and stared in bewildered fashion round the narrow cell.

"Come, pull yersel' together," persisted Abel. " You 'ave to get out o' this."

"Get out of what?" Harry questioned, still only half awake.

"Why out of this cell, man," said Abel in harsher tones. "You have to go to Bodmin to-day."

Harry was wide awake now. With something like a groan he sat up and yawned. But he took Abel's advice, and pulled himself together. "I will never show the white feather before this cowardly constable," was his thought; and slipping off the bed he stretched himself as well as his manacled wrists would allow, and then stooped and lifted the brown pitcher to his lips, and took a deep draught of the almost icy water.

"Rather weak stuff this, Abel," he said, laying down the pitcher.

"I've brought some bread with me," Abel answered gruffly, "but you can ait that on the way."

"Why it's not daylight yet," Harry answered.

"So much the better," was the reply. "I want to clear you out before the town's a stirrin'." Abel liked to speak of Restormel as a "town," it seemed to add somewhat to his own importance.

"As you will," said Harry. "It doesn't make any difference to me, as far as I know."

"But it do to me," was the reply.

"Am I to keep these bracelets on?" was Harry's next question.

"Aye!"

"Afraid of my bolting again?"

"P'r'aps so."

"Well, it was a rather shabby trick Nanny and I played you," Harry said with a laugh.

"You think so, do you?"

"And that chase last night," he went on, without heeding Abel's question, "was quite exciting; don't you think so, Abel?"

"Fur you I expect it was," said Abel gruffly. "A feller whose life's at stake feels queer, I reckon."

"You think so, Abel? Well, you have a vivid imagination, no doubt. But if it had not been for that hurdle I believe I should have beaten the lot of you."

"Ye're welcome to the b'lief," muttered Abel.

"Yes, you have the upper hand of me now," Harry said with a grim laugh, "and I am not going to complain. We shall say good-bye after to-day, Abel."

"Aye, you'll have another jailer to-night," was the reply.

"Well, I guess we shall not separate in each other's debt. I think we're about quits, don't you?"

"We shall be when th' hangman's done with 'e," said Abel grimly.

Harry ground his teeth and shuddered inwardly, but he answered jauntily enough,

"I hope he won't be such a bungler as you are, Abel. I should like a quick despatch, and then a long rest. Perhaps you'll envy me, Abel, when I am asleep. And perhaps you'll regret your eager haste in accepting such flimsy evidence."

But the constable did not reply. Opening the door, he led Harry out into the corridor, and then into the street.

Nathan was standing at the horse's head, the rein over his arm, his hands in his pockets, his knees bent, his teeth chattering.

"What in the name ov thunder 'ave 'e been doin' so long?" he growled, as Harry and Abel came upon the scene.

"Hold thy chatter," said Abel sternly, and proceeded to help Harry into the trap. The next moment he took his seat beside him, and gathered up the reins, while Nathan went round and climbed into the trap on the opposite side.

Restormel was still asleep. Above the rim of Carn Duloe the sky was beginning to pale with the first promise of rising day. A solitary light was burning in Trevose as they passed at walking pace. Harry wondered if the room was Mary's, and if she was still awake praying for his safety and escape.

He was feeling very wretched and ill. His teeth were almost chattering with the cold. He had bantered Abel, and tried to appear indifferent, but his heart was like lead. Life had become a desolation again, and death seemed the only friend he had left.

Before the morning's sun had kissed away the dewdrops, and awakened the woods to melody, Restormel was far behind them, and before them a seemingly interminable road leading to the place where the final scene of this little drama was to be enacted.

Restormel awoke unconscious of what had happened, but it soon began to be whispered abroad that the prisoner had been caught during the night, and was now on his way to Bodmin. Once started, the news ran like wildfire.

Mary Dunstan was setting out the breakfast-table, when her father came in from the farmyard.

"They've caught him," he said abruptly, and he flung his hat into a chair with an impatient gesture.

"Caught him?" she said, turning pale. "Do you mean——"

"Yes, I mean Harry Penryn," he answered hastily. "It was a most exciting chase, by all accounts, but they were too many for him."

But Mary made no reply, nor did she give any sign of what she suffered, save for a sudden pallor that swept over her face. Had she spoken she would have betrayed her feelings; had she even looked at her father she might have burst into tears. So she went quietly on with her work as though nothing had happened.

"I feel downright sorry," the farmer said after a little pause; "for hanging Harry cannot bring Jack back again."

"It'll be just murder," she said with sudden energy.

"I don't know," he said reflectively. "But I do think they often hang people who don't deserve hanging;" and the farmer took up his hat and went out again.

"Breakfast will be ready in a minute or two," she called after him; and then finding herself alone, she dropped into a chair and pressed her hand to her side, while her breath came and went in gasps.

She was quite herself again when her father returned. But the meal as usual was a very quiet one.

"It is only a week to-day," said the farmer at length, pushing back his cup and saucer, "since poor Jack disappeared. It seems like a year to me."

"So it does to me," she answered. "I suppose it is because so much has happened."

"Aye, it's been a full week," he said, "a very full week."

"The world can never be the same again," she answered, as though she were speaking to herself.

"Aye, it's very hard on us and the Vicar," he said, "very hard. And mother 'll be terribly troubled over this. I've said nothing to her about it yet."

"But she'll get to know," Mary answered.

"Yes, yes, we'll have to tell her, for she'll be asking directly;" and Mr. Dunstan got up from the table and left the room.

Two hours later Gladys Penryn rushed into the room unannounced.

N

"Oh, Mary," she said, rushing up to her, "Harry's been taken again."

"Yes, love, I know," Mary said, kissing her.

"Oh, it's wicked, it's cruel," Gladys replied between her sobs.

"I know it is," said Mary, caressingly. "But we must bow to the will of God."

"No, Mary," the young girl answered with swimming eyes. "Never say that again. I am sure it is not God's will. It is only the will of cruel people."

But Mary was silent, she felt the rebuke of Gladys' words. Moreover, she half felt the same herself.

"Pa is almost beside himself," Gladys went on at length. "He had hoped so much; and oh! we felt so confident last night. But now all our hopes are dashed."

"And have you lost hope also?" Mary asked.

"Oh, I don't know. I almost fear I have, though the peace has not quite gone out of my heart yet."

"Perhaps things may happen different to what we expect," Mary said soothingly. "At least let us try to hope so."

"Pa said this morning that he thinks now it must be the will of God," Gladys replied, after a pause. "Of course I could not contradict him; but it hurt me very much to hear him say so."

"It all seems very strange," Mary answered, going to the window and looking out. "But perhaps the light will shine out from behind the cloud again some day."

"Oh, I hope so," Gladys said, coming and standing by her side. "Oh, I hope so;" and then silence fell between them, and for a while they stood watching the swaying of the branches of a pear-tree in the rising wind.

"How the wind is getting up!" Mary said at length. "Father said last night we should have a storm."

"Why so?" Gladys asked.

"Well, you know, it has been reported that Treg-eagle has been seen again out on the headland, and they say he never appears except before a storm."

"But you do not believe that, Mary?"

"Oh, I don't know," was the reply. "There are so many strange things in the world, that one hardly knows what to believe."

"But Harry spent the night on the head," said Gladys, "and he saw nothing of Tregeagle; and so you may be sure he was the Tregeagle this time."

"I never thought of that," said Mary. "But it is singular the wind should get up just now."

But Gladys only smiled, and soon after took her departure.

At noon Mr. Dunstan came in looking quite excited.

"I knew it would be so," he said. "Didn't I tell you there'd be a gale?"

"Yes, you did say so, father," Mary answered, but ventured no further remark.

Steadily the wind rose all the afternoon, till by sun-down it was blowing great guns, while the wide Atlantic rollers were breaking with thundering crash upon the rocks around Tregeagle's Head.

Down at Pentudy and Porthloo the boats were drawn high and dry upon the beach, for everybody had heard of the appearance of Tregeagle, and all knew what that appearance portended. Sam Trewalsick, Dan Polslee, Barney Tabb, and many others kept out of doors all the afternoon, and swept the sea in all directions with a view to possible wreckage. Sam even ventured to climb the haunted slopes of Tregeagle's Head, that he might command a wider view of the main.

But if he saw any storm-beaten craft in the offing he made no remark on his return. Indeed he was quieter than usual, and just as it was getting dark he said he thought he would go indoors and have a smoke. But it was noticeable that Sam was seen in Pentudy no more that evening, and that Dan suddenly vanished soon after dark.

And still the wind rose and raved, and shrieked up the wretched street, and tore the thatch from the house roofs, and lifted the slates from the newer dwellings. While on the beach the great white waves fell with a crash that was terrible, and the wind catching the spray carried it far up the street, and splashed it like rain against the window-panes, and sent it hissing through chinks of the doors.

Only those who were steady on their feet, and strong to face the fury of the gale, dared venture forth into the night, and those who did venture forth could see nothing for the blinding spray. But it was reported that soon after midnight Tregeagle was heard crying in the darkness. Above the hissing wind and the thunder of the waves could be heard now and then wild, heart-breaking, despairing cries coming from the direction of Tregeagle's Head. Those who heard had no doubt as to the identity of the voice. It was the same old cry—wild, bitter, despairing; the cry of a restless spirit doomed to see the labour of his hands swept away by the pitiless gale, doomed to atone for his sin by unavailing toil.

As the morning advanced the storm began to abate, and by sunrise the strife of the elements was at an end. But on the foamy beach of Porthloo and Pentudy was evidence, abundant as it was sad, of the havoc it had played.

Then about noon a body was washed ashore, the body of a well-dressed muscular man, which an hour later Mr. Penryn recognized as that of his friend, Captain Will Paterson.

It was with strange and mingled feelings that the Vicar of Restormel looked upon the face of the dead. Oh, how he had hoped and prayed that his son might reach the *Gipsy*, and claim the protection of Captain

Will. Had his prayers been answered, he too would have been swallowed up by the sea. But would that have been worse than the fate that had overtaken him? He did not know. He was still in darkness, waiting and hoping for the dawn.

CHAPTER XXIII.

"HE KNEW THE WORST."

"So memory follows Hope,
And Life both.   Love said to me, 'Do not die.'
And I replied, 'O Love, I will not die.
I exiled and I will not orphan Love.'
But now it is no choice of mine to die:
My heart throbs from me."—E. B. Browning.

WITHIN a week of Harry's re-arrest the trial was over
and judgment given. Very little that was new came
out in evidence; some of the weak places had been
strengthened a little, and the chain rendered thereby
all the more complete. But practically the evidence
was the same as that given before the magistrates.
The only noteworthy feature of the trial was the speech
of Harry's "counsel." Mr. Trefry was a young barrister,
who was not yet overburdened with briefs, and so had
plenty of time to make a thorough study of the case.
Moreover, he had known Mr. Penryn and Harry a little
for several years, and was thoroughly satisfied in his
own mind that Harry was innocent. Hence he pleaded
not as one who was speaking against his convictions,
but as one whose heart and conscience were in his
work.

He took up a bold and striking line in his defence.
Submitting first that there was not a tittle of positive
evidence that the prisoner was guilty; secondly, that
there was an entire absence of motive; and thirdly, that

if there had been any motive, no sane man would resort to such an insane method of getting rid of his foe.

On these points he developed a speech of striking force and eloquence, and closed with a pathetic appeal to the jury to let their hearts as well as their reason have voice in this painful case.

"Consider the prisoner's youth," he said; "consider his previously unblemished reputation. Consider the intimacy and friendship that existed and still exists between the families of the deceased and the accused. Consider how easy of other explanation is the evidence set forth by the prosecution, and how impossible it has been found to produce any reasonable motive for such a deed. Consider the education and intelligence of the prisoner, and how unlikely it would be, even had he contemplated murder, that he would have resorted to such a clumsy method for its accomplishment. Gentlemen of the jury, to say that he is guilty of this crime is to say at the same time that he is insane, for no man in his right mind—even had he the heart for such wickedness—could be capable of such egregious folly. It has been suggested by the prosecution that he pushed the deceased over the cliff in a sudden fit of passion, but no tittle of evidence has been given in support of that gratuitous assumption; while we have shown clearly enough that the accused has never been given to fits of passion, and does not act on sudden impulses, his temper has always been rather sullen and slumberous than quick and passionate.

"Admitted for argument's sake that appearances are against my client, and that there is presumptive evidence of his guilt. I submit that presumptive evidence is not sufficient to condemn a man, and especially a man of such antecedents. Consider that he has not been reared amid surroundings calculated to blunt his moral sense, or to call into play the lower side of his nature. He has been reared in a Christian home, and taught from childhood to keep watch over his conduct, and do the right at all hazards. He is the only son of a Christian minister, his father's hope and stay, his sister's pride. In that home love has ruled, and peace from year to year has remained unbroken. In one of our great public schools he has taken an honourable position, and was entering with hope and pride on an honourable profession. I ask you therefore, gentlemen, is it credible that he should of deliberate purpose,—or so far change his nature as to yield to sudden passion—madly destroy all his hopes and prospects, nip in the bud love's young dream, cover with disgrace a name long revered, break the heart of his young and beautiful sister, and bring his father's gray hairs in sorrow to the grave? Gentlemen, the thing appears to me, and I think it will to you, quite incredible. How the deceased came by his death may never be known, but that the prisoner at the bar foully and cruelly murdered his friend is an assumption so outrageous, that I trust you will at once dismiss it from your minds, and that you will without any hesitation whatever bring in a verdict of 'Not Guilty.'"

If the jury had retired at that moment, it is possible that the appeal of Mr. Trefry would not have been without its influence; but the calm and unimpassioned summing up of the judge intervened, and so plenty of time was given them for reflection.

It was clearly evident what was in the mind of the judge. He meant no doubt to be strictly fair and impartial, yet he marshalled the evidence in such a way that it told heavily against the prisoner. Harry felt this to be so, and began to nerve himself for the worst, though he was not without hope that he would be given the benefit of the doubt, and set at liberty.

The jury were forty minutes in considering their verdict. To Harry it seemed an age; every moment was a concentrated point of agony. Yet outwardly he

betrayed no emotion. He paced the room to which he
had been taken to await the verdict with folded arms
and with a steady step, but he counted every heart-beat
in that agonizing time, and more than once feared that
his courage would utterly fail him.

To his warders his demeanour appeared that of callous
indifference, and on that ground they concluded that he
was guilty, and so showed him no sympathy whatever.

At length the long waiting came to an end, and amid
an exciting movement and buzz, he was hurried once
more into the dock. Then a silence that might have
been felt dropped down upon the scene.

The clerk stood up; the jury remained standing. At
the back of the room people craned their necks; women
who were present grew pale to the very lips; counsel
looked anxious and excited. The judge sat pale and
unmoved. Clearly the usual questions were asked. In
a voice somewhat tremulous, but painfully distinct, the
foreman of the jury gave the answer.

"Have the jury agreed upon their verdict?"

"We have."

"Do you find the prisoner at the bar guilty or not
guilty?"

A moment of breathless silence followed; the foreman
seemed swallowing a lump that had risen in his throat,
then came in a low and distinct voice the one word—

"GUILTY."

A moment of confusion—a palpable shudder—a deep
inspiration through a hundred lips—a suppressed groan
here and there, and then silence again.

The judge was speaking in grave, solemn tones,
telling the prisoner that he had been found guilty of
the awful crime of murder, and holding out to him no
hope of a reprieve. Had he anything to say why
sentence of death should not be passed?

Harry lifted up his head and looked the judge calmly
in the eyes. A great hush fell upon the scene.

"My lord, I am as innocent of this crime as you are," he said, and then dropped his eyes again to the ground.

Another moment of confusion, then sentence of death was pronounced in the usual form, of which Harry, however, scarcely heard a word. Then like one in a dream he walked back to his cell, glad to escape from the eager eyes of the crowd, and feeling in a dull stolid way thankful that the drama was ended, and that he knew the worst.

He "knew the worst," but he did not feel the worst that day; indeed, for the moment he was almost past feeling. He had suffered so much, the nervous tension had been so long and so keen, that now it was over, he experienced a dull relief which was almost pleasure after the previous pain.

All grief was over, all joy had come to an end; for him the end of the world had come. Nothing more could ever disturb him, or waken his interest. Pleasure and pain alike were past, and so he threw himself upon his hard bed, thankful for the sense of rest it yielded him; and closing his eyes, he was soon wrapped in a dreamless sleep.

His jailer finding him thus an hour later did not disturb him; for a moment or two he looked at him, as Abel had once done, and felt his heart soften as he did so.

"He don't look like a murderer," he said to himself; "'tis strange he should ha' done it."

Harry lay with his head upon his hand, his crisp locks falling carelessly upon his brow, his lips just a little apart, curved into the faintest shadow of a smile.

"Iss, iss," muttered the jailer, as he stepped quietly out; "'tis strange he should ha' done it."

CHAPTER XXIV.

"BE STRONG AND FEAR NOT."

"Through prison bars
    I catch the glory of the milky way.
The vivid stars
    In golden groups above the circus stray ;
To-morrow. Ah, to-morrow these poor eyes
Should look upon the lights of Paradise."

THE day preceding that fixed for the execution Mr. Penryn and Gladys drove to Bodmin to pay Harry a farewell visit. It was a sad journey, especially for the Vicar. Gladys was less depressed. With a perversity that had no foundation in reason, she refused even yet to believe that Harry would be hanged; her simple faith was pathetic in the extreme.

"I have prayed," she said, "that Harry may live, and God has sent a great peace into my heart, and so I know he will not die."

The Vicar did not like to damp his little daughter's faith, and yet he feared the effect upon her mind when she discovered how vain had been her belief.

"I would not be so confident, darling, if I were you," he said, with a sad look in his eyes. "If it's God's will that our Harry be taken from us, we must try to be resigned."

"But he is not going to be taken," she persisted with a bright smile. "God is going to spare him to us."

"I fear not, darling," he said, stroking her shining

hair with his long thin hand. "There is no hope of a reprieve."

"Oh, pa, you are unbelieving!" she said, smiling up at him.

"In matters like these we must be governed by reason," he said sadly. "Faith is belief upon evidence, and there is no evidence anywhere to lead me to believe with you."

"I don't think I understand what evidence is," she said, looking a little puzzled; "but I've got the proof inside. I feel it here;" and she placed her hand upon her bosom.

The Vicar smiled sadly and shook his head; but Gladys held on to her belief notwithstanding.

Very little conversation passed between them during the long drive to Bodmin. The Vicar was too over-burdened with grief to indulge in conversation. It was a bright sunshiny day, though there was a touch of frost in the air when they started in the morning; but the Vicar did not feel the sunshine, nor see the glory of autumn which lay on all the hills. The birds sang cheerfully in the brooding woods, and in the hamlets through which they drove the children laughed and made merry; but he did not hear the birds or see the children. He drove on hour after hour like one in a dream. One face was ever before him—the face of his only son; one bitter grief filled all his heart.

He had set himself a very difficult task, and he very much feared that he would not be able to carry it through. Over and over again he had said to himself during the last week—

"I must speak to my poor boy about his soul. I have my fears respecting his safety."

But though he had resolved to do this, he feared that his resolution would fail him when he came face to face with his son. To a man of a different temperament the task would be easy enough, and not only easy, but even pleasant. But Mr. Penryn was naturally a reserved man, with very little of emotion or sentiment in his nature. Harry was as reserved as he. Neither had been given to wearing his heart upon his sleeve, or to parading his deeper experiences before the world. Each felt in his own way that religion was a personal matter, to be *felt* and *lived*, but not prated about as though a matter of crops and stocks.

But now that his son stood on the brink of eternity, he felt that he must no longer forbear; that if he did, he would be traitor to his conscience and to his holy calling. If Harry had not made his peace with God, he must exhort him, counsel him, pray with him. And who could tell?—perhaps God might make him the means of leading his son out of darkness into the light.

Harry knew of the visit, and prepared himself for the ordeal. If he had consulted his own feelings merely he would have seen no one. He had given up everything, and felt that he was dead to the world and the world dead to him. By sheer force of will he had succeeded in reducing himself to a state of comparative apathy and indifference. He had so dulled his senses that he was only half alive. He would not think if he could help it. He would just exist in the dim twilight till the darkness closed around him, and sleep sealed his eyelids for evermore.

But to see his father and Gladys would be like coming back to life again—coming back to the bitter pain, to the sense of loss, and shame, and disgrace, that he had put away from him as something long past and almost forgotten. Still the agony could not be of long duration now. Another morning would see the end. Less than twenty-four hours, and all would be over, ended alike the joy and pain, and he would have entered into the invisible, and would be face to face with the realities of eternity.

His father saw him first, and alone, a privilege which he (the Vicar) was profoundly grateful for. They met in silence. Harry was the lesser moved of the two. He was pale and hollow-eyed, otherwise there was no change in him. He stood erect as ever, and about his mouth there was the old look of defiance which those who knew him little never knew how to interpret.

"And how is it with you, my son?" his father asked, as soon as he could control himself sufficiently to speak.

"I think I have nothing to complain of, father," he answered, after a moment's hesitation; "and considering the close quarters in which I live, my health is fairly good."

"Ah, Harry," and the Vicar's voice shook, "the health of your body is of little moment now."

"That is true, father. It will soon be all over with me."

"No, not all over, my boy. Do you think that you are about to be ushered into the presence of God?"

"Yes, I think of it sometimes, but I have no clear idea what it means. I tried to picture it to myself once, but I have given up speculating about it now. You see, father, I shall soon know."

"Yes, my boy, you will soon know; but are you ready for the change? Excuse me speaking to you so plainly, but oh, Harry, I must; this is my last opportunity."

Harry smiled wistfully and sadly.

"I will excuse anything to-day," he said. "You have been a good father to me, true and kind. I am sorry that I have been of so much trouble to you. But it is ended now."

"But, Harry, about the future?" the Vicar said with choking voice. "Have you made your peace with God?"

For a moment Harry hesitated.

"I do not know if I exactly understand your question,"

he said at length. "Between God and myself there has been no enmity that I am aware of. You have always preached that God loves us; I have tried to love Him. Is that a sufficient answer?"

"No, not quite. I want to know if you are trusting in Christ. Do you feel that you are safe?"

"Oh, yes, father," he answered with a smile, "I feel quite safe. I know I am in good hands."

"And you have no fear?"

"No; all fear has passed away. People will say to-morrow that I walked to the scaffold like a very hardened criminal."

"Oh, my boy, it is terrible!" said the Vicar with a shudder. "But I believe Christ will sustain you."

"He has sustained me hitherto," was the answer.

For a few moments silence fell between them, while they looked steadily into each other's eyes. Then the Vicar said brokenly, "Let us pray;" and together they knelt on the cold floor. But the prayer was an unspoken one. The Vicar tried his best to steady his voice and keep back the tears that choked him, but the effort was in vain. But the prayer was none the less real because unuttered, and each felt even while he knelt that the prayer had been answered.

They were still kneeling when the bolt was shot back, and the warder came to announce that the interview must end.

"We shall meet again," said the Vicar, rising, and falling upon Harry's neck in a passion of tears.

"Yes, father," was the whispered answer; "we shall meet in heaven."

Silently they grasped each other's hand, a long kiss followed, and then the Vicar staggered forth with bowed head and quivering lip, feeling as though life were at an end with him as well as with his son.

A few moments later the door was opened again, and Gladys came into the room like a ray of sunshine.

"Oh, Dodo," she exclaimed, calling him by an old pet name, and rushing swiftly towards him, "I am so glad to see you."

He did not reply,—he could not just then,—but he caught her up in his arms and began to kiss her, while his tears fell like rain upon her face.

"Don't cry, Dodo," she said cheerfully. "We shall have you home again very soon now."

"No, little Gladsome," he said, making a great effort to steady his voice; "I shall never come home to Restormel again."

"Oh, yes, you will," she said brightly; "for do you know, Dodo, I have been praying for you all the while, and God put a great peace in my heart, and it has never left me yet."

"God grant it may never leave you," he said, kissing her again.

"You are like pa," she said, "you won't believe."

"It would not be wise to entertain any such a delusive hope," he answered sadly. "And, besides, I don't mind going now. I have given up everything."

"Oh, Dodo, don't talk like that or you will make me cry," she said, her eyes filling. "And I have come to cheer you."

"My little Gladsome," he said, "you have cheered me."

"And when you come home—" she went on.

"Ah, Gladys," he interrupted, "to-morrow I shall be at home in heaven."

For a moment she looked at him as though she did not comprehend, then she said—

"Do you mean that these wicked people will hang you, Dodo?"

"Yes, Gladys," he said, with a slight shudder. "To-morrow, at dawn. It's not long now, is it? I want you to be awake and pray for me then. And don't fret, little sweet, it will soon be over, and then I shall be better off."

"And they will never let you come home again?" she asked, nestling closer to him.

"Never, my little Gladys; we say good-bye now. We shall meet no more till we meet in heaven."

"Oh, no," she said; "I can't believe that, and I'm not going to try."

"You will believe it to-morrow," he said sadly; "and you must try to believe that it is better so. Don't lose heart. Be cheerful, for father's sake, for this is a cruel blow to him. And tell Mammy Gaved that I thought of her to the last, and that she must try not to fret about me."

"Oh, but she frets all day long," Gladys answered.

"But kiss her for me, and tell her it was my wish that she shouldn't do so."

"Oh, she'll be bright enough again when you come home," Gladys answered.

"Ah, Gladys! But never mind," he said, after a pause. Then suddenly turning the conversation, he asked, "Have you seen Mary lately?"

"Who? Mary Dunstan?"

"Yes."

"Oh, yes; I see her nearly every day."

"And is she well?"

"I don't think she is very. She is like the rest, she is fretting herself ill about you."

"Is she troubling about me, do you think?" he asked, with a little gasp.

"I'm sure she is," was the answer. "In fact, Dodo, I believe Mary likes you better than she did Jack. And do you know, she sent a message."

"Did she?" he said quickly, a momentary brightness sweeping over his face.

"She said she wished she could come to see you," Gladys went on. "But then she could not leave her mother very well, and I don't think Mr. Dunstan would have liked her to come, though for my part I don't see why."

"I would like to have seen her," he said absently; "but it is too late now."

"But she said, 'Tell Harry for me, to be strong and fear not,'" Gladys went on.

"Did she say that?" he said, looking up.

"And she also said," continued Gladys, "'Tell him we don't forget to pray for him.'"

For awhile no other word passed between them. Outside they heard the regular tramp of the warder's feet as he paced up and down the corridor, and each knew that the period of their brief interview was swiftly coming to an end. Harry looked up at length.

"You will see Mary soon, Gladys," he said; "perhaps to-morrow, after it is all over."

"Yes, I shall see her to-morrow," she answered.

"You will remember me to her, and thank her for her message?"

"Remember you to her?"

"Yes, give her my love," he said, after some little hesitation; "and tell her she was in my heart to the last."

Before she could reply the door was thrown open again, and the jailer appeared. Harry caught Gladys in his arms again for a last embrace.

"Good-bye, little Gladsome," he said with quivering lips. "Be cheerful, for father's sake."

"My dear old Dodo," she answered. It was the name she gave him when she was just beginning to talk, and it had remained as a pet name ever since.

He tried to speak again, but his voice failed him.

"Don't cry, Dodo," she said, kissing him in her old childish fashion. "I have the peace still, so I know it will be all right."

He tried to smile through his tears as he shook his head. Then the door opened and shut, and he found himself once more alone; and throwing himself upon his bed, he burst into a tempest of tears. He soon recovered himself, however, and began to repeat to himself Mary's message, "Be strong and fear not," adding a few moments later—

"I must not give way now, when the battle is so nearly won."

CHAPTER XXV.

THE END OF THE STRIFE.

"I was ever a fighter, so—one fight more,
    The best and the last !
I would hate that death bandaged my eyes, and forbore,
    And bade me creep past.
No ! let me taste the whole of it, fare like my peers
    The heroes of old.
Bear the brunt, in a minute pay glad life's arrears
    Of pain, darkness, and cold."—R. BROWNING.

IT was four o'clock in the afternoon when Mr.
Penryn and Gladys left Bodmin for their long drive to
Restormel. They did not expect to reach home much
before midnight, for they would need a meal on the
way, and their horse would require a feed and a rest.
It would have been more merciful to the beast to have
remained in Bodmin all night, but the Vicar could not
bear the thought of such a thing. He wanted to get
away from the place as quickly as possible. Everything
about it was hateful to him. Already people were
coming into the town from all parts of the county,
eager to be in time for the " hanging," as they termed
it, on the following morning. The one straggling street
of which the place mainly consisted was beginning to
look quite lively. Shopkeepers were looking brisk and
cheerful in prospect of a busy day to-morrow ; nothing
ever brought so many people into the town as a
" hanging." Everybody hoped that the weather would

keep fine, in which case the success of the event would
be assured.

Some few people were disappointed that there was
not to be a "double" execution. Three years before,
when two brothers were hanged for an assault on an
old woman, the town was crowded from end to end,
and all the publicans and lodging-house keepers had
done such a roaring trade, and had been enabled to
exact such exorbitant prices, that they had never ceased
since to talk about it. During the past year there had
been no hanging at all, and the trade of Bodmin had
suffered accordingly. At present, however, things were
looking up. The criminal now awaiting execution was
no ordinary individual; his crime was of no ordinary
character. Indeed, everything about the case had
tended to deepen the interest which had been awakened
at the first, and to excite every atom of morbid curiosity.

The story of his escape from gaol had been told a
thousand times over, and in every part of the county,
and, like most stories of the kind, had grown considerably
in the telling. Harry had been represented as a young
giant in stature, strong as a lion, reckless and un-
principled in the extreme, and utterly fearless of both
God and man.

Mothers had already begun to frighten their children
with stories of his fearful exploits, and in a hundred
pulpits moral lessons of reproof and warning had been
drawn from his brief but shameful career. Those who
had been present at the trial had gone away very much
disappointed. Harry did not answer at all to the de-
scription given of him. Their conceptions of the
typical murderer had received a rude shock. Here
was no low-browed bully, no coarse-grained villain,
but a youth who, outwardly at least, was every inch a
gentleman, with a face clean cut as a Grecian statue,
and an eye and brow that betokened intelligence of a
high order.

Sundry village clergymen had gone away from the trial feeling that fresh light had been shed on some old texts. They understood more clearly than before how the devil could be transformed into an angel of light, and how even the very elect might be deceived. One clergyman preached a most moving as well as improving sermon on the words, "Look not upon his countenance, or the height of his stature, for I have rejected him," during the delivery of which the few handsome and educated youths in the congregation were made to feel decidedly uncomfortable, while numerous individuals, whom nature had not endowed with any excess of personal charms, began to feel that their very plainness might be regarded as a kind of "Hall mark" of respectability.

The result of all this was that Harry, if not the hero of the hour, was certainly the talk of the time. The very contradictoriness of the reports in circulation concerning him but tended to quicken curiosity. Everybody seemed eager to look upon the face of the most notorious criminal of the day, and thousands of people tramped the whole of the night that they might reach Bodmin in time to witness the hanging.

Gladys and her father riding homeward through the quiet lanes were constantly meeting little knots of people making their way with all possible haste in the direction of the town they had left. Gladys was greatly puzzled at this at first, for in their outward journey they had often driven for miles without encountering a single individual.

"Pa, where are all the people going to?" she said at length. "We did not see so many people when we were coming."

"They are going to Bodmin, my child," the Vicar answered with a very perceptible shudder.

"Is there a fair there, or something?" she asked innocently.

"Something, indeed, Gladys," he answered, with a choking sound in this voice; "but not a fair."

"Then what are they going for, pa?"

"My child, do not ask," he said, with a pained look in his eyes. "You surely can guess without my telling you."

"They are surely not going to see Harry hanged, are they?" she said, in tones of indignation.

"That is the object they have in view," he answered.

"Then I am so glad they will be disappointed," she said, with a look of triumph upon her face. "Won't they be mad when they discover they have tramped all the way for nothing."

"Alas! they will see what they have come to see," he answered with a groan.

"I don't believe they will," she said resolutely.

For a moment the Vicar was silent. Then speaking in low grave tones, he said,

"I wish, Gladys, you would give up this delusion of yours. It is better you should face the facts, and that quickly. I quite dread the shock you will receive to-morrow when the truth comes home to you, unless you accept the inevitable now. There is no escape for Harry. There *can be* no escape. To-morrow morning they will kill him, and you will have no brother, and I shall have no son." And the Vicar's voice ended in a sob.

"I can't help it, pa," Gladys answered, after a pause. "I shall believe it when they have killed him, but not before."

"But what reason have you for clinging to such a delusion?" the Vicar asked kindly.

"The only reason I have is that I *feel* it isn't going to be," she said, with a smile.

"That is no reason at all," the Vicar said, a little bit impatiently; and then the subject dropped.

Meanwhile Harry was pacing up and down his cell, and fighting his battle over again. He kept repeating to himself the words, " Be strong and fear not," but he found it a difficult task. A thousand memories had been stirred into life by the visit of his father and sister, and the old wounds had been opened afresh. He was living very acutely now. The old feeling of apathy had entirely passed away. Once more he was wide awake. The more he tried not to think, the more active became his mind; the more resolutely he tried to forget the past, the more vividly it came before his mental vision. Once more he felt the cruelty of his position, the injustice of the sentence, and the bitterness of the penalty he was doomed to pay; once more the feeling of life's sweetness swept over his heart, and the longing for love and freedom came back with two-fold intensity.

He had been trying for days and days past to play the part of a stoic, and on the whole had succeeded fairly well. But the visit of Gladys and his father had pricked the bubble of his philosophy, and once more he found himself kicking against the pricks, and longing to live with an unutterable desire.

After awhile he lay down on his hard bed, and began to dream of green fields and sunny lanes, and silent forests depths. He was back at Restormel again, sauntering in the shadow of the pine-wood, with Mary Dunstan by his side. On the path before them the sunlight flickered and danced, and over the hill-top came the murmur of the great shining sea. Oh, how sweet it was to live. He did not try to check his day-dream. Why should he ? If the play of his fancy could give him a moment's pleasure, or banish from his mind the dread thought of to-morrow, then surely it was wise to let his fancy play. So he lay with closed eyes, forgetful of his surroundings, till his jailer came to bring him his evening meal.

It was far on into the night before he fell asleep. He imagined at the beginning of the night that he would not sleep at all, that he would lie wakeful till the prison bell began to toll his doom. He had often in the last week or two tried to imagine his last night on earth. But now that it was actually upon him, he found the reality a very different thing to what he had pictured.

For a full hour he had knelt by his bedside in the attitude of prayer. But his mind often wandered, even while he tried to pray. Every form of words familiarized by prayer was redolent of memories of the past. Now he was back again in the dining-room of the vicarage, kneeling on the soft hearth-rug, resting his face on the chair, while his father's voice, low and monotonous, led their evening devotions, entreated pardon for the sins of the day, and prayed for protection during the coming night. So real did it seem, that he could almost feel Gladys by his side, and hear her soft breathing as she lingered on the brink of slumber.

Anon he was in the old church, with the wind sighing round the gables, and now and then rattling a loose pane of glass in the window above their pew. Away down the long aisles his father's voice rose and fell as he solemnly read the prayers, and the people in a faint murmur said " Amen."

Now all was still, save for the faint whisper of the wind outside, as it gently stirred the long grass upon the green hillocks where slept Restormel's forgotten dead.

" Oh, that I might be buried in the dear old church-yard at home," he sighed, while the tears filled his eyes in a moment, and fell in big drops on the hard mattress on which he rested.

He was keenly alive again now, and around him the bare prison walls.

" Oh, Father in heaven," he prayed, " forgive me for my wandering mind, and so fill my heart with thoughts of Thee, that all trivial things may be banished, and in the consciousness of Thy presence, and the sweet restfulness of Thy love, may I pass these last few hours of my earthly life till I come to Thee, no more to wander from Thy presence for ever and ever."

Then he rose from his knees and lay down, but he did not close his eyes, for to his imagination the darkness became peopled with the faces of those whom he loved. But no face remained long before him. His mind was too active, his nerves too highly strung for any mental picture to continue long.

Some thoughts came and went again and again. The picture of the quiet churchyard at Restormel, with its green hillocks and quaint and tipsy headstones, seemed to have a peculiar fascination for him.

"It won't matter when I'm dead," he said to himself, pushing his hand through his hair, and staring into the darkness. "It won't matter a bit where I'm buried. I shall know nothing about it. Only now it feels as though it would be sweet to sleep near the dear old home, where the birds could sing their morning's songs over me, and the damp west wind could wave the grass that would soon be growing green; where Gladys could come on summer afternoons and sit and read, and lay sweet-scented flowers from the vicarage garden; and Mary could stray sometimes, and perhaps linger a few minutes to keep me company. Oh, I think I should recognize her footstep even in my grave. And father would pause, I know, on his way to church; and dear old Mammy Gaved would come to ease her heart with weeping. Ah, well, it may not be. I shall be buried inside the prison walls, in unhallowed ground, where not even the birds will sing to me, and the footsteps of those who love me will never stray. Well, well, it cannot really matter. I shall know nothing about it. I only feel this now because I feel everything so keenly, but when the hangman has done his work I shall feel nothing; I shall sleep undisturbed for evermore."

So thoughts and memories kept chasing each other

through the chambers of his mind, till he became too
exhausted to think any more, and he fell suddenly into
a deep and dreamless slumber.

When he awoke the gray dawn was creeping into his
cell, and by his side stood his jailer.

"Come, sir, there's no time to be lost," said the man.
"You're to have a good breakfas' to-day; we allers
cooks 'em somethin' nice on the last mornin' to tempt
their appetites like. After you've done that, the chaplain will come to put the finishin' touches on 'e, as it
were; and then—why then of coorse the rest." And
without waiting for a reply he bowed himself out, and
carefully locked the door behind him.

"And so it's come at last," Harry said, as he got out
of bed and began to dress himself. But somehow he
felt very little concern. The old feeling of numbness
and apathy had come back again; the acute pain and
tension of the day before had produced its inevitable
result. There is a limit to all human pain; beyond a
certain point anguish becomes indifference. That point
Harry had reached.

He dressed himself with his usual care, but that was
the result of habit rather than of any fixed purpose in
his mind. He had scarcely completed his toilette, when
his jailer entered again, bringing the promised breakfast, which consisted of a jug of coffee, a steaming hot
beef-steak, and half a loaf of white bread.

"You'll have a tremenjus haudience," said the jailer,
laying down the tray. "There ain't been no sich crowd
since Mick Bunney was hanged for trappin' Squire
Newlyn's pheasants."

Harry looked up at him with a smile, but did not
reply.

"Don't 'e hear 'em a singin' an' shoutin'?" said the
jailer, with a pause; and over the silence of the prison
swept a sound like the roar of the distant sea.
"There's thousands an' millions on 'em," went on the

jailer. "They're crowdin' each other like pilchards in a siene. It'll be a grand opporchunity for improvin' the occasion; there's nothin' sich a crowd likes so well as a bit of a speech—a little sarmin like; it makes a hexcellent finish, and sends 'em all away in a good temper."

"You're very kind for suggesting such a thing," said Harry; "but if you don't mind I would like to have my breakfast now."

"Quite right," said the jailer. "The chaplain 'll be 'ere in twenty minutes."

"They shall not say I was too frightened to eat my breakfast," he said to himself, attacking the steak. "But after all what a farce it seems."

Yet notwithstanding the imminence of his doom he made a good breakfast, and felt all the stronger for the ordeal in consequence. A few minutes later the chaplain entered, and remained with him a quarter of an hour. He wanted Harry to make a confession of his guilt, and seemed very much disappointed as well as shocked that he persisted in declaring he was innocent.

When the chaplain had finished his ministrations the hangman was introduced, a low-browed, villainous-looking fellow, who came forward with a smirk and a nod, and proceeded at once to pinion his victim.

"I 'ope you bain't nervous," he said, with a brutal smile.

"Oh, not in the least," said Harry.

"That's right. I won't hurt 'e very much; I'll give 'e a longish drop, and you'll go off as quiet as anythink."

Harry was too disgusted to reply, and felt it rather a relief when a moment later the prison bell began to toll, and the door was thrown open, showing the way to the place of execution.

In a few seconds the procession was formed, Harry marching with head erect, and firm unfaltering step, between two warders.

Outside the roar of the crowd had died away into an ominous silence, so that the voice of the chaplain sounded painfully distinct, while the clang of the prison bell struck a chill to many a heart.

The sight of the black scaffold, with its dangling rope, sent a swift shudder through Harry's heart, and made him hesitate a moment; but he recovered himself instantly, and setting his teeth firmly together, he marched the rest of the distance without a tremor, and looking handsomer than he had ever done in his life before.

CHAPTER XXVI.

A DISCOVERY.

" What could I more ?
I warned thee, I admonished thee, foretold
The danger, and the lurking enemy
That lay in wait; beyond this had been force,
And force upon free-will hath here no place."

MILTON.

It will now be necessary to go back to the evening when Harry Penryn and Jack Dunstan parted company on the sands near Tregeagle's Head. The story Harry told on his return was strictly correct in every particular. Jack, not liking to be outdone by anybody, had resolved to perform the feat of walking round Tregeagle's Head. It had been done once at least; some people averred that it had been done many times, but of that there was no authentic history. But once during the present generation the feat had been performed, a fact well known to everybody, and Jack resolved he would prove himself equal to any man who had ever lived in Restormel or Pentudy.

He was one of those individuals that seem incapable of fear, while his love of adventure amounted almost to a passion. He would long since have left his home for adventures in foreign parts but for his invalid mother. Love of her held him like an anchor fast and firm. He knew her heart was bound up in him, that if he went away it would break her heart; and so for her sake he accomplished the bravest and most difficult feat of his life—he repressed the longing for adventure in foreign lands, and contentedly remained at home, doing his share of the work on the farm without a murmur, and appearing cheerful under every circumstance.

Mrs. Dunstan was naturally very proud of her son. He was so brave and yet so gentle, so fearless and yet so kind, so light-hearted and gay, and yet so full of a deep and tender affection for her, that it was only natural she should love him with all the strength of her mother-heart, and imagine there was not his equal in all the world.

The quarrel between Jack and Harry had not troubled her very much. "They will soon make it up again," she said in her heart. And when she learned that they had gone out together on Tregeagle's Head, she smiled with a sense of satisfaction that her prediction had so soon come true.

Out on the headland—where they ran races, and tried their strength and skill at wrestling—no allusion was made to the quarrel of a few days ago. They had each resolved to forget the little difference that had existed between them, and be as they had been from childhood—close and warm friends.

Jack had no thought when he left home of trying to walk round the headland. It was the sight of the exceedingly low tide that put the idea into his head. "Why, Harry," he said, stopping short suddenly in his walk on the sand, "it is the lowest tide of the year to-day; I had quite forgotten it. One might easily walk round Tregeagle's Head on the rocks. And, by Jove, I'll do it too."

"What an idea!" said Harry.

"Why, it has been done," said Jack, raising his hat and pushing back his hair, "and what has been done can be done again."

"But what's the good of it?" questioned Harry.

"Oh, I don't know. One might get a good look into Tregeagle's cave, perhaps get a glimpse of old Tregeagle himself; and then it'll be something to be able to say you've done it."

"Oh, nonsense," said Harry. "I'm sure the game is not worth the candle."

"Worth it or not, I'm going to risk it," Jack answered with a laugh, "so here's off. I'll be back to Restormel almost as soon as you, perhaps sooner." And away he bounded, leaving Harry standing alone.

"I wouldn't risk it if I were you," Harry called after him.

"Oh, there's no risk worth mentioning," he answered back, and a few minutes later Harry saw him leaping from rock to rock, keeping close to the cliff all the while.

For a considerable distance he found no difficulty whatever; the low tide had left the sand and shingle between the rocks quite dry. It was not until he neared the extreme point of the headland that the difficulties of the journey began, but even these to an agile youth seemed hardly worth considering. Here the water was sobbing quietly among the rocks, and laving with musical plash the foot of the cliff.

"If I slip, the worst I shall get is a ducking," Jack said to himself. "But I should like to do the thing dry-shod if possible."

On accomplishing half the distance he turned and faced the cliff, giving at the same time a low whistle. Above him the beetling brows of the cliff overhung considerably; right and left the shallow waters sobbed and sang among the rocks; behind him the deep ocean, guarded by the sentinels, that now towered high above the water; in front of him a broad high cave, the sandy floor of which slanted up, while the roof sloped steeply down to meet it.

"Bah," he said to himself, "that cave is a fraud—the floor and roof touch each other twenty yards from here;" and he gave a leap on to a large rock that stood within its entrance, and then sprang upon its hard sandy floor.

Appearances, however, are sometimes deceptive. The roof and floor did not touch each other, as he had thought. He had not proceeded far before he discovered that the outer cave terminated in what seemed a broad low opening, or entrance to another cave.

"I shall have time to see what's beyond that low doorway, at any rate," he said to himself. "I don't think the tide has turned yet," and he paused for a moment and listened.

Outside the wavelets were tinkling musically on the narrow pebbly strand, and falling back with a low surge among the rocks that guarded the entrance.

"Oh, I shall have plenty of time," he said to himself, and he stooped down and passed through the low, broad opening, and soon found himself in another cave, or rather a series of caves, that seemed to branch away in all directions.

Standing still, and raising his face to the roof, he gave another whistle, but this time of surprise instead of disappointment. He was standing under an immense dome, which seemed to rise a hundred feet above his head. But what surprised him most was, that the whole place was suffused by a rich, beautiful light.

"Evidently there is another way to the outer world than that by which I have come," he said to himself, "for the light seems to come from the top. I must find out the secret of this if I can."

He was not long in discovering that this central dome was surrounded by irregular galleries and steep passes, and what seemed for the moment almost a network of tunnels.

"Well, this is an adventure," he said to himself, as

he commenced to ascend a steep zigzag gallery, lit by openings into the dome. "I wonder if this place is wholly natural, or if some of these caves and galleries were made by the old Phœnicians who worked these cliffs for copper and tin?"

At length he paused; he had ascended at least fifty feet from the level of the beach, and found himself standing on the floor of an upper cave of considerable dimensions. Directly opposite, but separated by the gulf of the dome, was another cave running seaward, which terminated in two round holes which pierced the cliff into the daylight.

Here then was the secret of the light. These round holes were the eyes of Tregeagle, which he had heard people talk about, and through them now was streaming the rich golden light of the west, flooding the cave, indeed flooding the whole series of caves, and rendering every object distinctly visible.

"Well, this is curious," he said to himself, "the stories about this old headland being honeycombed with caves is true after all. I must have a good look round while I have the chance," and turning his back on the eyes of Tregeagle, he began to explore the cavern in which he now found himself. This was not at all difficult, for the western light shone straight past him, and enabled him to see his way with tolerable distinctness.

He had proceeded about twenty-five or thirty yards, when he paused and gave a low whistle of surprise; he found that the cave had expanded to about twice its previous size, and that on every hand there was evidence of its being used as a store-house or dwelling-place, or perhaps both.

He was now so far from the eyes of Tregeagle that the light had become very dim, while most of the objects in the cave were in complete shadow; but he soon got used to the dim light, and after a few moments was able to determine with tolerable accuracy the contents of the place.

The floor was covered with pieces of wood, evidently broken planks from wrecked vessels that had been washed into the cave. This irregular planking was strewn with rugs and skins of various descriptions, while the walls were adorned with articles of a similar nature. Piled up in various corners and recesses were boxes and bales and barrels of all shapes and sizes; in one corner was quite a small stack of brandy-kegs—and not empty either, judging from the odour given forth; in another corner was a large barrel filled with some black stuff which seemed very much like powder, while scattered in all directions was wreckage of various descriptions, but of no particular value.

Nearly opposite where he entered was suspended a large piece of tapestry, which hid the entrance to another cave, or more correctly, perhaps, a continuance of the same. But Jack did not attempt to penetrate the darkness beyond; that might be done some other time, if he were ever fortunate enough again to effect an entrance.

To the left of what he termed the doorway, in a narrow recess not unlike a chimney corner, were the burnt-out embers of what seemed a comparatively recent fire, though how the smoke escaped was not clear, for there was no opening above it.

For a moment Jack stood still with a puzzled look upon his face; then it suddenly occurred to him that he had heard of smoke being seen issuing from the crown of Tregeagle's Head. Here was evidently the explanation: the smoke found its way upward through crack and crevice until it reached the upper air; and what had so alarmed the fisher-folk of Pentudy, and filled them with superstitious dread, was but evidence that some unknown and perhaps unsuspected smugglers were having a good time of it out of sight.

Who were the smugglers? that was the question that leaped to his lips in the first moment of his discovery; but he had no time to debate the question just now, though he fancied in two guesses he could hit upon some of the men, even though he could obtain no positive proof.

But smuggling was evidently not the worst part of their business. Whoever they were, there was proof enough that they were wreckers as well as smugglers; and wonderfully well was the place adapted for that nefarious business. If they could only succeed in luring vessels on to the sentinels, a good part of the cargo was certain to be washed up into the lower cave, where they would be able to secure it without discovery and without difficulty.

"The Vicar's right, after all," he said to himself, with a look of pain upon his handsome face. "He has always stuck to it that the race of wreckers had not died out, and here's proof of it in abundance; but we'll soon unearth them now, that's a comfort. But I must be moving, or I shall get a ducking;" and he cast another glance about the place previous to taking his departure.

"Whew!" he said, as his eye alighted on several bunches of candles hung against the wall close to the fireplace; "and, by Jove, here's a flint and steel and a box of tinder. Evidently the occupants of this place know how to make themselves comfortable. But I must be off, that's certain."

And he turned quickly on his heel and hurriedly left the place. The light through the eyes of Tregeagle was not nearly so brilliant as at the first, and when he reached the dome he found it full of a gray haze. On looking down he uttered an exclamation of horror. Instead of a level floor of yellow sand, a surging cauldron of foamy water met his gaze.

"Good heavens!" he said. "The tide cannot surely have got to that height yet!" and he hurried quickly down the zigzag path until his feet touched the water.

Here he paused and gave a low groan. Through the broad low opening the big Atlantic rollers were sweeping in with a thundering roar, and had already risen almost close to the roof. To attempt to struggle through that rush of surf he knew would be but to court destruction. Even if he got into the outer cave the rocks by this were covered, and to attempt to swim around the headland among the breakers would be an impossible task.

Evidently there was nothing for it but to retrace his steps to the upper cave, and wait as patiently as he could for the low tide of the morning.

CHAPTER XXVII.

"Though plunged in ills, and exercised in care,
Yet never let the noble mind despair;
When pressed by dangers, and beset by foes,
The gods their timely succour interpose;
And when our virtue sinks, o'erwhelmed with grief,
By unforeseen expedients heaven brings relief."

PHILLIPS.

BEFORE retreating into the smugglers' cave, Jack made one or two efforts to reach the eyes of Tregeagle. He thought that if they were large enough to admit of his crawling through, he might be able to climb up the face of the cliff to the crown of the headland, and so make his way home before his mother got alarmed. But all his efforts ended in failure. He could discover no way by which he could cross to the other side of the central cave, the dome of which rose high above where he stood, creating a gulf that was absolutely impassable. To cross the floor of the cave, and attempt to find a way up on the other side was also out of the question, for the shingle was already covered with a surging flood of foaming water to the depth of five or six feet, and which was rising higher and higher every moment. It was quite possible that, right or left, there might be a gallery or tunnel leading

round the dome; but if such a way existed, he was
unable to find it. Besides which, he knew not what
unseen pitfalls might lurk in those dark caverns, and
so concluded he could not be too cautious in his
explorations. Then, too, the light was not so good as
when he first entered the cave. Evidently the day
was rapidly declining, and very soon the place would
be wrapped in total darkness.

So he made his way with cautious footsteps back
into the smugglers' cave, while the darkness deepened
and became more oppressive at every step he took.
In spite too of his natural courage and love of adventure,
he began to be a little bit alarmed; he could not
hide from himself the fact that he was a prisoner,
trapped by the tide, and that he might find it a much
more difficult matter to retrace his steps than he had
imagined. The door by which he had entered was
only passable at extremely low tides, and when the
wind was blowing off the land; at other times the
water evidently never left the floor of the central cave.
Hence, if he failed to escape at the next low tide, which
would be about seven in the morning, he might be
kept a prisoner for a month; and if at the next full
moon the weather should be stormy, he might not
be able to escape then.

Evidently the situation was one of extreme gravity.
He tried his best, however, to make light of it, and
almost succeeded in persuading himself that the only
thing that troubled him was the anxiety his mother
would feel at his absence.

"Well, never mind," he said to himself, "it won't
be for very long. I'll be home to breakfast; and then
all their fears will be at rest."

But though he spoke brave words, there was all the
while an uneasy feeling at his heart, and he heartily
wished himself out of a place so uncanny. He was
not particularly superstitious, nor, as a rule, very

much troubled with nerves; yet somehow the whole
atmosphere of the place was suggestive of ghosts and
hobgoblins. Was it not the chosen home of Tregeagle
himself? Did not his foul and tortured spirit haunt
these caverns incessantly? and might not he appear at
any moment? And besides Tregeagle, what legions
of sailors had been battered to death on the cruel rocks
outside. How often had their swollen corpses been
washed into the central cave, had rocked on its riotous
waters, or lain stranded upon the floor. Pah! the
whole place reeked of dead men, and their bones
were rotting all about him. What if their spirits
haunted these gloomy caverns? Some of them had
been lured to their doom by cruel wreckers, and had
died with curses on their lips. And if their restless
spirits still haunted these dark recesses, who could
wonder?

He chided himself again and again for harbouring
such thoughts, but they would come, in spite of all
he could do. He had already provided himself with
a light, but its feeble and fitful flame only served
to make the darkness visible. In every recess dark
shadows lurked, and suggested all kinds of horrible
things, while from out the darkness hoarse voices
spoke, and moaned, and sobbed, as though a thousand
ghosts peopled these realms of gloom.

As the evening wore on the cavern became chilly
in the extreme. This suggested a fire, a welcome relief
to his gloomy thoughts. Thanks to whoever made the
cave their rendezvous, there was no lack of fuel. Quite
a stack of driftwood was piled up near the fireplace,
so that there was no present reason, at least, why he
should suffer from cold.

He laid his fire very carefully; first cutting a bit
of deal plank into thin splinters with his pocket-knife,
and laying them together on the hearth, then adding
larger pieces of broken and inflammable wood, and

finally adjusting some pieces of oak in a way that the flames might easily play upon them.

The trouble was well repaid by the result. When the brimstone match was applied, the splinters of deal quickly caught fire, and soon the cheerful crackling of the wood was heard above the low sob of the waves, which surged and moaned in the caves below. The smoke from the fire slowly spread itself across the roof of the cave, and hung in dark folds like a pregnant rain-cloud in an autumn sky,

"Well, well, this is a little more cheerful," Jack said, pulling a chunk of wood towards him, and seating himself before the cheerful fire. "I shall be able to tolerate this till morning, at any rate, though I am getting desperately hungry. I wonder if there are any victuals in this establishment?"

After awhile he rose from his seat, and taking the candle, which had begun to burn dim in the firelight, commenced a search for food.

"Goodness gracious," he said to himself, after he had gone a few steps, "this is a regular store. Calicoes, prints, silks, rugs, skins, a good deal damaged, evidently with salt water, but valuable still. But I can't eat calico unfortunately, so I must look further. Ah, I must be careful with my candle, or this barrel of powder may give trouble. Phew! there's brandy enough here too to demoralize the whole of Pentudly and Restormel to boot. Pah! how the stuff smells. But what's this?— a box of raisins, as I'm alive. Well, I shan't starve just yet, that's a comfort. And here, by Jove, is a barrel of flour, with the top knocked in. Not exactly eatable in its present form, though there's no knowing what one may come to. But here turns up something more in my way, a case of ship's biscuits. They look rather stale, 'tis true, but hungry men shut up in caves must not be too fastidious; and here, by Moses, is a stack of dried codfish. Good gracious, I wonder how long these things have been accumulating? But I'll not search any further just now; I'll see if I can't make a supper on hard tack and raisins."

And he returned to his seat before the fire, intent upon appeasing his hunger. It proved a very dry morsel, for he had discovered nothing in the place to drink, unless he tapped one of the brandy kegs, which he had not the least disposition to do.

"If I am to get out of this place I must keep my head cool," he said to himself; " so no meddling with raw spirits for me."

When he had eaten as much as he could of the biscuit, he heaped some more fuel on the fire, and then sat down with his face in his hands and his elbows upon his knees, and gave himself up to reflection.

The eerie creepy feeling which oppressed him at first had in a large measure passed away. Since the fire had been lighted the place looked infinitely less dismal than before; indeed, for a cave it was decidedly comfortable. Then, too, he had got accustomed to the endless sob and moan of the sea as it surged in the lower caves; while his fear of Tregeagle had almost completely evaporated.

Yet notwithstanding this he was still very anxious. He dreaded the possibility of the wind changing during the night, for he knew in that case he would be a prisoner for an indefinite period, even if he ever got out again.

As the evening wore on the surge of the waves gradually died away into silence, broken only now and then by a deep low moan, that pulsed solemnly through the echoing caves. But for the cheerful crackling of the fire the stillness would have been painfully oppressive.

Jack sat perfectly motionless, staring into the fire, and watching in a listless fashion the tongues of flame eating their way into the slowly yielding oak.

Suddenly he started and raised his head, while an eager, anxious look came into his eyes.

From somewhere, but from what direction he could not determine, came a sound the like of which he had not before heard—a soft, gliding noise, as though a ball of flannel had been dragged along the floor, or had quickly slid down a steep passage, and stopped suddenly with an almost imperceptible thud.

"I wonder what it can be," he said to himself with knitted brows, and turning his eyes in the direction of the tapestry which covered the entrance of the unexplored caverns.

"Hist! there it is again," he said, starting to his feet, as a sound of muffled footsteps fell distinctly on his ear.

"Evidently I am not alone in this place," he whispered to himself, a cold perspiration breaking over him. "Either real people live here, or it is haunted."

"Good heavens! the sound is coming nearer," he said, taking the candle in his hand, and backing toward the powder.

Behind the curtain of tapestry, but still far away, came distinctly enough now the sound of approaching footsteps.

Though by no means a coward, Jack felt as though his courage was oozing through every pore. Indeed he had a difficulty in keeping his knees from knocking together, so great was his terror. Whether ghost or human being, whether Tregeagle or some monster of the sea, he felt himself perfectly helpless and defenceless before its presence.

Suddenly the muffled sounds became clear and distinct; there was a rush of cold air through the cave, which bent and swayed the tapestry. The next moment a large hand was seen drawing the curtain aside, followed a moment later by the tall figure of a man, which almost completely blocked the opening.

It would be difficult to decide which looked the more astonished, Jack or his visitor. The new-comer, however, was the first to speak.

"The devil——," he gasped, as an evident preliminary to some further remarks.

"No, there you are mistaken," said Jack, recovering his courage at the sound of the man's voice.

The man let fall the curtain and took a step forward.

"I know your voice," he said, "and I think I know your face."

"Very likely," was the reply. "My name is Jack Dunstan, and yours Sam Trewalsick."

Sam swore a great oath, and looked disconcerted.

"Young man, I'm sorry for you," he said at length. "I wish you'd been the other fellow."

"Who d' you mean?"

"The passon's son."

"Why do you wish it had been him instead of me?"

"Because I'd be glad to have the chance of quietly putting him out of sight. You're a better sort."

"Well, what's that to do with it?"

"You've found out our secret."

"Yes, you smuggle, perhaps worse."

"Just so! Our fortune is 'ere in this place. Several on us is in it; so we couldn't let you loose. You might promise not to split on us, but—" And Sam shook his head.

"Well, and what is the moral of all this?" Jack asked quietly.

"Well, youngster," Sam answered reflectively, "we'll 'ave to quieten you. I'm sorry, I don't deny it, but there's no 'elp for it. Ef I was disposed to let you off the others wouldn't. We should never feel safe ef you was free. No, it won't do. You'll never 'ave to leave 'ere again. We'll give 'e time to repent, an' all that, but we caan't 'old out no 'ope of life."

"Then you'll murder me?"

"Well," and Sam spat two or three times, "it will be easy to drown yer. An' some ov the tides will wash yer up on the beach. It'll seem quite natural."

"Will it?" Jack said with a shudder.

"Quite. We'll give 'e no onnecessary pain. But hark! 'ere comes some ov the other fellers, so you'd better prepare yerself."

CHAPTER XXVIII.

SMUGGLERS AT WORK.

"No help ?   Nay, 'tis not so !
Though human help be far, thy God is nigh :
Who feeds the ravens hears His children's cry.
He's near thee, wheresoe'er thy footsteps roam,
And He will guide thee, light thee, help thee home."

ANON.

A FEW seconds later the curtain was pulled aside, and Dan Polslee and Billy Trewalsick entered. For a moment Dan looked as if he were about to faint with fright, and his lantern jaws became deadly pale ; but Billy took in the situation at once.

" Hello ! so it's 'ere you be, is it ? " he said, addressing Jack.

" Yes, it's here I be," Jack answered, a little bit scornfully.

" Well, you've got into a nice 'ole, that's all I 'ave to say," Billy replied, " an' one you'll not find as easy to get out on as yer got into.   Yer frien's 'ave gived yer up—they're jist returnin' to Restormel ; so yer may as well consider yerself dead fus' as last."

" Thank you," said Jack ; " but I'm not in the habit of saying ' die ' any sooner than is necessary."

" But ye'll 'ave to say it this time," said Dan, who had by this time recovered himself, and was now anxious to cover his cowardice by a greater show of bravery than

"With a curl of his lip, and quick as thought, Jack stuck the flame under Dan's nose."—P. 251.

usual. "Folks as come in 'ere unaxed don't go out widout permission."

"Indeed," said Jack, with a smile of scorn.

"Iss, indeed," said Dan, coming close up to Jack, and staring defiantly into his face.

"What, lantern jaws, art anxious to have the candle inside?" Jack said, with a curl of his lip, and quick as thought he stuck the flame under Dan's nose.

With a yell that was almost blood-curdling Dan sprang back, and fell over a piece of wood with a great racket, striking his head violently on the floor in his fall. The effect was so comical that Sam and Billy went off into a violent fit of laughter, the latter twisting himself into all imaginable contortions, and holding his sides as though in pain.

The laughter of his friends only added fuel to the fire of Dan's anger, and leaping to his feet, and seizing a long strip of wood, he began to execute a kind of war-dance, brandishing the wood in the most menacing manner of which he was capable, and steadily edging nearer his foe.

Jack stood his ground unmoved, and regarded his opponent with a cynical smile. He still held the candle in his right hand, but watching his opportunity he quickly changed it to the left, and seizing Dan's weapon as it came dangerously near his head, he wrenched it from his hand, and lurching forward, drove the end of it against Dan's stomach with a force that would have been fatal to his enemy had it been sharp.

The end of the stick, however, being only blunt, no worse effect followed than the sudden deprivation of his breath. With a great gasp he sat down on the floor with a bang, and looked for the moment as if he were about to give up the ghost.

For a second or two there was the most profound silence, while Dan rolled round his goggle eyes in a wild, imploring fashion. A deep inspiration followed, and the words, "Oh, lor!" and then Billy went off again into an uncontrollable fit of laughter.

At length Dan struggled to his feet a second time and propped himself against the wall.

"I'll be quits wid yer yet," he said, with a diabolical leer. "Thou thinks thou'lt git out, but thou never wilt. Thou'lt drown, but not before thou'st been made to suffer."

"If thou dost not shut thy lantern door, and keep thy noise to thyself, I'll twist thy neck for thee," Jack answered, with sudden anger. "Dost think I'm afraid of such a monkey as thou art?"

"Monkey, eh?" Dan hissed. "Ah, but we shall see. When thou art strugglin' and dyin' thou'lt wish thou hadst been more civil."

"Come, come, cease your chatter," said Sam, with an oath. "It's quite time we was a movin' these kegs. Now, Billy, pick up this top one an' be off."

Instantly Billy caught up a keg of brandy and disappeared, going in the direction of Tregeagle's eyes.

After a few minutes Dan came forward, picked up a second keg, and followed Billy. Another minute or two and Sam prepared to follow suit.

"Now, youngster, don't you attempt to follow," said Sam, and he marched away into the darkness.

In a few minutes he was back again, and disappeared with another keg, and so on for seven or eight times in succession.

When about a dozen kegs had been removed Sam did not return again for a considerable time; but Jack could hear the voices of the three men very distinctly coming from the direction of Tregeagle's eyes; while every now and then came faintly the sound of other voices which he did not recognize.

It was quite clear, however, what the smugglers were up to. The tide was now at its height, and a boat getting free of the sentinels had drawn close up to the cliffs under Tregeagle's eyes. Sam, Billy, and Dan were lowering the kegs of smuggled brandy into the boats through the eyes of Tregeagle. This would be landed later on in some quiet creek, and carted away during the night into the country.

"The whole thing is certainly ingenious," said Jack to himself; "evidently the Vicar has been right all along. But let me get safely out of this place, and we'll put a stop to the performance for ever."

But there came the rub—how was he to get out? He saw clearly enough the force of Sam Trewalsick's words and Dan Polslee's threat. It was to the smugglers' interest to silence him, nay, their very safety depended upon it. They might be unwilling to murder him, but only by murdering him could they insure their own safety.

Still he was not going to give up in despair. There was a way out of the cave other than that by which he had come in, and unless these men killed him at once he might yet be able to find it, that is, supposing he did not escape at low tide next morning, which he had now little hope of doing; the smugglers would most likely prevent that.

At length the sound of voices ceased, and he heard the sound of footsteps again, echoing through the gloomy caverns. Throwing a few more pieces of wood on the fire, and lighting a second candle, he took up his station once more by the powder-cask and waited.

Nearer and nearer came the footsteps, then suddenly ceased; then he caught their echo again; but they seemed retreating instead of advancing. Now they were coming nearer again, but seemingly at the opposite end of the cavern, now they were dying away once more. At length silence, save for the moan of the wind through Tregeagle's eyes, and the low surge and sob of the water in the lower cave.

Still the minutes dragged on and on, and no other sound broke the stillness. Steadily he kept his eye

Q

fixed on the open entrance of the cave, expecting every
moment to see one or other of the smugglers enter ; but
no one came.

" Well, now, what's the meaning of this ? " he said to
himself with knitted brows. " I wonder what devilry
these fellows are concocting ? Perhaps they intend to
surprise me, or wait till I'm asleep, and coolly murder
me then. Anyhow, I'll not sleep to-night," and he
shifted his position uneasily, still keeping his eye on
the entrance of the cave.

Still the minutes dragged slowly on, then noiselessly
the tapestry was drawn back once more, and Sam
entered. Jack turned his head with a start.

" Ah, you thought we had left you, eh ? " Sam remarked carelessly.

" Nay, I hardly thought you were as considerate as all
that," Jack answered ; " but I thought you would enter
by the open door."

" Exactly so, but I didn't you see. But would it not
be safer if you would keep away with that candle from
the gunpowder ? "

" Exactly so," Jack answered, with mock gravity.
" But where are the others ? "

" Well, I presume they're in Pentudy by this."

" And why do you stay here ? "

" To keep you company."

" I'm not afraid of being alone."

" That may be so ; but we're hardly likely to let you
escape at low tide, though I don't think there's much
fear, for I reckon the wind's shifting round to the west."

" Ah, that's bad for me."

" Nay, neither bad nor good," Sam answered. " You'll
never leave here alive, whichever way the wind gets."

" You think so, do you ? "

" I'm sure on it."

" Then perhaps you wouldn't mind telling me when
I'm to be murdered, and how ? "

"Well, the truth is, that ain't decided yet. We ain't in no perticler 'urry, unless you wish to hook it from this 'ere sinful world," and Sam laughed as though he had said something particularly funny.

"We might all the lot of us 'hook it' together," Jack said, with quiet scorn.

"In which way?" said Sam.

"Well, if I were to drop this candle into this barrel of powder, we should both of us depart at the same time."

"Don't be a fool," Sam said, turning pale.

"Oh, I don't intend to send you off alone," Jack said, with a laugh; "I can wait till the others are here; and as it's settled I'm to be dispatched, we might all of us go up like a rocket."

"I wish you would come away from that powder," Sam said at length, looking uneasy. "I promise 'e nothin' will be done to 'e to-night, or to-morrow, for that. We'll give 'e good time to repent in, there now, so make yerself comfortable."

"Oh, I am quite comfortable," said Jack, "except that I'm rather thirsty."

"Well, I'll get 'e somethin' to drink," and Sam took an old kettle and disappeared into the darkness.

He evidently knew his way about in the dark as well as in the light. After a while he returned with the kettle full of spring water.

"We can have some grog if yer would like a little," he said; "there's lots o' brandy left."

"No, thank you, I'd prefer the water without the brandy," Jack answered.

"Well, wait a moment till I get out a mug. You see we've lots o' things here. We've 'ad many a feast here o' summer nights. It's allers cool here."

"I should think so," Jack answered.

"I'll get 'e somethin' to eat d'rectly," said Sam. "I ain't got no grudge agin 'e; I'm main sorry for 'e, I be. I wish it had been the other feller; he's allers a spyin' about, he is. But you've got 'ere, that's your misfortin. It's a pity, a great pity; but there's no 'elp for it now. So I 'ope you'll be comfortable."

"I'll try," Jack answered.

"That's right; now for a bit of boiled cod. Would yer mind fixing up that crock stand? Splendid fireplace this to draw, though there ain't no chimbley to it," and Sam laughed again.

After supper the two men wrapped themselves in rugs and lay down on the floor in front of the fire; but neither of them slept, each seemed more or less suspicious of the other. As soon as the light began to struggle through Tregeagle's eyes Sam got up and replenished the fire; then he took the kettle, and went off for a fresh supply of water.

"Yer quite safe," he said to Jack on his return; "the wind's blowin' haaf a gale from the west. Ye couldn't git out by the lower way now if ye were a shark."

"Well, it doesn't matter much since there is an upper way," Jack answered.

"Which way you'll never find," said Sam.

"Perhaps so," Jack answered; and then the subject dropped.

The day passed very slowly; to Jack it seemed almost an age. He made no attempt to explore the caverns around him. Sam was evidently not disposed to let him go out of his sight, yet he did not give up hope of effecting his release sooner or later, though he kept the hope to himself.

About seven o'clock it was low tide again, and Sam took him to have a look at the way by which he entered. It was quite true that he could not escape even if he were a shark, for the rollers were rushing through the low opening with terrific force, and breaking themselves into spray on the jagged rocks.

"I guess you'll not try to git out that road?" Sam said, with a laugh.

"Not to-day, at any rate," Jack answered; and he turned on his heel and marched back into the cave.

He expected every moment that Sam would follow him, but, to his surprise, he did not come. After a while he went back to look for him, but he was nowhere visible; he had disappeared as completely as though he had fallen into the surging cauldron of the lower cave and was drowned.

"Well, so much the better," Jack said half aloud; "I expect he's on his way to Pentudy, if he has not reached there by this. It's funny if there is a way out which I cannot find. I'll get a candle and commence the search at once."

And he returned again to the cave, and went at once to the corner where he had left the candles hanging; but they had disappeared, not a candle was to be found anywhere. Evidently Sam had removed them, and he was left to make his explorations in the dark.

CHAPTER XXIX.

LEFT ALONE.

" A thousand fantasies
Begin to throng into my memory,
Of calling shapes, and beckoning shadows dire,
And airy tongues that syllable men's names,
And sands, and shores, and desert wildernesses."

MILTON.

FOR a whole week Jack was left alone, a prey to the most gloomy apprehensions; every hour of those dreary days and nights he expected to hear the sound of returning footsteps, while he had little doubt that when the smugglers did return they would murder him without further delay.

After the first day or two he began to lose hope, and by the end of the week he was in despair, while a wretched cold he had contracted made him feel so ill and miserable, that he almost wished sometimes the smugglers would return at once and complete their murderous work. He ached in every limb; his hands were cut, and his body covered with bruises, caused by numberless falls in his attempts to find his way out of his prison. The wonder was that he was alive; here he had struck his head against a projecting piece of roof, and there he had fallen into an unseen pit. For hours he had crawled about in impenetrable darkness, having lost his reckoning altogether; now and then he had lain down, saying in his heart he would go no further, he would just remain where he was and die.

But love of life is strong, and especially so in the young, and after he had rested awhile he would continue his blind search again, but always with the same result. Two discoveries only did he make—the first a small pool of fresh water, kept ever full by a constant trickle down the rocks; and the second, the way to the eyes of Tregeagle. It was Sunday morning when he made his second discovery—that dreary Sunday of cloud and rain which we have already described. He was very much surprised when he got close to the eyes to find how large they were—three or four men might have easily clambered through them at the same time; but when he pushed his head and shoulders through and looked around him, above him, beneath him, all hope of escape in that direction vanished for ever. Above were the beetling brows of Tregeagle, projecting almost horizontally for five or six feet; below the hollow cheeks fell sheer to the surging sea. Right and left the smooth, weather-worn rocks offered not a single inch of foothold anywhere.

Yet, nevertheless, it was pleasant to sit in the open, with the daylight all about him, and the great restless, wind-swept sea rolling away before him into infinite space. He did not forget that it was Sunday morning, and once or twice he fancied, when the wind lulled for a moment, that he could hear the faint tone of Restormel bells.

Every now and then he called at the top of his voice, "Help, help!" but the wind seemed to blow the words back into his teeth, and he very much questioned whether people could hear him even if they stood upon the brink of the cliff above his head.

But no one stood there on that rainy Sabbath day, and so no one heard him; yet he continued to call, in a despairing sort of way, hoping almost against hope that sooner or later some answering voice would respond.

It seemed very strange to be able to stand there in the free air, and yet be so absolutely a prisoner; to be almost within sight of home, and yet be unable to reach it; to be mourned as dead by those he loved the best, and yet to be unable to send even a message to assuage their grief.

He did not heed the driving mist and rain as he sat there hour after hour, and so he became chilled to the bone almost before he was aware. He started up at length, feeling stiff and cramped, and began to grope his way back to the cave.

"I hope my fire has not gone out," he muttered to himself; "how stupid of me to forget all about it."

He was only just in time to save it; the resinous wood had burnt itself down to a little heap of white ashes, that only glowed faintly red when stirred. To slice a bit of deal into shavings with his pocket-knife was his first operation, but even then the fire was only saved from extinction by the exercise of the greatest patience and ingenuity.

"I must not do such a stupid thing again," he said, when at length the fire began to leap up merrily once more.

Towards evening he went out to the eyes again, and remained there far on into the night, calling at intervals for help that seemed destined never to come.

By the following morning he was so hoarse he could hardly speak, so he remained in the cave most of the day, and by nightfall had rigged up another curtain, and hung it across the entrance; this considerably heightened the temperature of the place, and lessened the necessity for so large a fire.

By the following evening his voice had nearly recovered its usual tone, so he went again to the eyes, and cried and called till nearly midnight, with the result that he became hoarser than ever; indeed, for several days after he could scarcely speak at all.

Now and then he saw a fishing-boat far out in the distance, but none of the boats came near enough for him to make himself either heard or seen. Wave his hat or handkerchief as much as he might, who would notice him—a small speck on the great face of the almost endless line of cliffs? So the days and nights passed on; he had no regular time for eating or sleeping, and day was so much like night, except when he was out in the eyes, that he was in danger of losing count of the days.

Fortunately there was no lack of provisions of a certain kind, while now and then he succeeded in catching a lobster or crab, which he boiled in an old crock that had evidently been used before for similar purposes. He managed to get some table salt by filling his kettle with sea-water, and letting it evaporate over the fire. Nor was there any lack of small shell-fish, such as cockles, limpets, and mussels.

So a week passed away, and Jack had nearly given up all hope of leaving his prison alive. It was nearly midnight, and he was seated before the fire, his elbows upon his knees, his face in his hands. His thoughts were of the gloomiest character; they could hardly be anything else. He was almost wishing that Trewalsick and the rest of them would come and put him out of his misery; this solitary confinement, without hope of release, was worse even than death.

Suddenly he started; a grating noise fell upon his ear, while at the same moment the curtain swayed toward him, and a cold breath of sea-air swept through the cave.

"Hem," he said to himself, "the exit is blocked by some kind of door; if I'm not murdered to-night I shall have an idea to go upon." The next moment he had seized a flaming stick from the fire, and was standing again close to the powder cask. Almost at the same moment the tapestry curtain was pulled back, and Sam Trewalsick entered.

"What, living yet?" he said.

"Yes, I'm like the Irishman, I can't die for the life of me," Jack answered.

"Ah, well, we shall 'ave to help you, I expect," Sam answered, "though I'd rather not. To light a couple o' fires in the eyes, and fool the ships on to the rocks, and let a lot o' foreign sailors drown, ain't the same as killin' a neighbour in cold blood. The truth is, I wish you'd kill yourself, an' save us the trouble."

"Very likely I shall, if I'm kept here long enough," Jack answered.

"Well, there ain't no 'urry as I knows on," said Sam, musingly; "though we should feel more safe like if you was out of the way."

"I thought perhaps you had come to do the business to-night," Jack answered.

"Oh no, I only comed to see if you was 'ere, and alive; I didn't know whether p'r'aps the gale t'other night had blowed you away."

"Oh, no, I scarcely felt it in here; and I'm getting so used to the roar of the sea, that a little more noise than usual does not trouble me much."

"No, you're purty much out o' the world 'ere; a case o' bein' buried alive, eh? An' yet there be purty big stirrings above. The trial 'as been a rare do—lots o' fun with it. An' the way he locked Abel in an' got off was a caution. However, he was nabbed at last, and by this he's safe in Bodmin gaol."

"What do you mean?" said Jack; "I have not the remotest idea what you are talking about."

"Of course not," Sam said; "I'm quite forgettin';" and he proceeded to give a full and particular account of the arrest of Harry Penryn, the trial, his escape from the lock-up, and his recapture.

Jack listened with open mouth and flaming cheeks.

"And you never told them I was alive," he said at length, as soon as his indignation would permit him to speak.

"Well, 'ardly," Sam said, pushing a large quid of tobacco into his mouth; "our business was to make 'em b'lieve you wasn't alive."

"Why so?" Jack asked, indignantly.

"Well, you see, we know'd in the fust place as 'ow you wouldn't be alive long," Sam answered slowly; "an' in the second place, we didn't want folks a-rootin' about Tregeagle's 'Ead in search ov you, as they would ha' done had they thought you was locked up here in one ov the caves; so Billy an' me fitted up a little story as just settled that matter."

"You fitted up a story?" Jack asked. "What do you mean?"

"Oh, you want to be knowin' too much," Sam answered with a leer. "But I can tell 'e, there's been rare doin's. But the case was clear as day. You'd killed his dawg, he'd vowed to kill you—that were point one; he was seen chasin' you on the 'Ead—point two; he catches you, and there is a struggle on point of cliff —point three; something is seen a-fallin' over by a fisherman about that time—point four; after struggle, only one man seen on the 'Ead—point five; body of deceased discovered out in deep water—point six; prisoner skulks 'ome in the evenin' alone, as if not wantin' to be seen—point seven; when charged, tells a goose an' gander kind ov a story that ain't no sense in it—point eight. Bless me, I'm a good lawyer spoiled, don't yer think so?"

"Do you mean those were the points of evidence?" Jack asked eagerly, without heeding Sam's questions.

"Them's them to a hair; an' ov course the magistrates couldn't do nothin' else but send 'im up to 'Sizes on charge of murder."

"And you permitted such a thing to go on?"

"In course I did; couldn't 'elp myself. If this place was discovered it 'ud be a gone job wi' me."

For a moment Jack was silent, then he raised the smouldering piece of wood he held in his hand, and blew at it until it brightened into a flame.

Sam looked at him curiously, and then asked,

"What are 'e a-doin' that for?"

"I'm thinking I'd better put this to the powder, and blow you out of time," Jack answered. "A fiend like you is not fit to live."

Sam sprang back, with an oath.

"Ah, coward!" Jack hissed; "you're ready enough to do other people to death."

"Nay, but I'm not," Sam answered. "I've told 'e I'm sorry, an' I ain't a-going to do the job myself; the lot's fallen on Dan Polslee and Jerry Beer. Jerry's away at present, but he'll be back as soon as weather bates a bit. Dan's itching for 'im to come; his nose ain't a-stopped smartin' yet."

"May it never stop smarting to the day of his death," Jack answered. "But tell him he may expect a warmer reception the next time he comes."

"Well, I don't expect he'll be comin' again till he comes wi' Jerry," Sam answered. "But don't you be a-bearin' ill-will agin me. I consider I've treated yer well; I've 'lowed you to stay 'ere burnin' fuel, an' eatin' wittels, an' I've brought wi' me a loaf of new bread to tempt yer appetite, there now. I tell 'e again, I'm main sorry for 'e, but it caan't be 'elped, so don't you be bearin' no grudge agin me."

Jack almost laughed, in spite of himself; such an odd mixture of kindness and cruelty he had never seen before. Then a thought struck him.

"How do I know the bread is not poisoned?" he said.

For a moment Sam looked grave, then his face brightened.

"I'll eat a piece with you if yer like."

"Good," and Jack threw the piece of wood into the fire. "We'll have supper together," he said.

"Agreed," responded the smuggler.

After supper Sam remarked that he would go to the eyes and see if any boats were loitering about, and he lifted the curtain and disappeared.

Jack sprang to his feet and attempted to follow him, but he saw no more of Sam that night, nor for many a long day after.

CHAPTER XXX.

HOPE AND DESPAIR.

"Oh, hope! sweet flatterer! thy delusive touch
Sheds on afflicted minds the balm of comfort—
Relieves the load of poverty—sustains
The captive, bending with the weight of bonds—
And smooths the pillow of disease and pain."

GLOVER.

"FOILED again," Jack muttered to himself when at length he had succeeded in finding his way back into the cave once more. "But his going out at the end opposite that by which he entered is a mere ruse intended to foil me. How softly the villain can thread his way through those passages. But I'll not despair yet. It's a dead certainty that there's a door in this direction which opens and shuts. If I can only find that, then freedom!" And his eyes sparkled in the firelight at the thought.

For the next three or four days he scarcely went near the eyes of Tregeagle. He spent nearly all his time groping like a mole in the darkness, and sometimes getting lost in the interminable tunnels which honeycombed the headland.

On the fifth day he made another discovery which for the moment filled him with hope and exultation. Behind the tapestry curtain was a fairly straight tunnel extending some fifty or sixty yards, and ending abruptly in a wall of rock. On the right-hand side of the tunnel the wall was unbroken, but on the left it was pierced by a dozen other tunnels and passages. Which of these passages led to freedom? He tried them all in turn, and more than once got lost in their tortuous recesses.

On the day in question, however, he felt his way to the very end of the straight tunnel. It might be there was some narrow continuation of it which had escaped him, perhaps some carefully-contrived doorway which had eluded his search. Carefully as a blind man might, he felt with his fingers in all directions, pushing his hands into every crack and fissure, and pulling at every stone that seemed at all loose.

At length his labour was rewarded. A big rock, as he pulled, seemed to swing towards him. At first he imagined it was mere delusion, but soon he became certain that the rock was moving. Then a current of air moved slowly past him.

" I've got it now," he said, excitedly. And truly for the moment it seemed as if he were in sight of freedom; the huge piece of rock was so nicely balanced, that as he pulled it moved slowly on its hinges, while if he let go, he discovered it would fall gradually back into its place again.

In a few minutes he had the door wide open, but, alas! all was darkness beyond. Still that did not alarm him very much, he felt convinced that he had at last found the road to freedom.

In less time than it takes us to describe he had crawled through, and the heavy door closed slowly behind him. Stretching out his hands, he discovered he was still in a tunnel of about the same dimensions as the one he had left; indeed, the one seemed but a continuation of the other.

For about a dozen yards he groped his way slowly, then the tunnel suddenly widened into what seemed a fairly large circular room. Very carefully he felt round with his hands, then a groan of despair escaped him.

On every side rose up a wall of smooth rock, without a crevice in it anywhere. The only opening was above him—he could not touch the roof at any point.

"I see how it is," he said to himself. "I'm at the bottom of a shaft, and so am as much a prisoner as ever; I may as well give up first as last;" and he sat down on the floor and gave way to a passion of tears.

After awhile he returned again to his cave. "If I am to die I may as well die here," he said, and he threw himself on some skins before the fire and fell fast asleep.

When he awoke his fire was nearly out, besides which he was desperately hungry and cold; so he set to work at once to replenish his fire, and then to get something to eat. Having accomplished that to his satisfaction, he did not feel nearly so despairing as he had done. Indeed, his hope seemed to revive with the reviving fire, and when the meal was ended he resolved to prosecute his search once more. Nothing, however, came of it. The days and nights passed away until he almost lost count of them.

He never seriously entertained the thought that Harry would suffer in consequence of his disappearance. He began to think after awhile that Sam was merely hoaxing him. Had he known that even at that very moment Harry was lying under sentence of death, his misery would have been a hundred-fold greater.

It was the evening before the day appointed for Harry's execution that Jack, utterly despairing, went out to sit in Tregeagle's eyes. Over the restless sea he watched the daylight fade, watched the fishing-boats in the offing grow vague and indistinct in the gathering gloom; watched the stars come out one by one in the great lonely dome above him; watched the sea-gulls

hie away to their hiding-places, till not a white wing
was left to cleave the air.

Once or twice he called "Help, help!" but his voice
was lost in the deep surge of the sea, and there was no
heart left in him for further effort or cry. Any sort of
visitor would have been a relief to him at the moment;
even Tregeagle himself would have been welcome. He
had been alone so long that he almost feared at times
he would lose his reason. He wondered why the
smugglers did not come and carry their threat into
execution. Even death was less to be dreaded than a
continuance of this hopeless misery.

He did not notice that all the light of day had faded,
and that the great sea had become invisible in the
deepening gloom. Suddenly he started at the sound of
a footstep near him; the next moment he recognized
Sam Trewalsick's voice.

"So you're not dead yet?" he said.

"No," Jack answered, "but I wish I were."

"Then why don't yer throw yerself into the sea?
It 'ud be a easy way out on it, an' drownding ain't at all
'ard dyin'."

"I have thought about it," Jack answered, "but I've
not had the courage to do it yet."

"Well, if yer don't do it soon ye won't 'ave the
chance. Jerry Beer returned this mornin', and we've
fixed to-morrer for the job."

"You've fully resolved to murder me, then?"

"We don't call it murder," Sam said, uneasily. "It's
a case ov necessity. Ef you escape, what's to become
ov us?"

"I quite understand," Jack answered, with an effort.
"I hope I'll be ready for you to-morrow."

"I thought I'd give 'e fair warnin'," Sam said, after
a pause. "An' you might like to know that the passon's
son is to be polished off at same time."

"What, Harry Penryn?"

R

"Aye, he's to be hanged to-morrer mornin' for a murderin' you; funny, ain't it?"

"Funny!" exclaimed Jack, clenching his fists in impotent anger. "It is wicked beyond words to express."

Sam laughed sullenly. "It jist sarves 'im right," he said. "He's allers been rootin' round 'ere trying to ferret out our secrets. Now we've stopped his little game, an' I 'ope it'll be a lesson to his faather at the same time."

But Jack did not reply. He sat staring out into the darkness, a prey to the most agonizing thoughts.

How he blamed his folly now for trying to walk round Tregeagle's Head! How he wished he had taken Harry's advice! Why had he not thought that if anything happened to him, Harry would be blamed? If he were prepared to jeopardize his own life, he ought not to have jeopardized the life of his friend. By his stupid folly he had wrecked half a dozen lives. His father and mother and Mary would never cease to grieve; while Mr. Penryn and Gladys would feel disgraced for the rest of their lives; and—worst of all—Harry would be hanged like a common felon for a crime he never committed.

"Oh, heavens," he groaned, "my punishment is greater than I can bear." Then a sudden revulsion of feeling came over him. "No, no," he said, "it cannot be. It is too horrible. God would not allow such a wrong to be committed. Sam is only hoaxing me." And turning his head toward his companion, whom he could not see in the darkness, he said, "This is rather a ghastly joke of yours, Sam; you need not try to torture me in mind as well as in body."

But Sam did not reply.

"Come, say you are only hoaxing me," Jack pleaded in earnest tones.

But no answer came out of the darkness.

"Ain't you there, Sam?" he said, starting to his feet.

But still no answer.

"Oh, fool that I have been," he said, clenching his teeth, "to have let him escape the third time without following him." And he began to grope his way back to his cave.

"I almost deserve my fate," he muttered, "but I did not think he would slip away after that fashion. But there; it's my fate, I suppose. So I must make the best of it. To-morrow is to be the grand *finale*. Let me test the powder," and he threw a grain upon the fire.

"Whew, that barrel will make a grand flare up. And now for supper. Bless me, I'm getting quite reckless." And he proceeded to replenish his fire, preparatory to cooking his supper.

CHAPTER XXXI.

THE WITCH TO THE RESCUE.

"There is some soul of goodness in things evil,
Would men observingly distil it out."—SHAKESPEARE.

"What can I pay thee for this noble usage
But grateful praise? So heaven itself is paid!"—ROWE.

MEANWHILE the witch of Carn Duloe had not been inactive, but so far all her scheming had been in vain. More than once since Harry had been in Bodmin Gaol she fancied she had heard cries for help coming from the direction of Tregeagle's Head; and in conversation with the fisher-folk of Pentudy and Porthloo, she found there were rumours afloat of Tregeagle having been heard again, with the consequent expectation of further destructive gales.

"I must probe this to the bottom if I can," she said. "I like the boy, and I believe he is innocent; and if I can but succeed in saving him, I shall establish my influence more strongly than ever."

But when the eve of the day of execution was reached, Mrs. Flue, like many others, was almost in despair. She had spent days and nights in trying to explore the better known caves of Tregeagle, but so far nothing had come of her efforts.

On the night in question she was sitting on the edge of the cliff on the Porthloo side of the headland, leaning against a large granite rock, while her eyes wandered across the billowy stretch of turf in the direction of

Pentudy. Why she sat there she hardly knew, except that she was weary with her efforts, and the rest was grateful. She was wondering too if there was anything else she could do. She did not like being foiled, and yet there seemed no means of confirming her suspicions.

Suddenly she started, and caught her breath with a quick gasp. Not many yards away a large lump of the spongy turf seemed to be moving. What could it mean? It was as though an invisible hand was raising a trap-door. A moment later a dark object appeared at the edge.

"Pah!" she thought, "it's only a rabbit coming out of its burrow, looking half as big again as it ought to in this uncertain light. But, hist!" and she drew closer to the rock.

It was no rabbit, but the head of a man. A moment later the shoulders came into view, then his body. Slowly he crept out from under the lid of turf, and after a swift glance around him rose to his feet.

He did not expect to see any one at this late hour, for he knew no one cared to come on to the headland after nightfall. Still it was always well to be cautious, so he threw a large cloak he carried over his head, and glided away like a headless ghost in the direction of Pentudy.

Mrs. Flue drew a long breath.

"So that's you, Sam Trewalsick, is it?" she said, half aloud. "Well, I'll try what rabbit-burrowing is like now; likely I shall find something worth while at the bottom of that hole."

And she crept forward on her hands and knees, keeping her eyes fixed on the spot where Sam's head first appeared.

There was nothing peculiar about the place; the lump of turf was like a hundred other lumps scattered in all directions. At its lower edge was a hole, which had the appearance of an ordinary rabbit burrow—it might be a little larger than most of the burrows, that was all. But when she put her hand into the hole and attempted to raise the little hillock, she found it opened like the lid of a box, and revealed a much larger opening than any one would ever have suspected.

"I must find the bottom of this," she said; and she crept in feet foremost, and found a small tunnel slanting downwards at an angle of about forty-five degrees.

As soon as the lid dropped she found herself in pitchy darkness, but she was not of the nervous sort; steadily she slid or crept downward, until she reached the level floor of a small cave. Here she proceeded to get a light, for she had brought a plentiful supply of tinder with her, as well as a number of candles.

When her candle was well alight she looked around her. At right angles from the hole down which she had crept was another tunnel much larger, and with an almost level floor. Cautiously she made her way along this tunnel for some considerable distance, then suddenly stopped. At her feet lay a coil of knotted rope, and beyond it a dark and, for all she knew, a bottomless abyss.

"Hem," she said, "I see one end is made fast by a large iron clamp. So far satisfactory; Sam has climbed up this hole and pulled his ladder after him. I wonder if he were afraid of some one following him? Well, I'll have to descend by it—a risky thing rather for one my age; but the hole is not deep, judging by the length of the rope."

And she threw it into the pit, and heard the end strike the bottom.

"Now I must fasten my candle to my bonnet," she said—a feat she quickly accomplished; and grasping the rope with her strong, sinewy hands, she slid over the edge of the pit, and by the aid of the knots in the rope descended easily to the bottom of the pit, which was not more than twelve or thirteen feet deep.

Here she took the candle from her bonnet, and hurried along the tunnel she saw opening out before her, but only for a few yards; the way ended abruptly in a wall of rock.

"I've taken the wrong turn, evidently," she said; and she quickly retraced her steps to the bottom of the pit. But though she looked in all directions, she could discover no other way out of it.

"There must be a way somewhere," she said; "and what's more, I'll find it if I have to stay here till doomsday."

And she moved forward again along the tunnel, but much more slowly than before, but only to be confronted a second time with the wall of rock.

"Bah!" she said, "if the boy is not discovered to-night it will be too late. I'll shout; if the lad is living in any of those caves perhaps he'll hear me." And standing with her face against the wall of rock, she cried—"Ahoy! ahoy! ahoy!" in a shrill, clear voice.

Jack, who was busily engaged scooping out the shell of a crab with his forefinger, started, and then leaped to his feet.

A second time came from behind the tapestry curtain the call, muffled and indistinct—

"Ahoy! ahoy! ahoy!"

Instantly he pulled the curtain aside, and shouted at the top of his voice—

"Hallo! who's there?"

"Mrs. Flue," came the answer. "How can I get to you?"

"Wait a moment," he replied, as he rushed madly along the tunnel. "Oh, glory! I'm saved at last."

"Are you Jack Dunstan?" called the witch, from behind the stone barrier.

"Aye, aye, or all that's left of him," he answered; and he seized the stone and swung it back on its hinges, and a moment later he was standing in the grateful light of the witch's candle.

For a moment she looked at him in silence, while her eyes filled with tears, then in a choking voice she said—

"Since the Lord has been pleased to use me as His instrument, perhaps He will yet have mercy upon my poor old soul;" and she brushed her hand swiftly across her eyes.

"I don't think you need fear on that score," he said. "But now tell me the news. Is mother still living? and is it true that Harry has been sentenced to be hanged for murdering me?"

"Thy mother is still living," the witch answered gravely; "but Harry is to be hanged to-morrow morning unless some one can reach Bodmin in time to stop the execution, which I fear is now impossible."

"No, not impossible, surely," he said, with a sudden gasp. "What time of the night is it?"

"I know not," she said; "but it must be getting late. It has been dark these many hours."

"Then let us hurry," he said. "I will go to Bodmin myself. Jet will carry me in five hours, unless some accident happens."

"I did not think of thy mare," she said. "I know she is swift of foot, but I fear me her strength will fail in so long a journey."

"Let us hope for the best," he said, as he climbed swiftly up the knotted rope.

A minute or two later the witch followed, her strength and agility being not only a surprise to Jack, but to herself also.

"Now follow me," she said; and she strode swiftly on before him. Up the sloping hole she crept with the fleetness of a cat, paused for a moment when she pushed her head into the open air, then crept boldly out upon the spongy turf.

A moment later Jack stood by her side; then hand-in-hand they hurried along the headland in the direction of Restormel. Oh, what bliss it was to be free again; and how fragrant was the country air after the salt sea breeze!

"It's like being in heaven," he said. "I hope I'm not dreaming."

"Nay, thou'rt wide enough awake," she answered. "But keep cool, thou'lt need all thy nerve."

"I know it," he said; "but how can I keep cool? Think how delighted dear mother will be, and Mary, and the dad."

"Thou must not think of them just now," she said. "Thy duty is to save the lad. Think of him."

"I am thinking of him also. Oh, what a lot of suffering I have caused by my foolishness! It will be a lesson to me for the rest of my life."

"Aye, aye," she answered. "Want of thought is at the bottom of a great deal of the world's misery."

They were reaching the brow of the hill by this, and so far they had not met a single creature. A few minutes later Restormel lay dimly outlined beneath them; but the village lay in darkness, not a solitary light glimmered anywhere.

"I fear it's very late," said the witch. "Let us hurry, for every moment is precious."

For the rest of the way scarcely a word was spoken. Down in the shadow of the pine-wood they hurried with long and rapid strides; over the stile Jack leaped without touching it, and the witch almost as quickly followed. Across the fields they almost ran, till, panting and out of breath, they emerged into the long deserted street.

How their footfalls echoed, walk as silently as they would, but no one seemed to heed them. The great angel of sleep brooded over old and young alike, drying the tears of the mourner, and hushing the sighs of the distressed. The weary ones forgot their weariness, and the bereaved ones their heart-ache; the aged no longer remembered how near the end was, nor did the young picture the long and tortuous way they had to travel. Joy and sorrow alike was forgotten in the kindly shadow of the great angel's wings.

Trevose, like all the other houses, was wrapped in silence and in darkness.

"Which is thy sister's room?" the witch asked.

"That to the left," said Jack with a gasp, for his heart was beating so violently he could scarcely speak.

"Keep behind me," she said; and taking a handful of sand from the garden path, she flung it against the window.

A few moments of breathless silence followed, and then a second handful was thrown. A moment later the window was thrown open, and Mary Dunstan's bonny face was dimly seen.

"Who's there?" she asked.

"It's I," said the witch. "Keep cool, I have good news for thee."

"Jack?" she gasped.

"Yes; he is alive and well. Now call thy father, and get down-stairs as quickly as possible."

"Oh, God be praised!" she said, clasping her hands; but she did not wait to close the window.

In a few moments Farmer Dunstan, with an old dressing-gown thrown over him, opened the door and confronted the witch. Jack kept in the background.

"What is the meaning of this?" he said, trembling with excitement.

"Thy son is alive," she said.

"Art sure, woman?"

"As sure as that thou art standing there," she said.

The next moment Jack rushed forward, and the farmer caught him in his arms, crying,

"Oh, my son—my son!"

Then Mary appeared upon the scene, her eyes swimming with happy tears.

"Now," said the witch, "there's no time to be lost; if yonder lad is to be saved you must make use of every moment. You, farmer, get the mare saddled; and you, girl, get him something to eat, while he gets out of his dirty clothes and greets his mother, for she will be wondering by this the meaning of the hubbub."

"I will break the news to her," the farmer said; and he rushed up-stairs three steps at a time. Jack followed quickly after, and was soon locked in his mother's arms.

Joy never kills, they say. Certain it is it did no harm to Mrs. Dunstan; on the contrary, it seemed to inspire her with new strength and energy.

By this time the whole household was astir, and lights gleamed from almost every window. Jet was saddled in an incredibly short space of time, and led round to the back door. She seemed to know something strange had happened, for she trembled visibly, as though thrilled with an unspoken excitement.

"Let me go," said the farmer, as Jack appeared in the doorway. "You are but a shadow, my boy, and I fear your strength will not hold out."

"Nay, nay," he answered; "they will not believe at Bodmin unless they see me in the flesh. Besides, you are too heavy for Jet to carry such a distance. If I am but a shadow, so much the more hope of my being in time."

"Then God speed thy journey," said the farmer.

"Amen!" Jack replied.

Then Jet set up a loud and joyous whinny, and began to paw the ground with her fore-feet. She had recognized her master's voice, and seemed unable to contain herself with delight.

"Jet, my darling!" Jack said, patting the faithful creature's glossy neck.

And for answer she rubbed her nose against his hand again and again.

"Thou hast a long journey, my darling," he said, laying his face against her neck; "and all depends upon thy fleetness of foot. May God speed thee and me."

And for answer she tossed her head high in the air, and began to paw the ground again, as if impatient to be off.

The next moment Jack had leaped into the saddle, and the farmer led the way to the yard gate; Mary, the witch, and all the servants followed.

"Now God speed thee," said the witch; "and meanwhile I will go and explore Tregeagle's Cave."

"Be careful," Jack answered, "for they will be desperate when they discover I have escaped, and they go to the cave in the morning."

"I do not fear them," she answered. "Now, away."

For answer he waved his hand, and a moment later he had vanished in the darkness.

CHAPTER XXXII.

FOR DEAR LIFE.

" Soft as a bride the rosy dawn
    From dewy sleep doth rise,
And, bathed in blushes, hath withdrawn
    The mantle from her eyes ;
And with her orbs dissolved in dew,
    Bends like an angel softly through
      The blue pavilioned skies."—WELBY.

A RIDE of more than forty miles, alone, and on such an errand, was enough to quicken the beat of the stoutest heart. Jack, weakened by exposure and loss of sleep, was in anything but a fit state to undertake such a journey. He tried to hide from the loving eyes that watched him closely how weak and nervous he was, while he assumed a confidence and courage he did not feel.

He could not hide from himself the fact that the odds were greatly against his reaching Bodmin in time to save his friend. To begin with, he was only imperfectly acquainted with the road, having travelled it only once, and that several years before ; and if at any parting of the way he should take the wrong road, the mistake would probably prove fatal to his enterprise. And then, if Jet should cast a shoe, or should stumble, or her strength should fail before the journey was completed, he would only arrive to learn he was too late ; and even if all went well, and there was no mishap of any kind, it seemed scarcely possible that his fleet-footed mare could cover the ground in the time allotted.

He said nothing of this, however, to any one. Harry was in danger of suffering the cruelest death, and all through his folly, and no effort he could put forth to save his friend should be wanting; so, setting his lips tightly together, he waved his hand and rode away into the darkness.

For several miles the road lay along the valley; then it crossed over a range of hills, and struck the coach-road or " turnpike " on the opposite side. On the whole the road was in good condition, and fairly direct, though one might easily drift in the wrong direction where roads branched at an acute angle.

"Steady, darling, steady," Jack said, patting the mare's neck, directly his back was turned on Restormel, for Jet seemed eager to dash away at a furious gallop.

"Not so fast, my beauty," he went on, holding the curb rein with a firm hand. "You will need your strength later on, and so must not waste it now. There, that is better," as the mare settled into an easy swinging trot.

Jet seemed to understand her master's words, for she gave a knowing snort, and shook her mane to the breeze.

"We will save him if we can, Jet," Jack went on. "It is for dear life we journey to-night. By dawn of day we must be in Bodmin town, and there's no time for resting on the road. Now lift up thy feet well. There, I will loose the rein. Bonny Jet, bonny Jet."

So he talked to the beautiful creature, keeping time to the beat of her hoofs.

Onward and onward they sped, past cottage, and farmstead, and mill. The trees swept past them like tall shrouded monsters; the hedges seemed running a race with the fields; and Jet, with her ears bent forward,

"Jet and her rider were far in the distance."—P. 263.

never slackened her speed for a moment. With a long swinging pace she came to her strength, and quickened that pace with each passing minute, till the beat of her hoofs, like the click of a mill, sounded clear and distinct in the shadowy night.

Old people in cottages close to the road rose quickly on elbow, and knitted their brows, wondering much who the rider could be, and what could be his errand in the morning's small hours, when all decent folks should be asleep in their beds; then sighed as they remembered the hanging at dawn, and how a brave life would suddenly end at the hands of the hangman and the end of a rope; and sighed still more heavily that people could wish to witness a spectacle so terrible, and take a night's journey to be in at the sight.

But Jack gave no thought to what people would think. With fast-beating heart and brow furrowed deep, he was debating the chances of covering the road between now and the dawn.

The hill they climbed slowly till the summit was reached, then Jet was given her will. What a gallop that was down the long slanting road, while the hedges flew past like a swift-flowing stream! At the foot of the slope a gate blocked the way, the keeper being snugly asleep. But Jet was on fire, and would not delay, but leaped the tall barrier like a bird of the air, and sped on with a clatter of hoofs that woke every echo that slept in the hills, and awoke all the birds in their nests.

The keeper jumped up with an oath and a growl, and tugged at the window, forgetting the latch; then rushed down the stairs and threw open the door, but Jet and her rider were far in the distance, though the echoes of her footfalls were still in the air.

In the first hour's ride ten milestones were passed, and Jet was as fresh as at starting. But in the next stage a wrong turning was taken, and a mile was lost in retracing their steps, and a hope taken out of the heart of the rider.

But Jet never faltered or bated her pace—she seemed like a creature possessed; and Jack, full of love for his faithful companion, kept patting her neck, and whispering low words of hope and strong admiration. She knew as well as a Christian the words her master kept speaking, and answered him back with a toss of her head and a shake of her beautiful mane.

At one of the gates was a weary delay, for it blocked the road near the top of a hill, and Jet hadn't strength to clear it. The keeper was old, and angry, and slow, and vowed he wouldn't hurry—no, not for the king; and when Jack told him he bore a reprieve for the prisoner who was waiting his doom, he said he was sorry, for thousands had gone, had tramped all the night to be there in time, and 'twas a shame they should be disappointed.

Jack tossed him a sixpence as he passed through the gate. "I meant to have given thee more," he said, "but thy churlishness deserves no reward." Then he bent in his saddle, and patted the neck of the beautiful brute who bore him. "Haste thee, my bonny, beautiful Jet," and she needed no further bidding. Yet as the third hour drew to its finish, it was clear her strength was failing. Her breathing became heavy and laboured, and she swayed in her headlong gallop. Jack cheered her with word and the touch of his hand, but he knew all the while she was doing her best, and would be faithful even to death.

At length the gray dawn—pale, fitful, and sad—crept slowly along the crown of the hills, and smiled on the earth as a mother might smile whose heart was broken with sorrow. Jack always had welcomed the glow of the dawn, had hailed its approach as a friend out of heaven, a new gift from God, sweet, beautiful, pure. But to-day its soft footfalls struck a pain to his heart, for the prison was yet many miles in the distance, and at dawn, or soon after, his friend was to die.

"My darling, keep heart up;" and he bent in his saddle. "Keep heart up, my darling, or all will be lost." And the beautiful creature, though all but exhausted, showed her will by galloping faster.

Foam-flecked and dripping, with nostrils extended and breathing irregular and laboured, swaying this way and that way, with eyes almost blinded, the dumb faithful creature sped on. Like the click of a mill her hoofs still resounded, and the houses flew past one by one — past farmstead and cottage, past cottage and farmstead, ever on, ever on. What a gallop was that! How the villagers wondered and talked of a spectral horse and its rider, and prophesied earthquake and war!

But the dawn was increasing. Up the steeps of the east and over the pale heavens went galloping the heralds of day. Northward and southward the clouds caught fire, and burned crimson red for awhile, then paled and grew faint in the brightening day, and vanished before the king's coming.

"Thou art giving thy life, my darling," Jack said, and he patted her neck once more. "Keep heart, oh, keep heart, for the race is near run. And see! there's the jail in the distance." And lo! the gray walls of the prison loomed dimly, and surging around was a black human sea. Hark! the roar of the voices, like the surge of the ocean or the swaying of pine-trees when tossed by a storm.

"On, on! darling, on!" But in vain he caressed her; she had given her best, was giving it still. Did she know she was dying for the sake of her master, and for the sake of his friend who was waiting his doom?

Still onward she galloped, ungraceful, ungainly, with head hanging low, and eyes glazed and sightless. The hill was against her, but she was grit to the last. Did

she hear that great roar—that tempest of voices as the
door was thrown open and the prisoner appeared ?

"Now give us a speech!" "Aye, give us a speech!"
"Confess the foul murder ere you go to your doom!"
"But isn't he handsome?" "Whoever would ha'
thought it?" "It's sad for his parents!" "It's sadder
for him!"

Harry caught these brief sentences bandied about
by the crowd, but he moved not a muscle, though he
felt all their sting. Should he speak to these people—
declare he was guiltless? He might win their compassion, perhaps some would believe him. Life was
beautiful still, though he stood on a scaffold, and beautiful earth as he looked far around him; and fain he
would linger though a few moments longer, and feel
the warm sunshine and the sweet breath of heaven, and
gather strength to meet bravely his doom.

Then a roar from the great human sea spread around
him, smote his ear with a stab of terrible pain. "Come,
give us a speech; now improve the occasion," and they
yelled and gesticulated like people demented.

But how could he speak? His heart grew rebellious.
Speak to people half-drunken, besotted, compassionless?
Pander to curiosity morbid and vulgar? No, never.

"Now, hangman, I'm ready," and he stepped to the
toe-line, and quickly the noose encircled his neck.

Then a whisper—a murmur far out in the distance;
then a cry that soon grew to an ominous roar. Away
down the street a horse with its rider was struggling to
reach the black surging crowd. Foam-covered, dripping,
staggering, swaying, galloping still with an effort despairing; while the rider stood up in the stirrups and
shouted—"Stay the hands of the hangman, I bring a
reprieve." And the word was caught up, and sent on
and on, till the crowd thundered out, "A reprieve! a
reprieve!"

Then the black sea divided, and the horse with its

rider staggered into the centre; and Jack leaped on the saddle, and waving his hat, shouted,

" Harry, you're saved."

And the crowd roared again with a roar like the ocean, and Jet opened her eyes and lifted her head; then sighing as gently as a child that was tired, fell sideways stark dead.

CHAPTER XXXIII.

HOME AGAIN.

" 'Tis sweet to hear the watch-dog's honest bark
    Bay deep-mouthed welcome as we draw near home ;
'Tis sweet to know there is an eye will mark
    Our coming, and look brighter when we come."—BYRON.

THERE was at least a score of people in the crowd
from Restormel, Porthloo, and Pentudy, and among
the rest Abel Tregonning and Nathan Fraddon, so that
Jack had no difficulty in establishing his identity. Yet
notwithstanding this the officials were not at all disposed
to set Harry at liberty. They would need an order
first from the Home Secretary, they said. And but for
the High Sheriff of the county, who happened to be
present, and who had less respect for red tapeism than
most of the local authorities, the chances are Harry
would have been kept in prison another week. As it
was, an hour after he had been led out on the scaffold
to die the prison doors were thrown open to him, and
he marched forth into the sunshine a free man.

At first he feared he was dreaming—it was all so
sudden and unexpected. But the cheerful chatter of
Jack, and the loud hurrahs of the crowd, soon convinced
him that he was wide awake.

In Jack's cup of gladness there was only one bitter
drop, and that was the death of Jet. The beautiful
creature still lay where she had fallen. Jack could not
keep back his tears as he looked at her, and patted her
neck again that was now stiff and cold.

"We will have her buried at home," Jack said to Harry, blowing his nose violently.

"Aye, that we will," Harry answered. "She gave her life for me."

"And gave it willingly," Jack interposed. "She seemed glad to do it. And, bless her, she knew when you were saved, and died without a groan."

An hour later they had made all arrangements for the removal of poor Jet to Restormel, and were seated in a carriage behind a pair of splendid horses, with their faces once more towards home.

In Restormel the day was one of intense anxiety and excitement. What had happened, or what was going to happen, no one knew. Soon after daybreak the whole district had been alarmed by a terrific report, louder than the loudest thunder, and more startling than any shock of earthquake ever known. In Porthloo and Pentudy the shock was most severely felt, and fishermen out at sea declared that Tregeagle's Head rocked for a moment or two like a vessel in a storm; that huge splinters of rock flew from it in all directions, and that from the crown a shower of stones flew up to a tremendous height.

In Restormel people rushed out of their houses with white, terror-stricken faces, and gathered in groups in the street to discuss the strange phenomenon.

"What was it! Where was it! What did it portend?"

Then a whisper got into circulation, though no one knew how, that Jack Dunstan was alive; that he came into the village long after midnight with the witch of Carn Duloe; and that in the small hours of the morning he rode away on black Jet to Bodmin, hoping to be in time to stay the execution.

The Vicar, who had joined the crowd in the street, heard the whisper, and grew pale as death; then he rushed off to Trevose to make inquiries.

Mary met him at the door.

"What is this I hear about Jack being alive?" he gasped.

"It is quite true," she said. "Have you not seen father? He has gone to the vicarage to tell you."

"The Lord be praised," said Mr. Penryn, as he staggered into the house and dropped into a chair.

"It's very wonderful," said Mary, shyly. "Oh, I do hope he was in time."

But when Mary told him what time Jack started he looked very grave, and pressed his hand to his side.

"I fear it is vain to hope," he said. "It is hardly possible he could cover the distance in the time."

There was no telegraph in those days. They could only wait and hope till Jack should have time to return. They knew he would not keep them in suspense any longer than he could help.

But as the day wore on the tension became almost intolerable. Gladys spent her time in the churchyard among the graves—she could not bear to look into her father's white anguished face; while Mrs. Gaved's startled eyes almost frightened her. Yet in her heart she never doubted; she believed that God had spoken to her, and her simple childish faith overleaped every obstacle. Her father watched her walking among the graves in the pale autumn sunshine, but he never attempted to go to her. Her bright face smote his heart with a nameless pain; her faith seemed almost irreverent presumption. So they kept apart from each other and waited; the one with eager confidence, the other with dread foreboding.

In the village the interest was divided between the return of Jack and the strange behaviour of Tregeagle's Head. People who had been sufficiently venturesome to go on the peninsula came back with a puzzled look in their eyes and a wonderful story on their lips. They declared that the conformation of Tregeagle's crown had been entirely changed—that where once there had been a rocky elevation there was now a deep depression, and that out of this hollow smoke and vapour rose incessantly.

This story was received with varying degrees of credulity, and led to an infinite amount of talk and discussion, and in some instances to angry recrimination.

As the afternoon wore on everybody crowded into the street to await the arrival of Jack, and speculation became rife and animated as to whether he would return alone or bring Harry with him. In some instances indeed—though it is with sorrow we confess it—wagers were laid and accepted.

Mr. Penryn was in a strait betwixt two—not knowing whether to saddle his horse and ride toward Bodmin, or wait at home; and so while he hesitated the time wore on, and the crowd in the street became more dense all the while, for people came in from Porthloo and Pentudy, and from all the country side.

A stranger would have wondered what such a crowd could mean, and why every eye was turned in one direction. In the trees boys climbed till there was no longer any room for them; on the top of walls and fences they sat thick as bees.

And still the afternoon wore on, and the sun began to dip behind the fir-wood, and to fling long shadows across the valley, while the rugged slopes of Carn Duloe burned red in the westering light.

Little by little conversation had flagged, till now it had ceased altogether. People could no longer talk with such a weight of suspense upon their hearts. With white eager faces and loudly beating hearts they stood still and waited.

At length a shout was raised by some one away out beyond Trevose, which sent a thrill through the crowd from end to end. But as yet its meaning was not understood, and a painful stillness followed.

Then another shout was raised, but this time it did

not die away in silence; faint at first, like a single voice far in the distance, it soon began to swell and roll nearer, till by and by it grew into a roar.

Then the roll of wheels was heard, and the click of horses' hoofs. And the boys in the trees shrieked, "They're coming," and the men and women caught up the cry; and still nearer and nearer came the roll of wheels, till the crowd surged back right and left that there might be room for the carriage to pass. A moment later, and the foam-covered horses leaped into sight. A moment of awful suspense followed, and then a shout went up that rent the very heavens.

People talk of that shout till this day. And how strong men became blinded with tears, and women sobbed for very gladness, and children hid their faces in their mothers' aprons for very wonder and joy. And how the horses were taken out of the carriage, and men drew it in triumph through the street, and shouted till they were hoarse. And how bareheaded the Vicar rushed through the street to meet the strange procession, and leaped into the carriage while it was yet in motion, and fell on his son's neck in a paroxysm of speechless joy.

All this and more the people talk about yet. There never was known in Restormel such a day as that. The people were almost frantic with excitement. The very fact that they had wronged Harry in thought so much in the days gone by seemed to increase their enthusiasm now. They dragged the carriage up and down the street, till both Harry and Jack begged to be released.

Then they tramped off to Carn Duloe—hundreds of them with faggots of furze upon their backs, and by midnight a huge bonfire was blazing on the mountain's crown, and shedding a lurid light on all the country round.

To describe the scene within the vicarage that

evening would be impossible. It was long past midnight before prayers or rest was thought of, and when at length they knelt down, and the Vicar tried to pray, his voice failed him.

"Oh, Lord, we thank Thee," he began, "from our hearts we thank. Thee. We have doubted, but Thou hast been good, and hast given him back to us, who——" Then his voice broke, and ended in a sob. But each one prayed in his and her room that night, and gave thanks to God.

To Harry it was like heaven being in his own room again, with the wind singing in the fir-trees above him, and all the fear taken from his heart, and the shadow wiped from his name. It was far on into the morning before he fell asleep, and then it was to dream of Mary— sweet, blissful dreams, that did not end when he opened his eyes to the light of another day.

Was it accident, that when afternoon came he should meet her in the shadow of the pine-wood, and that they should stray together up the sun-flecked avenues?

Was it unnatural that he should tell her of his prison dreams, and of the beautiful hope he had cherished so long, and how he lived in the memory of that hope long after it had gone out in darkness and despair?

Was it strange that her hand should tremble on his arm, and her eyes grow liquid with tears, while beautiful blushes stole up her neck and mantled her cheek and brow?

Was it wrong that their lips should meet in a passionate kiss, and that they should vow that only death should separate them?

I do not think so. But then I am old-fashioned, and believe in love, and like to see young people happy.

It was the old old story they told that day; and when they returned together to Trevose, both Mr. and Mrs. Dunstan gave them their blessing, and Jack declared that nothing in the world coul l have pleased him better.

And now our story is nearly done. Of Mrs. Flue nothing was ever heard again. That she went to explore Tregeagle's cave there can be no doubt, but she returned no more to her familiar haunts. And with the witch there disappeared also Sam Trewalsick and his son Billy, Dan Polslee, Mark Jory, and Jerry Beer. They were all seen in Pentudy on the night Jack effected his escape, but before dawn they had vanished, and were never heard of again.

But when Jack Dunstan had told his story there remained but little if any doubt as to their fate. Who fired the gunpowder was long a matter of speculation, and opinion was divided as to whether it was done purposely or by accident.

That the powder was kept there for the purpose of destroying all traces of their nefarious traffic in case of discovery there was no question whatever. But no one was alive to explain the mystery of the explosion.

When Jack, accompanied by a number of local authorities, attempted to find their way to Tregeagle's cave, they found the tunnels almost completely blocked by large heaps of débris. They managed to crawl on their hands and knees for a considerable distance, but only to discover that the roof of the cave had completely collapsed, and that the contents had been buried beyond hope of recovery.

For a long time people avoided the headland more persistently than ever, but as the years passed on they got the better of their fears, especially as Tregeagle was no more heard of, and stormy nights had no longer the painful accompaniment of human voices crying in the darkness.

Carn Duloe also lost its gruesome reputation. And when the witch's hut fell into ruins, it was discovered she had laid a bell wire from a bend in the road to her hut, so that any one approaching would tread on a spring, and so give the signal within her dwelling.

The collapse of Tregeagle's cave proved the death-blow to many long-cherished superstitions. People talk of Tregeagle still, but the legend is no longer believed. Even the fisher-folk of Pentudy and Porthloo have long since outgrown most of their superstitions.

Jack's painful experience taught him a lesson he never forgot. He was still as bright and fearless as ever, but he avoided foolhardy adventures, especially when he learned that Gladys Penryn felt an interest in his well-being.

Harry's career was a most successful one. Soon after he was called to the Bar he and Mary Dunstan joined hands for life, and a happier couple never journeyed through life together. He was still quite a young man when he took silk, and but in his prime when he was elevated to the Bench.

It is said he was the most compassionate judge ever known in the Western Circuit. The memory of the time when he stood a prisoner at the bar he could never wholly banish, and so if there was any bias in his judgment at all, it was always on mercy's side.

THE END.

Price 2s. 6d. each.

SELECT BOOKS.

In crown 8vo, cloth gilt.

THREE FAVOURITE WORKS BY THE REV. J. H. INGRAHAM.

THE PILLAR OF FIRE; or, Israel in Bondage. By the Rev. J. H. INGRAHAM, LL.D. With Illustrations.

"This volume takes up the Hebraic history at the time of the sale of Joseph into Egypt, and closes with the promulgation of the Two Tables of the Divine Law from Sinai."

THE THRONE OF DAVID. From the Consecration of the Shepherd of Bethlehem to the Rebellion of Prince Absalom. By the Rev. J. H. INGRAHAM, LL.D. With Illustrations.

"This volume illustrates the grandeur of Hebraic history when 'The People of God' had attained, under the reigns of David and Solomon, the height of their power and glory as a nation."

THE PRINCE OF THE HOUSE OF DAVID; or, Three Years in the Holy City. By the Rev. J. H. INGRAHAM, LL.D. With Original Illustrations.

"This volume illustrates the decadence of the Hebraic power, and the final culmination is presented in our Saviour."

These Works serve to illustrate the three great periods of Jewish history, and throw considerable light upon the Bible narratives by bringing before the reader much that is important and interesting with regard to the social life of the peoples who were then engaged in making history.

WORKS BY THE AUTHOR OF "ZENOBIA."

ZENOBIA, Queen of Palmyra : A Tale of the Roman Empire in the Days of the Emperor Aurelian. By the Rev. WILLIAM WARE. With Steel Illustrations.

AURELIAN; or, Rome in the Third Century. Being Letters of Lucius M. Piso from Rome, to Fausta, the Daughter of Gracchus, at Palmyra. By the Rev. WILLIAM WARE. With Steel Illustrations.

JULIAN; or, Scenes in Judea. By the Rev. WILLIAM WARE. With Steel Illustrations.

These three volumes are of the highest literary character, and will be found to give the reader a clear and enjoyable insight into the period of history dealt with.

THE BOYS OF HOLY WRIT, and Bible Narratives. With Original Illustrations.

"Records of the youth and boyhood of Scriptural characters, from Cain to St. John the Evangelist."

FEMALE CHARACTERS OF HOLY WRIT. By the Rev. HUGH HUGHES, D.D. With Original Coloured Illustrations.

"The story of the lives of more than twenty of the mothers and women of Israel is told in this volume by a loving hand."

Price 2s. 6d. each.

WORKS BY THE REV. E. P. ROE.

FROM JEST TO EARNEST. By the Rev. E. P. ROE. With Original Illustrations.

"A charming love story, in which a girl's playful jest leads to serious but finally happy consequences."

BARRIERS BURNED AWAY. By the Rev. E. P. ROE. With Original Illustrations.

"An exciting story of the destruction of a city, and of how the barriers between love and pride were removed. The heroine is a finely-drawn character."

OPENING A CHESTNUT BURR. By the Rev. E. P. ROE. With Original Illustrations.

"A delightful tale. . . The heroine is a very charming maiden."

NEAR TO NATURE'S HEART. By the Rev. E. P. ROE. With Original Illustrations.

"A tale of the beginning of the American war of independence."

A KNIGHT OF THE NINETEENTH CENTURY. By the Rev. E. P. ROE. With Original Illustrations.

WITHOUT A HOME. By the Rev. E. P. ROE. With Original Illustrations.

"A deeply interesting and pathetic tale of a family struggling with poverty."

HIS SOMBRE RIVALS. By the Rev. E. P. ROE. With Original Illustrations.

"A powerful love story of the period of the Civil War in the United States."— *Literary World.*

A YOUNG GIRL'S WOOING: A Love Story. By the Rev. E. P. ROE. With Original Illustrations.

"Mr. Roe writes with charming ease, grace and intelligence. Every page is worth following carefully. The sweet girl-heroine becomes an object of sympathy and admiring regard."—*Daily News.*

FAVOURITE WORKS BY THE AUTHOR OF
"THE WIDE, WIDE WORLD."

SAY AND SEAL. By ELIZABETH WETHERELL. With Original Illustrations.

"If any man make religion as twelve and the world as thirteen, such a one hath not the spirit of a true man."

ELLEN MONTGOMERY'S BOOKSHELF. By ELIZABETH WETHERELL. With Original Illustrations by J. D. WATSON.

"A suitable work for village libraries."

THE LAMPLIGHTER. By Miss CUMMINS, Author of "Mabel Vaughan." With Original Illustrations.

UNCLE TOM'S CABIN: A Tale of Life among the Lowly. By HARRIET BEECHER STOWE. Fully Illustrated.

DUNALLAN; or, Know what You Judge. By GRACE KENNEDY, Author of "Father Clement." With Original Illustrations.

Price 2s. 6d. each.

"DARING DEEDS" LIBRARY

In crown 8vo, cloth gilt.

THE WARS OF THE ROSES; or, York and Lancaster. By JOHN G. EDGAR, Author of "Sea Kings and Naval Heroes." With Original Illustrations.

"A book written to attract the English boys of to-day to a remarkable epoch in the history of their country."

SEA FIGHTS, from Sluys to the Bombardment of Alexandria. By Mrs. VALENTINE. With Original Illustrations.

"Stories and descriptions of the most interesting sea fights of the British Navy, designed to give some idea of the great and glorious records of our country's sea-empire."

LAND BATTLES, from Hastings to the recent Battles in the Soudan. By Mrs. VALENTINE. With Original Illustrations.

"Brief sketches of our most famous land battles."

DARING DEEDS, and TALES OF PERIL AND ADVENTURE. By JAMES S. BORLASE. With Original Illustrations.

TWO YEARS OF SCHOOL LIFE. By Madame DE PRÉSSENSÉ. Edited by the Author of "The Heir of Redclyffe." With Original Illustrations.

"An admirable story of school life."

TRUE STORIES OF BRAVE DEEDS. Edited by Rev. G. T. HOARE. With Original Illustrations.

"Some noble examples of manly courage, which are so profitably studied by the young, are here depicted."

THE BOY'S BOOK OF HEROES. By HELENA PEAKE. With Illustrations.

"An interesting record of the heroes of other days."

THE LIFE AND ADVENTURES OF ROBINSON CRUSOE. By DANIEL DEFOE. With numerous small and full-page Illustrations by ERNEST GRISET.

THE SWISS FAMILY ROBINSON. New and unabridged Translation by Mrs. H. B. PAULL. With upwards of 200 Illustrations.

WILLIS, THE PILOT; or, The After Adventures of the Swiss Family Robinson. With Original Illustrations.

TALES OF OLD OCEAN. By Lieut. C. R. Low. With Original Illustrations.

"Stirring tales of life at sea."

THE BOY WITH AN IDEA. By Mrs. EILOART, Author of "Cris Fairlie's Boyhood." With Illustrations.

"An amusing and well-written story for boys."

SEA KINGS AND NAVAL HEROES. By JOHN G. EDGAR, Author of "Cavaliers and Roundheads," &c. With Original Illustrations.

"The achievements of men who at various times have made their names known to fame as sea kings and naval heroes are here depicted."

Price 2s. 6d. each.

"DARING DEEDS" LIBRARY—*continued.*

MEN OF NOTE: Their Boyhood and School-days. By ERNEST FOSTER. With Original Illustrations.

"A most interesting account of the early days of a few of the great men of the present and past century."

"As a school prize no more appropriate book could be desired, and it has the merit that it would be heartily appreciated by the recipient. Mr. Foster's descriptions are pithy, and the various incidents are well written and interesting."—*Wigan Observer.*

THE LIFE OF NELSON. By ROBERT SOUTHEY. With Original Illustrations.

"The best eulogy of Nelson is the faithful history of his actions; the best history that which relates them most perspicuously."

BARON MUNCHAUSEN: His Travels and surprising Adventures. Illustrated with Thirty-seven curious Engravings from the Baron's Own Designs and Five Woodcuts by GEORGE CRUIKSHANK.

ÆSOP'S FABLES. Translated by SAMUEL CROXALL, D.D., and Sir ROGER L'ESTRANGE. With Applications and Morals by the Rev. G. F. TOWNSEND and L. VALENTINE. With 110 Original Illustrations.

THE ARABIAN NIGHTS' ENTERTAINMENTS. New Edition, Revised, with Notes, by the Rev. GEORGE FYLER TOWNSEND. With Original Illustrations.

GOD'S SILVER; or, Youthful Days. By the Hon. Mrs. R. J. GREENE. With Original Illustrations.

"Full of interest and admirably portrays the aspirations and fancies which animate the youthful mind."—*Times.*

MARTIN NOBLE; or, A Boy's Experience of London Life. By JOHN G. WATTS. With Original Illustrations by GUNSTON.

"Martin is simply a frank, manly lad, who does his best under all difficulties, and he secures the reader's sympathy from the first. It is a brisk, cheerful story well told."—*Pall Mall Gazette.*

A NATURALIST'S NOTE BOOK.

EVERY DAY IN THE COUNTRY. By HARRISON WEIR. With 400 Original Drawings for Every Day and the Months, and Eight Coloured Plates by the Author. With Interleaving for Memoranda. In imperial 16mo, cloth gilt, gilt edges.

"A charming little record for a naturalist. A more perfect or useful handybook of everyday incidents that occur in the natural history world it would be difficult to procure."—*Nature.*

THE CRESCENT AND THE CROSS; or, Romance and Realities of Eastern Travel. By ELIOT WARBURTON. With Original Illustrations. In crown 8vo, cloth gilt.

"As a volume treating of the romances and realities of Orientals, places and things, it ranks pre-eminent. It is a book to learn from; it presents the history of the East in its most interesting style, and treats of Eastern subjects in a manner calculated to impress the reader with their grandeur and importance."—*Belfast Morning News.*